For my father and for Joel – making the connection

Thanks to Faith Evans, for her tireless dedication; to Beverley Cousins, for insightful yet unintrusive editing; and to Paul, for everything.

Nowhere's Child

FRANCESCA WEISMAN

MICHAEL JOSEPH
an imprint of
PENGUIN BOOKS

MICHAEL JOSEPH
Published by the Penguin Group
Penguin Books Ltd, 80 Strand, London WC2R ORL, England
Penguin Putnam Inc., 375 Hudson Street, New York, New York 10014, USA
Penguin Books Australia Ltd, 250 Camberwell Road,
Camberwell, Victoria 3124, Australia
Penguin Books Canada Ltd, 10 Alcorn Avenue, Toronto, Ontario, Canada M4V 3B2
Penguin Books India (P) Ltd, 11 Community Centre,
Panchsheel Park, New Delhi – 110 017, India
Penguin Books (NZ) Ltd, Cnr Rosedale and Airborne Roads,
Albany, Auckland, New Zealand
Penguin Books (South Africa) (Pty) Ltd, 24 Sturdee Avenue,
Rosebank 2196, South Africa

Penguin Books Ltd, Registered Offices: 80 Strand, London WC2R ORL, England

www.penguin.com

First published 2003
I

Set in Monotype Garamond
Phototypeset by Intype London Ltd
Printed in Great Britain by Clays Ltd, St Ives plc

A CIP catalogue record for this book is available from the British Library

ISBN 0–718–14615–8

PROLOGUE

She disappeared hours ago.

You've been here so long, humped and stooped behind the refuse, you might almost have forgotten why you came. The sick-sweet stink of the place swells inside you, and your hooked knees and shoulder blades strain against cramp.

The discomfort is so great, the watching through squinting eyes and the waiting, that you're almost ready to give up, abandon the whole idea. Who, after all, could ever have guessed it would come to this? And then, just as you unfold your elbows and steady your sore, bent thighs, there is the sound of a door creaking open then closing again.

She sways into view at the edge of the pavement.

Wine has blunted her senses, made her stupidly bold. She must have heard your footsteps, and the rustling rubbish as you straightened, but she's blasé and untouchable, snorting out tendrils of smoke. Still, your footsteps keep up with her, break her rhythm, draw level. They do not quite match hers. She turns back again.

Freezes.

For a second, she thinks of running, makes an amateur lunge for it. Her torso jerks forward, but your wild arms bring her close. She steps backward, begging.

– Please. God, please. No.

You step closer, bringing her into your body like a lover. Your palms press tight upon her collarbone and the blood starts to drain. The surface of her throat purples and her nostrils funnel air with a high, peculiar whistling.

– Please. No. I'm sorry.

She's down on the ground now, her legs kicking out gracelessly. Film glazes her dulled eyes. Her lips slacken fatly, like unfashioned plasticine.

1

A stream of bile smears her chin, a liquid filth stains her underskirt.

– Oh, God. Please. I haven't said anything.

Her pleas fail to soften you as you bring out the small knife. The blade works beautifully, like an extension of your fingers, not like rigid steel at all but strong and agile as a snake. You carve through the soft, shallow flesh and her sad, thin legs spasm. The blade travels downward, chasing the trail of the breastbone, slicing the rise of flesh either side, still stirred by faint breaths. Blood crimsons the blouse where it strains over her nipples.

Now back up for the last lap: past the dead pout of her lips, following the jut of cheekbone and brow bone, skirting nostril, then eye. The open mouth belches a warm, putrid gas. The blade zig-zags the eyelid, scoops lightly at the jelly.

One whimper, one final twitch beneath the pelvis. And then it's over. She's gone, face turned down on the pavement. A dustbin lid tumbles and clatters, the corpse merges with its surroundings; the indeterminate rotting stink, the oily film in the gutter. She's become a messy meal for feral cats, a curiosity for pigeons.

A curtain stirs, is drawn again: a distant car stereo crescendos, then fades.

And then the quiet street is empty. No one the wiser.

PART ONE

I

1984

Kit lived with his mother in the small quiet house which nestled at the apex where the road curved round. Its brittle windows shone like shrewd eyes in the sunshine. Whilst playing in the garden he'd sometimes peer inward and watch his mother's shadow move in the low-ceilinged hallway.

He didn't begin his search in earnest until he was past twenty, but his sixth sense started working well before then.

Kit developed a habit of watching his mother, of monitoring her progress from rarely more than seven paces. He marked the curve of her neck as she bent to wash the dishes, the plunge of her fingers into the thick, soapy water. He followed the pattern of veins on the back of her hands as she crouched to lace his shoes, or tucked his shirt into his waistband. Often he'd wake early and listen for her footsteps: for the gurgle of the shower and her sweet, throaty singing. She loved to listen to the radio and sing along with it, and once he caught her unexpectedly in her pyjamas skipping round the room.

When she realized he was spying she came to an abrupt halt, but then carried on, only more softly now, scooping him up in her arms so that he travelled the room giddily with her. He reached out with small, four-year-old fingers and touched the softness of her skin.

On a cold autumn morning he woke well before breakfast. His stomach howled as noisily as the bathroom pipes in winter and his mouth watered with the wish for butter melting into toast. Weak, dappled light strained on the other side of the curtains, and on the tiny L-shaped landing the floorboards creaked twice.

In unslippered feet, Kit slid from the bed. He wandered half-blind through a pattern of shadow. Opening the bedroom door was like lifting a veil of secrecy. From down the narrow stairs, which had in those days seemed endless, he heard half-muffled grunts followed by a few beats of silence, then a sing-song goodbye and the clink of the front gate. Without understanding, he felt exposed to vague danger. He held his breath and retreated, not quite closing the door. And, like a creature from cartoons he'd seen, he peered through the crack.

His mother came bounding up the stairs in a long, flowing robe. Her cheeks were flushed pinkly as though she'd been walking through air-frost. As her bare feet hit the landing, she let her long robe fall open. Her pale body startled him: the strange pointiness of the breasts with their blatant, rosy nipples; the shallow dip of her belly towards a triangular shock of hair. She trailed a heavy, sweetish smell, like the flower beds in summer. Kit dived for the bedclothes as his room door flew open.

Shocked by his own trespass, his breath quickened to hiccoughs. His mother drew near to the bed and pulled down the blankets. Her face hovered above his: sharp-nosed and upside down, the inverted cheeks strange and squashy, the brows heavy and knitted. He wished he could say sorry, but only the hiccoughs came out.

'What's this, little man? Have I caught you spying on me?'

He thought of a nursery rhyme book with a boy whose thumbs had been cut off with giant scissors. Her nail was sharp on his cheek and her breath hot and stale. The finger hovered and pressed, ready to scratch or perhaps pinch him.

'Do you know what happens to nosy children? Who comes and gets them?'

Kit tried to squirm down to the dark cocoon beneath the blankets. His hiccoughs were high and rough now, hurting his chest. But then his mother's hand loosened and her heavy brow lightened. Her face broke into a smile and she gave a long, loud laugh. He didn't understand, but suddenly his breathing grew easy. He let her crowd in and cradle him in the crook of her shoulder.

Although men often stopped to stare at her in the street, Kit's mother appeared to lead a solitary existence. In the small neighbourhood where they lived at the edge of the suburb she kept herself to herself and there were things she would not do. She did not stop for long chats with the fruit seller when she went to buy apples, or drink cups of tea in the cafe with the other women who had pushchairs.

Once Kit went with his mother to a restaurant a long way from the neighbourhood. He asked her where they were, and she vaguely explained 'town', but didn't add anything further and appeared somewhat distracted. None of the women here had pushchairs and some wore long coats and tight gloves. The two or three children present had soft voices and clean faces. One tall woman walked past and gave such a sour look that Kit wondered if her food had been rotten and she had pains in her stomach.

'Support the workers against Tory privatization, love?' asked a young man who had just breezed in off the streets, wearing a hairy black jacket and clanking a large plastic jar. The tall woman's face crumpled so Kit knew her stomach must now be in agony, and Kit's mother raised her eyebrows, and then laughed softly and slipped the young man a coin.

'The other half, eh?' he said, and blushed just detectably,

and carried on staring at her. Kit thought his mother looked pleased, but her smile faded to a far-off lost look, and she quickly gathered their coats to leave.

Kit learnt of buses and trains which led to Town, away from the clusters of slow shops and orange bricked houses, far from the park with its low trees and beds of trimmed shrubs. But it was to prove a very long time before he went there again himself.

Now and again his mother took a bus into Town alone, and left him for the afternoon with a sitter called Miss Dickenson. Miss Dickenson had pink skin and white, wispy hair; there were a few whiskers on her chin and she had poor hearing. He asked Miss Dickenson where his mother was, but she didn't say much apart from a casual, hand-waving reference to shopping.

'Can I go too?'

Miss Dickenson sucked her teeth (which might have been false) and adjusted her glasses which were made of pink plastic.

'You'd better ask your mother. Are you allowed to eat Mars Bars?'

'Will I get punished?'

'Ah, not just this once.'

His mother scolded him if she caught him with sweet, sticky traces, but it was worth it for the lingering after-taste of chocolate in his mouth. He would always worry, though, that if he had the chocolate then by some quirk of fate he would be deprived of the soft toys or matchbox cars his mother would come home with. Then again, sometimes she'd come empty-armed and he'd wonder why she'd bothered to go shopping at all.

Once, in the living room, he asked if she would take him. She turned her face to the window and started fiddling with her hair. When she turned back to him, her skin was all reddened, and she lifted him, and kissed him.

'Maybe. When you're older.'

Kit never looked much at his reflection until just after he started nursery school. The boys in the playground were the ones who made him do it. Two of them, Danny and Robby, as he sat apart watching them. Their games were raucous and bloody-kneed, their shins covered in grazes. He preferred to watch the pigeons and the sunlight in the trees, but they pulled him to his feet and gurgled with laughter. One of them spat at him.

'Stinky Kit. Kit stinks!'

They circled their eyes with their fingers, and gurgled harder and nastier. Miss Jones came and scolded them, and shook her head sadly.

'Children. *Children!*'

She took Kit inside and he was allowed to go home early.

Later, he stood staring at the mirror in the bathroom. His eyes stared back, wide and clear: one green and one blue. If he lowered his lids and squinted, his vision would blur, and his face became a mess of features in strange, terrified disorder. They were as senseless as the letters on the flashcards or the fearsome snickers of schoolchildren.

From the kitchen, up the stairway, came the sound of rushing water, roaring in and washing over him as he stood drowning in the moment. Half-blind, he hit the mirror, yearning to straighten his reflection.

'Kit,' called his mother, 'are you ready to come down?'

His eyes widened; the vision sharpened: he was normal once more. So what if one of his eyes was a different colour to the other.

His mother had the clearest eyes, he could stare at them all day.

*

Kit's eyes caused him problems in more ways than one. Looking at the black letters on the flashcards, which were used to help the children learn words, he could sometimes turn quite dizzy. Other children sat straight-backed and expelled strange sounds like *C-A-T*, sometimes even making words Kit recognized and then sitting with puffed-out chests, smiling. But Kit saw only a chaos of dots and angles that made his eyeballs go fuzzy. There was a sad afternoon when he tried to guess a word, but all that came out was a simian grunt. Other children snickered, and not for the first time Miss Jones had to rescue him. She breathed deeply, and clicked her tongue, and bit the end of one long nail off.

Numbers were altogether easier, and gave Kit far fewer headaches. He knew, for example, that his mother was reading a book called *1984*, and had no trouble in observing that this was the same pattern of numbers as those on the front of newspapers.

'What's all this?' he asked his mother, tugging at the sheaf of words and pictures she hid behind.

'It's stuff about us, our world.'

Later, when he saw her with that book, he said, 'Is this about us?'

'Well, perhaps, in some ways, yes.'

Kit loved to watch his mother reading, to see her complete, satisfied, quiet, as she sat with her feet curled under her, her pink and white features softening. If he snuggled up close, she would move blindly to accommodate him, arranging her body by instinct so they could nestle like animals.

When it first happened Kit hardly minded about the Park Incident, but he understood that for his mother it was something of a watershed. For years afterward she would continue to speak of it. *The Park Incident* became a shorthand for all things strange and dreadful. When talking to Miss

Dickenson she would occasionally refer to it, and say the words so quietly as to appear to be mouthing. Both women would shake their heads in grave, sober agreement.

For Kit it had just been an extended weekend. An afternoon in late spring, and a walk in the park: the woolly clouds picked out by pale halos of sunshine. There were one or two women in long coats, like the ones they'd seen in Town, but most were sighing, flustered and pushing buggies heaving with yowling infants. The soil was damp with fresh rain and the young flowers vivid. Kit held his mother's hand as they threw crumbs to the ducks.

But at the end of the path which ran in a crescent round the water, his mother stopped abruptly and stood rooted to the spot. Opposite her were two women, also accompanied by offspring. They exchanged glances meaningfully, as though in silent conversation. Their unfamiliar heads bobbed vigorously, and they hissed in whispers like children. One of them pointed.

Kit looked up at his mother and saw her bottom lip trembling. Her colour had risen, her chin thrust forward and upward. She yanked him about face, her fingers so tight round his wrist that the skin chaffed and tingled. They walked home so fast he could barely keep up. When he stole a glance up at her, there was a large tear on her cheek.

When autumn came that year, school life grew stranger. He had to go to the big school next to the nursery, where some of the oldest children were not even that much smaller than his mother. They still had lessons with flashcards, which continued to make him feel sick, and there were low tables set out in rows with a big board at the front.

Some days grown-ups from school would come and talk to him privately, either outside the classroom or afterwards at home. Occasionally they'd bring some of the nauseous flashcards, on other afternoons there'd be picture books or toy animals. When he was given the chance to contemplate and tell his own stories he quite enjoyed these slow times and the peace away from the other children. But the appointed schoolperson this particular day would insist on distracting him, and asked him barrages of questions while he'd tried to play with the animals.

'Are you happy at school? How are the other kids?'

He made up brief, colourless answers to keep the questioner at bay, and carried on drawing up the toy-animal battle lines. His mother sat with him, weaving her fingers.

'What sort of things have you been doing? Anything special?'

Kit thought the question stupid, but to pacify the schoolperson he decided to talk about the Park Incident. He cleared his throat and began.

Slowly, and then more quickly, his mother unweaved her fingers. She straightened her legs, then her back, and then stood up off the sofa.

'Kit. I've just remembered. There's somewhere I must go today. I must give you your bath and then take you to Miss Dickenson. You're really terribly grubby, you know.' She turned to the schoolperson whose jaw had unhinged, bewilderedly. 'I'm so terribly sorry. I simply forgot.'

The poor confused schoolperson was as good as yanked off the sofa, knocking over her tea as a result of the sudden change of plan. Kit watched the dribbling liquid form a moist, tawny stain.

But he never got his bath, or got taken to Miss Dickenson. When he questioned his mother later, she said she'd made a mistake.

Men came and went like ghosts in that small, quiet household. On the rarest of occasions they would come round for supper and drink wine with his mother, whilst he would have grape juice. Under the influence of alcohol, her skin went pink and dewy, and she'd throw back her head, laughing, showing the long curve of her throat. Whichever man was round would sit silent, waiting intently, making Kit feel invisible.

But most of the time, it was the men who were invisible. They'd arrive late at night and leave early in the morning. He'd hear the landing boards creak and jumbled groans from the bedroom. Sometimes unfamiliar, opened bottles would spread a spicy scent in the bathroom. Or there'd be a used razor blade by the basin. That would be all.

Kit grew accustomed to the distant, midnight moaning and he learnt to shut it out and hide beneath the bedclothes. But one Sunday before dusk he heard stifled, anguished murmurs – similar, but different – coming from his mother's room. The men never came in daylight. Fear quickened his breathing.

He trod swiftly to the bedroom and, though the boards creaked their usual warning, as he inched the bedroom door open his mother sensed no intrusion. In fact, he could barely see her at first, and in a brief thrill of panic he wondered if the room were, in fact, empty. But then there she was: he caught sight of her outline, kneeling on the rug on the other side of the bed, face hidden by her hair and her upper body rocking. Her thick reddish locks parted at the back of her scalp, and he glimpsed the long, pale stretch of neck sliding towards her shoulders. Her forearms cradled her belly as though her insides were hurting.

She still didn't notice as he stepped even nearer and it was then that he caught sight of the box on the carpet. Golden, shiny streaked walnut wood, like a miniature treasure chest: unlocked, he could see, with a small, silver key. Both inside and out there were papers and pictures, many strewn about on the carpet, words both printed and handwritten. The letters went fuzzy, as usual, but still he strained to see more.

And then nearer, nearer, and it finally happened. His steps disturbed the peace and his mother bolted upright.

Her face, jerked towards his, was as shocking as a mask: eyes red-rimmed and puffy, lips swollen fat and quivering. Blue-black streaks of tears stained her ivory cheeks. She unfurled her body and bent her long face towards him.

'Don't ever, ever, creep up on me like that again! If you go into people's bedrooms don't you know you should knock first!'

Kit stepped back, baffled, a lump rising in his throat. He looked helplessly at the witchwoman his mother had become, then at the pale window past her shoulder and at the paper-strewn floor. She crouched, swift and feral, but with a sharp creaking of joints, and swept up the fragments and photographs and returned them to the little chest. She wore a low-cut, light jumper and he saw the outline of her breastbone ridging the surface of her skin. She jabbed a finger at the box, and then somewhere close to his nose.

'And don't you ever stick your nose into other people's private things. Curiosity killed the cat. Don't you know you shouldn't snoop?'

Her breath had shortened, the way it did when she'd smoke too many of the cigarettes she pretended she'd given up; or when he came upon her smoking secretly, and she'd stub the butt out furiously. She clutched the little box to her breast, and then locked it with the key, before stashing it behind some clothes on the top shelf of the wardrobe. Well out of reach. Safe with its secrets. Hot pinpricks of tears smarted at the backs of his eyeballs.

Later, when he was pretending to sleep, she came in and said sorry. She stroked the hair on his forehead and sang a quiet, wordless lullaby. But he kept his mouth downturned and refused to wake up.

*

One of his last, clearest memories of the small, quiet house was a long winter's afternoon when he was day-dreaming of spring and his fifth birthday. He'd been round at Miss Dickenson's while his mother went on one of her increasingly rare excursions. He spent much of the afternoon padding about and asking lots of questions.

'Where's my mother now?'

'Do *you* ever go to Town?'

Miss Dickenson didn't answer, but made lots of high, laughing noises and kept looking at her watch and offering him boiled sweets. They nestled in a long-stemmed glass which she as good as placed in his lap. Eventually, after a final glance at the watch face, she smoothed her skirt over her knees and looked unmistakably jolly.

'Time's up, young gentleman. Time to go home.'

Walking back, Kit's stomach skipped lightly, as he pictured thick paper shopping bags and myriad presents. But once at the house, from the very bottom of the path, a quiet hush descended and the air seemed to go colder. Through the shallow bay windows he saw two shadows moving. He knew his mother instantly from the bird-like swoop of her neck: her arms folded high on her breasts gave a clear sign she was nervous. The other figure was less clear, but soon swam into focus: a tall, straight-backed man, who also had his arms folded. They both stood, stiff as sticks, facing each other.

Miss Dickenson rang the bell and Kit counted seconds silently. His mother opened the door and pulled him in without kissing him. She paid Miss Dickenson hurriedly with scrunched up paper and coins.

'Go to your room,' she said, crouching, but still not touching him.

When too much time had passed without a real welcome, he decided to clamber back down and tip-toe to the kitchen. He couldn't forget the rage he'd incurred previously, but his stomach was growling and his bedroom was cold besides. He went halfway down the stairs and then came to a halt.

His mother and the man had moved into the hallway. She held the door open, her back to the staircase, one set of nails rasping at a high spot on her shoulder. Winter evening blasted inwards and nipped at Kit's fingers. The man stood tall, looking downwards, his thin lips wide and parted. Though he couldn't say why, Kit knew this wasn't a smile. Both voices were high and sharp, but he couldn't make out words.

Finally, after a particularly shrill outburst from his mother, the man stepped backwards, head shaking, still wearing the same non-smile. 'If that's the way you want it.' Then he turned and was gone.

She slammed the door on him so hard the potted peace lilies shook. Then she swung round, and pressed her back to it, as though all her frail weight was needed to keep the man out. Her breasts rose and fell beneath her thin, scratchy jumper. Only then did she see Kit halfway down the stairs. He held his breath, braced for the swell of her anger. But she opened her arms, smiling, and let him run into them.

Next morning he awoke to a cold-fingered shaking. It was Sunday, too early for breakfast, and they never went to church. But she stood at his bedside, coat buttoned to her chin.

'Come on, Kit. Hurry. We've got to get moving.'

Eyes sticky with sleep, he was led to the washbasin, his face sponged with freezing water. The chill of the tiles thrilled the bare soles of his feet and he wondered at being allowed to stand here without wearing slippers.

Downstairs in the kitchen he at once saw things were different. A frosty stillness had settled and everything was tidy. As though his mother had spent all night awake and spring cleaning. As she drank coffee quickly he saw the dark rings round her eyes. When she rinsed the cup out her thin fingers were trembling.

Back in the bathroom her voice grew thin with impatience. She wiped the last of the toothpaste from the edge of his mouth, and then parcelled him back downstairs where he was ordered to wait.

Then he saw the soft bags and cases lined up by the front door. The house echoed with cupboards slamming and drawers rattling empty. When his mother returned and stood by him, she was hot, and puffing softly. He locked gazes with her.

'What's going on?'

She ruffled his hair, soothed the unspoken fear.

'Nothing to worry about. We're moving away.'

2

1980

They find her in the morning.

The temperature has dropped sharply: an Indian summer's nosedive into a dawn of thin, grey drizzle. Some of her skin has gone a strange, freezing lilac, and much of the blood is washed away by the rain.

Smallbone gets the call early. He reaches for the receiver as he struggles from a dream which beats to the imagined rhythm of his wife's gentle snoring. Brian Redhead's on the radio blabbing on about Seb Coe winning gold last month in Moscow. *But with the Soviets still in Afghanistan, has sport been politicized for ever?*

Smallbone blinks awake into the morning, wishing he could care less. The sheets look dowdy and creased, the same grey as the light. Not for the first time, he is swamped by a nostalgia for dazzling, fragrant linen and Margaret's fleshy, slothful waking.

He recognizes the telephone voice, but cannot retain its name.

— *Yes, uh huh.* He's mumbling, trying not to sound too rude.

— *A body, sir. Suspicious circumstances.* His stomach growls for breakfast.

— *East London, sir. Just past Stratford.* But has he remembered to replenish the stock of Nescafé?

— *Nasty one. Stabbing. Female. Youngish. Someone needed urgently, sir. Before we move the body.*

Well, he won't be long. The sudden chill makes him hungry, and appetite smothers all else but the remnants of his dream. He unfolds his long body and hauls himself out of bed.

Margaret left a month ago, and in that time he has seen Julie only once. Settling in, you have to suppose: new school, new friends. Not that his darling daughter had anything but a robust disdain for it all.

She'd taken to playing Pink Floyd's *The Wall* incessantly, till the monstrous beat throbbed inside his skull, and he took an oddly personal insult at those mindless, destructive lyrics. He'd have to keep yelling at her to turn it down. Who could've guessed he'd miss it so much now?

The thick belt of flesh around his middle has started to fall away. Chrysalis-like, a new self is emerging. Leaner, more muscular, as though the years are being pulled back. Typical, really, because he's in no mood to enjoy it. He stumbles to the bathroom and reaches for a razor blade.

A bleary-eyed reflection frowns at him with reproach. He ignores its accusation, leans forward to wash and shave. Just before he finishes, he makes the smallest of cuts beneath the chin. He dabs the spot with a towel and watches as the threads of blood spiral down the plughole.

– *Nasty one. Female. Stabbing.* Let's hope there won't be too much blood.

It wasn't always like this, of course. Not ten, eleven years ago, when still in his late twenties he'd just started to play a part in the major investigations. AMIT were the big boys, it really was a step upwards. Everyone else doffed their caps to you, and every fresh, bloody corpse brought a rush of adrenalin.

His first ever was a ninety-year-old, cut up in her own home. The sight of it was horrible, poor old sod's body punctured all over, her nightdress pushed up and her face covered by a pillow. She'd been dead a while when they found her, and there wasn't just blood, but pus and putrid stuff everywhere, leaking from the cuts and open wounds. The sight and the stench of it made him want to vomit.

But it was exciting, too. They followed the trail of blood and it led all the way next door, and they found him there, the neighbour, straight-backed and arms folded, sitting on his bed. He'd been staring into space as though waiting for their arrival, his bloodied clothes folded and ready in the wash-basket in front of him. Great piece of detective work. Really tricky, that one.

Half-dressed, Smallbone makes his way to the kitchen. It's still odd not to have to negotiate stairs littered with girls' shoes and hairbrushes. He peers inside the fridge and cupboards, but finds little more than bread. No classic English breakfast then. Toast'll have to do. He makes coffee too quickly, without measuring the spoonfuls properly. His face puckers in disgust and he pours it out and starts again.

The pager beeps twice, and he goes over to the telephone.

– *Any ETA, sir?*

– *Yes, yes. Not long now.*

What difference does it make, really? The poor bitch isn't going anywhere. And even when they get there, if they manage to make good their chase, get all the clues in the right order, what after all, will it come to? Some smart-arse defence lawyer will leap up to save the culprit, quoting textbook stuff about evidence, abuse of process and what not. Whatever. It's nothing but a game. Why hurry breakfast for that?

The kettle hisses again, the second cup is much better. He gulps it gratefully, savours its warmth on his tongue. Sometimes, in the early days, when he'd be all hyped and nervous, Margaret would stand behind him like an angel at the breakfast table. Her fingers would play beneath his hairline, knead the hard muscles in his neck.

– What good are you to anyone if you don't look after yourself?

– Calm down, eat your breakfast. You won't be too late to save the world.

Perspective, that was her thing, Margaret, when he'd been itching to get on with it. To nail the murderous neighbour with the giveaway, bloody laundry. Barely out of his teens, that one had been. Almost a child still. A smackhead, craving and desperate, starving for his next fix. He broke down and confessed quickly, cried all night in his police cell. His parents had known the old woman, used to cook her lunch on Sundays.

Not too late to save the world? He's not saving bloody anyone. Murderers, victims, loved ones: they're all of them damned, all of them.

First off, he has her down as an outsider.

The heavy, tweedy skirt rides ragged over her knees, neither covering nor exposing them, unsure of the fashion. A dowdiness in death as there was, perhaps, in life. Opaque, tan tights obscure her true skin tone; surprisingly slim ankles slip into solid, sensible shoes. There's a smell of real leather. A country girl perhaps; or you could imagine her in a library. Bolstered by quaintness. Not quite modern.

Smallbone squats creakily to inspect the downturned face. The jaw is half-turned, one slanted cheek visible. He leans closer, then stops. A thick, congealed bloodline runs from cheekbone to mouth. Mercifully, the one exposed eye is shut, so it's impossible to tell exactly, though it looks like it's been gouged. He wipes a hand across his mouth. Who could guess if she was pretty?

He bends as close as possible without gagging, and then feels it for the first time. His stomach flutters with a fleeting stir of recognition. Her forehead is unlined, her skin startling in its clarity. Not long out of school, just a few years older than Julie. As he steadies his posture, his palm spreads on the pavement. His skin is getting knobbly and blue-veined, with some uneven, brown patches. But hers stretches smoothly over a web of slim bones, and those nails left unsoiled are polished and filed. Not such a frump then.

The clatter of an East London morning swells dully about him. From a block away, there's the repetitive bellowing of market stalls. Junior officers stand guard by the luminous cordons. Others don plastic gloves and start to comb the damp pavement. There's a boy hovering beside him whose name he can't remember. He points at the woman's clutchbag.

— *Get that. Be careful.*

The boy is less gentle than he should be, and the mess of flesh rocks slightly. Even though the girl is supine, it's as if she's missed her footing. He thinks of her running for a bus and slipping: in that moment, clumsy, graceless. But then again, he could be wrong. Where the dirtied fabric of her clothing has torn and clung, slim, shapely limbs emerge from beneath. The lower half of her body is less damaged and twisted. An exposed thigh curves seductively up under her skirt . . .

His own thinking startles him, and he turns sharply leftwards.

— *Got anything for me?*

The junior officer's rummaging, and Smallbone draws closer. His skin warms as he fingers a string of bright jewellery. Real diamonds, it looks like. Who would have thought it? Apart from that, there's some loose cash, a pocket mirror, lipstick. Comb, tweezers, women's things. But no credit cards or driving licence. Only thing approaching a means of identification is a laminated plastic card with bold black block letters. But the letters are smudged and faded, and so have become quite unreadable. Like a name tag for conferences which no one can decipher.

He turns back to the body, and then it happens a second time. A white hush rushes in his ears, like that old-style adrenalin. When the junior moved the corpse, he must have altered her balance: one forearm has swung forward, and the skull has rocked sideways. Not much, but enough. The coarse, mud-brown plaits that coiled round her scalp looked at first part and parcel of her general frumpishness. Now the coil is tilted sideways. A hairline peeps from beneath. The strands are silky, bright blonde.

She'd been wearing a wig.

One of the boys on door-to-door enquiries has taken a break, gone out to fetch coffees. Now he's on his way back, carrying a broad, cardboard tray. The air in front of him steams with the heat of the drinks. Smallbone takes a cup and sips, crunches at the residue of sugar. He quizzes the boy, briefly, but gets replies in the negative. Others are noticing the wig, the corpse starting to look odder. Like a half-undressed drag queen. There's a purr of an engine, and he wipes his hand on his overcoat and walks up to the cordon.

— *Smallbone! What have you got for me?*

— *Dr Brett! Come with me.*

The doctor has a cold and a big smile on his face. His skin is a grey-brown, perhaps from his fluishness. He's not wearing gloves, and the rubbing of his hands makes him appear a tad gleeful. He sniffs loudly and keeps humming, then flexes his joints showily as he sheathes his fingers in plastic.

— *OK then, chaps. Let's take a look.*

There are sugar granules crusting at the bottom of the cup, but the last of Smallbone's coffee tastes peculiarly sour. His throat tightens as the doctor turns the body. First the collarbone emerges, piebald with bruising, then the swell of the sliced breasts where the sodden shirt clings. But the other side of her face is untouched by the knife.

23

Several officers gasp, let out awestruck expletives. Small-bone's fingers stiffen and the plastic cup falls away.

Dr Brett's grey skin blanches, his glassy tones flatten.

– *Good God! Fuck me. Who'd have thought it?*

Smallbone's coffee repeats on him, and he feels all sick and sorry. Yet grim as it all is, he can't stop imagining the headlines:-

'Top Model Found Hideously Slashed And Dumped in London Gutter'

3

1977

She had been watching him now for almost a week.

Following him with her eyes for days before they spoke. He was tallish, and lacked the oily sheen of acne that afflicted most boys, and there was a dangerous green-eyed glint to his crooked-toothed smile. Plus a faint scar on his right cheek, a hint of something wild once. It went without saying all the girls fancied him.

He must have had a name, but she hadn't learnt it just yet. Before, they'd had a system at Hollybush where for several days each new arrival walked round with a name tag. Clipped to the V-neck of their jumpers, screaming their identities. She'd had it when she'd first come, and had to endure the endless stupidity of boys marching up with purposeful myopia and thrusting their noses somewhere close to her breasts.

'Oh, hello, Mi-*ran*-da.'

They said it snickering, as though its musical lilt made her stuck up and posh, which was mad because she was a nowhere child, just like the rest of them. Still, their pitiful lips quivered as they hovered near her nipples, and she knew she'd never let their scrofulous cheeks any closer. Not long ago, she'd walked half-crouching, arms hunched over her breasts. Now she stood straight, shoulders back, chest thrust forward. Like the girls in a ballet class from a telly programme she'd watched once. She wore her copper hair side-parted, half covering her face. In the streets, saliva gathered on the lips of old men and schoolboys.

*

Most of the kids at Hollybush were a bit of a waste of space. They liked football and crap LPs and penny arcades. With punk rock sweeping the city, many tried to wear safety pins. One girl pierced her own nose and had to be hospitalized. The staff held a meeting in the common room about the do's and don't's of punk. Safety regulations – big deal, yawn, yawn. Not yet fourteen and nonchalant, Miranda sat in a corner, and flexed her pale upper arms, just to show she'd got the point.

Voguish, jolting staccato wasn't really her thing. They'd probably have laughed and called her square, if she hadn't been so beautiful. Her preference was for melodic things, and she liked to read poetry. She often sat in her room, when Candy wasn't there, or took long afternoon walks down by the canal. In those first days after his arrival, her mind became a fever of love-phrases, and she wrote some of them in her notebook and recited them softly.

> *If ever any beauty I did see*
> *Which I desired, and got, t'was but a dream of thee.*

It wasn't that Miranda hadn't had her fair share of admirers. Mr Davis, her last foster father, had thus far been the most ardent. The Davis household was a place she'd have much rather forgotten, having it in mind as a collection of dark stains and noises. There was always a plastic cloth on the kitchen table smeared with jam and half-fried fat. Mrs Davis made beans on toast at some point almost every day, and every time she served up, Mr Davis would ask for more. *Don't be mean with beans, Mum*, he'd say, and wink at Miranda. He waited for her amused approval, but she gave only a light, sour smile, and then Mrs Davis would ruffle his hair, and shoot her darts of dislike.

The house had constantly felt crowded, no matter who

was in or out, and the walls of her bedroom were a sick, peeling green. She slept in a wobbly top bunk, with four-year-old Jamie on the bottom, and he still wet his bed regularly yet never got told off for it.

She had to leave because Mr Davis surprised her in the bathroom. She must have forgotten to lock the door, or perhaps the lock had not been working. Thirteen years old then, her milk-white chest still skinny. She'd taken off her vest so as to wash beneath the armpits, lathered up the crumbling Palmolive and had heard the door groaning heavily.

Mr Davis came up from behind, so the first thing she'd seen was his reflection. His face was distorted by the steam and the chips on the mirror. Initially he'd looked shocked, and she thought he'd turn and go. But then all movement seemed to stop, and the warm air hung still between them. He reached out softly and closed the bathroom door.

Up close, his skin was rough and dark with pin-pricks of stubble. He had on aftershave, or hair lacquer, and that and his warm beer breath smelt all stale and pungent. He put his mouth on to her breasts and poked his fingers up inside her, sliding aside her knickers, which were greyish, because Mrs Davis couldn't get her whites right. Miranda stayed quiet and uncomplaining, swallowing disgust like vile medicine, keeping her sickened, angry gaze on a mouldy crack in the ceiling. Eventually, he finished with a low, jolting moan.

Much later, when it had all gone on for too long to keep quiet about, she cried loudly whilst speaking to Mrs Lincoln, the social worker. Mrs Lincoln shook her head and gave her a tentative hug. Mrs Davis screamed at her with narrowed eyes and called her a witch. *Always odd, with her fancy ways and reading*, was how she'd described Miranda. Mr Davis appeared to stop shaving altogether and acquired eyes like a blood-hound's. There was some sort of investigation. Miranda found herself outward bound.

*

Hollybush House was in a posh part of town. It had pointed gables and ivy, a gravel drive and big bay windows. A few years back, it had been a hospice, and before that, a prep school. And still before that, a real family had lived in it. It didn't matter to Miranda that inside it was impossibly shabby – the rec room carpet, for example, a quite disgusting burnt brown. The zoo wasn't far off, the park even nearer. If you skirted beyond the neighbours' houses, in no time you reached the canal.

Kids who lived in nearby houses went to snobby paying schools, and there'd be frequent visits from neighbours with petitions complaining of 'disorderliness'. The neighbours wanted to hold summer street parties to celebrate the Queen's silver jubilee, and you could tell they were alarmed at the thought of including the Hollybush contingent. Not that they needed to worry unduly: the nowhere children preferred to go down the King's Road with Krazy Kolour in their hair. They chattered about which of their body parts they might put a ring through next, and taunted passing rich kids with every fresh curse they could muster. Residential workers like Richard called the petitioning neighbours tossers.

Yet to Miranda there was an almost Victorian orderliness to Hollybush, like the orphanages described in novels by Noel Streatfeild. There were meals at fixed times, and curfews each night. The ones like her, who didn't have learning difficulties or a serious criminal record, went to a real school nearby. Others stayed in for study periods under strictest supervision. The dangerous ones weren't allowed out except with one of the workers. The most dangerous of all got beatings, and if, after that, they still didn't behave, they got sent somewhere else and were sometimes never heard of again.

Miranda chose her moment carefully. Anyone else would have thought it just coincidence.

'I hate you! I *hate* you.' She listened as the voice wafted upwards through the shadows. 'Tosser. Wanker. I hate you.' It shuddered with emotion.

It was Sunday afternoon, a rest period at Hollybush. Some of the kids who knew their parents had actually gone home for lunch. The big house echoed with absences. The voice shuddered again. Miranda rose from the quiet place on the stairs where she'd been sitting.

She approached him slowly, from behind, where he sat in the open doorway. The hot June day spread out beyond, and the yard was thick with rubbish smells. His shoulders moved beneath his shirt, but she couldn't picture what he was doing. The voice broke thickly between words, almost into sobs. It was odd to hear a man cry, though sometimes Mr Davis had.

'I'm sorry. Is something wrong?'

He jerked round and blushed deeply, his torso and shoulders stiffening. The surprise on his features thrilled her, sending a rush into her stomach. 'I didn't see you there.'

'I was sitting on the stairs reading, and I heard you. I thought – is something the matter?'

She stepped closer, her legs bare beneath her skirt and her unshod feet soundless. The warmth and the stillness gathered stickily on her skin. He made an abrupt movement with one arm, as though to throw something away. But still he edged aside on the doorstep without being asked, and she folded her naked legs in front of her and sat down there next to him.

'Aintcha got nowhere to go to dinner then?' He looked outwards, not at her.

'No. I had to leave my foster home. Got no parents to go to.'

'Me neither. 'Squiet today.'

They stared out at the concrete, and beyond that the wild

grasses punctuated by dandelions. She held out her hand formally. 'By the way, I'm Miranda.'

A look of astonishment crossed his face, as though he didn't know where to put himself. But after a few seconds he cleared his throat, took her hand, and answered.

'I'm Mark.'

Mark. A good name. A little ordinary, but quite refined. Even a touch Roman. 'Very pleased to meet you, Mark.' His skin was quite exceptional for an adolescent boy, and his features regular, flawless, just as good close up.

'Miranda. That's a posh name. Where'd you get that then?'

'I don't know. I've never met my real mother.' She leaned back on her elbows, tilting her face upwards to the sun.

'Me neither.'

'Well, that's something we've got in common.'

Through eyes half-closed against the glare, she could sense him watching her, and she sucked in her stomach and puffed out her rib-cage. But when she opened her eyes properly, he was rummaging for something furiously, not looking at her at all.

'Is something the matter, Mark?'

'No! Why d'you ask?'

'Before I said hello, I thought you were talking to someone.'

'Who says?'

'I heard you.'

'Come off it, there's just me here.'

'So you were talking to yourself?'

'I was *not*. Look, can't you just mind your own business.'

'Sorry, d'you want me to go?' She stretched her legs beneath her skirt.

'No – it's all right. I – just mind your own business, OK?'

Miranda shifted on her elbows so she was almost horizontal. 'My foster mum didn't like me so I got kicked out and sent here. What about you?'

'Fighting and stealing. Disruptive. Nearly went on remand once. D'you get called Mandy for short?'

'Ugh – Mandy, I hate that. If anything Randy's better.' He raised his eyebrows and she giggled. 'But I prefer to be called Miranda. You got dorm mates?'

'Todd. He's all right.'

'I share with that girl Candy. You know her? She's got brown hair and freckles and she's always reading *Jackie*.'

'Got any fags?'

'Don't smoke.'

The heat gathered around the dandelions and covered the grasses in a blur. Miranda flexed her toes and calf muscles sideways and hit something sharp upon the concrete. She gave a little yelp of pain and then a small bubble of scarlet stained the whiteness of her ankle.

'Ouch! What the fuck – ?' She drew her feet hastily inwards, but not before she'd seen it. He jerked forward, blushing furiously, but by then it was too late.

'Mark – is this yours – what the bloody hell – ?'

He wiped a sheen of sweat from his upper lip, for the first time looking oily.

'Look – it's nothing – '

'But what – '

'Don't you ever stop asking sodding questions?'

He was angry, but it was useless, for she was holding the strange thing now, and he sat there, sweating madly, while she glanced from it to him.

'Well,' she said at last. 'I thought boys weren't supposed to play with dolls.'

Still, you had to admit, this was no Barbie or Cindy. It was a male figure carved of wood, unclothed and unformed. But the soft wood of face and body was freshly scarred everywhere, and where one of the eyes should have been there was a new, shallow hollow. A couple of small pins lodged in the wooden mouth. She recalled his shuddering near sobs.

'Mark! Is this – ?'

'Look, shut up, will you? It's just something I made in woodwork.'

'But it's brilliant, Mark. You're doing your own voodoo!'

She swivelled her body towards him, so he could see down her dress top. 'It looks like Mr Davis, my ex foster Dad. He came in once when I was in the bathroom. He tried to touch me, you know . . .' Mark's eyes had widened suitably. 'That's why I had to leave. Not really because of my foster mum. Though she was horrid too. Can you stick some pins in for me.'

'No pins left.'

'What were you doing before then?'

'Just cutting it with this.' He took out a tiny penknife. Miranda held her breath, and several seconds passed in silence. Then she swivelled closer.

'All right. Carve him one for me.'

Mark wrinkled his forehead, then laughed. 'OK, here's to you, Mr Davis. Dirty little wanker.' He dug the blade of the knife between the stumpy wooden legs. 'That'll learn you where to put it.'

'What about you? Who are you getting back at?'

'Dennis from the boys' home. He made me do a robbery and then pretended not to know and when I told he took my trousers down and beat me with a belt buckle.'

'That's awful,' said Miranda solemnly. 'Worse than Mr Davis. Come on, let's stick the knife in a few more times for Dennis.'

'Die, you silly cunt!'

'Drown in your own spew!'

'Eat shit and pins for breakfast!'

'May you get raped by Princess Anne!'

The yard filled with snorts of pleasure, then quickly turned still. Footsteps sounded in the hallway, drew closer then receded. Quick as a flash, Mark hid the knife in his pocket, and slid the wooden totem back into its hiding place. Then he moved his face closer, and stole a glance down her dress front.

'Miranda.' He was almost whispering. 'Promise not to tell anyone.'

His breath was strangely sweet, his full lips pouty, like hers.

'I won't tell a soul.' She was so close she was touching him. 'Not a soul, Mark. This is our secret.'

For days after that, they spoke only casually, but exchanged meaningful glances at opportune moments. When next weekend came round, they met in the hallway. Mark spoke in a low voice, like some sort of secret agent.

'D'you want to meet me later? Go out somewhere together?' He shifted from foot to foot; she felt the strange rush in her stomach.

'Is wooden Dennis coming?'

'No – let's make it just us two.' They smothered squeals of laughter.

'Shall we walk by the canal? I know some good places.'

'Two-thirty. After dinner. Meet you at the gatepost.'

The hot summer was continuing, and the canal water was still. They followed the tow path round the edge of the zoo, where the air shrilled with birds' cries and the howls of wild monkeys. Pleasure barges floated by.

'If I save up some money, I'll take you on one of them.'

'You'll never have enough.'

'Yes I will. Wanna bet?'

'Done,' said Miranda.

'Done,' agreed Mark. They pressed their moist palms together.

'Miranda – can you come here a minute?'

She moved her body into his. 'There's something in your hair.' He placed his fingers behind her ear lobe. 'Hold on – '

'Is it gone now?'

'Let me just – a little closer – '

He kissed her ear, then her cheek, then moved round to her lips. She opened her teeth, so he could swivel his tongue in. He pushed his hand beneath her dress and she felt her breath growing shorter. Several lurid yelps and wolf whistles rang out from a passing pleasure barge. When she opened her eyes her vision was dancing and blurry. Mark looked at her seriously, and she stared boldly back at him.

'I love you, Miranda.'

And then he pulled her so close it hurt.

4

— The trouble is, sir, we don't know who she is.

The Guvnor's eyes bulge with savage dissatisfaction. His
rubbery jowls work frantically over the last of a boiled sweet,
the pale flesh of his jaw stretching and shrinking by turns.
Smallbone looks at his shoes and swallows. He might just
as well have said, *The trouble is, sir, our main witness lives on
Mars.*

Still, you've got to see the point, it does seem bloody
ridiculous. Here you have a model and a starlet, how can you
not know who she is? The cruel, casual heap of cuttings lies
accusingly on the desk: a naughty schoolboy's hoardings, or
a dirty old man's secrets.

There she is, the girl, in a recent glossy fashion shoot,
hugged by a long turquoise glittery sheath. Terribly glam, like
something out of *Dallas.* Her pipe-cleaner body is sucked
in and thrust out, so she curves for the camera, breasts
suspiciously prominent. Their sudden swelling had generated
a good few lines of newsprint. The colour of her eyes is
shaded by the black paste of her lashes.

And there she is again at a long, oblong dinner table,
laughing uproariously beside some older, tubby, bald geezer.
Her wide open mouth shows two or three silver fillings. An
assortment of semi-familiar faces floats in the background.
In another, she doesn't look beautiful: she's not primped or
poised for the picture. But she holds herself upright and with
a coy, sly smile. Like she likes what she's got and reckons
you'll like it too.

For Smallbone's cash, the only really nice shots are the

earliest. When she still looked schoolgirlish and innocent. Not that she is – was – old now. She must've died at – what? – nineteen? Early twenties, most: perhaps even younger. In some of the first snaps she looks almost indecently young, so that Smallbone gets little goosebumps looking at her, like he's sneaking a glance at child porn.

Crazy, her almost meteoric rise to fame. Not much more than a year ago she was doing a little bit of pretty girl pouting for a few mags read by – who? can't be anyone more than ten-year-old girls and teen boys. Those desperate, furtive, fumbling moments in the bedrooms of adolescents. And then she made that single, so ubiquitous even he could practically sing the chorus off by heart. *Here, There and Everywhere* – you could say that again. Posters, chat shows, even some stupid advert for toothpaste, her smile and her voice inescapable. Not for the likes of Julie, who's much too sophisticated, and for his money the voice and the song are tinny, samey and forgettable. But there's just some folks who get right there, underneath the public skin. Even if they never do anything, they just can't bear to be forgotten.

There's one of the earliest photos of her, from well over a year back. She hasn't acquired that archness yet: she looks little more than an infant. Blue eyes wide, frank and open; fine hair a mousy blonde. A gangly, leggy teenager with a smattering of freckles, suddenly tall but still childish in the too grown-up clothes they gave her.

From the little they've found out, looks like her real name's Louisa Laverty, but the public have only ever known her as Sacha. Nothing more. One of those shorthand, one-word diminutives that denotes instant celebrity. Lulu. Twiggy. Made up to spark association. A little bit Euro in this case, because of the blonde, blue-eyed, candy looks; or maybe a touch Eastern bloc, because of the big lips and sharp cheekbones. Truth is – you've got to laugh – she's probably from Essex.

Except right now that's precisely, embarrassingly, what they don't know.

The Guvnor leans as far forward as his ample stomach allows him. His fishy eyes swim with a flat, rheumy moisture. His open mouth shows an orange smear on his tongue – the trace of the boiled sweet, which has sweetened his breath.

– *Smallbone* – his voice a rumble – *no prannying around on this one. I don't need to remind you . . .*

And Smallbone grinds his teeth because, no, he certainly doesn't need reminding. If you owe a favour to your friends you feel weak, maybe slightly resentful: but a favour to your enemies and you're watching your back for life. The Guvnor leans away from him, puffs out, pats the broad stomach.

– *'Don't know' is NEVER good enough. Get out there. Find out.*

Revisiting the drag where the whole sorry mess happened, Smallbone senses at once that it's not getting any easier. There's flat, matt, city rain all over the pavement, covering the concrete in a liquid film half dust and half dirt. He's got a junior with him – Raff – who's learning the ropes: posh, fast-track type, with a voice good as plummy.

– *Weather's broken, looks like.*

Smallbone parks the motor, hating the dullness of his own voice. Somewhere deep in his belly there's an ache for the memory of summer.

– *Surely has,* says Raff, except the 'surely' sounds like 'Shirley'. Smallbone rolls his eyes. They get out onto the pavement.

A day later and a body shorter, the stretch of god-forsaken road looks bleaker than ever. There's sodden headlines on the billboard outside the newsagents near the corner – 'Top Model Stabbed To Death In East London Gutter'. It looks all sordid and out of place as the blazered schoolkids skip by, popping into the shop for Lucozade and Maltesers.

Smallbone flares his nostrils for the hunt, Raff treads clumsily after him. They skirt a pile of shit and the contents of an overturned litter bin, bumping each other's flanks awkwardly as they meet on the other side. Smallbone's head tilts towards the smeared shop-front of the red-and-blue all night chippy.

— *We'll be starting in there. Just a bit of basic groundwork.*

But the man behind the counter wipes his greasy hands on his apron and shakes his head sadly from shiny side to side.

— *Sorry, guv. Can't help. Innit awful? Gorgeous lass.*

The neighbourhood gossip in the flat above the laundry pokes her head from behind curtains and offers tea and jaffa cakes. Smallbone and Raff sit on armchairs with faded, floral covers, and the gossip beams at Raff a lot and occasionally touches his knee. But she never saw or heard anything, and when questioned closely, she sinks back into the chintz and pulls down thinning eyebrows.

— *You hear all sorts of things these days. But you don't go poking your nose in. Me, I'm not one for snooping for things I'd rather not find.*

The thin, brown-faced man at the newsagents blinks at them blankly. The chubby bloke in the butcher's doesn't look up from his meat cleaver. The lime cordons round where the corpse lay stay damply stretched in place, but no scenes-of-crime officers ever come away smiling.

At lunchtime, they eat in the corner cafe. There are coffee stains on the table and business is slow. The gaff's owner looks cross, like he just wants them to go away. Their plates of egg and salami are all pale and runny. Smallbone has a pang of a flashback to Margaret — their last restaurant meal together — and pushes his plate aside. Raff is looking seriously pained and unpractised: Smallbone suppresses a chuckle – must be more used to caviar.

A bald man with glasses slurps milky tea loudly, steals a greedy glance over his shoulder, then pretends not to have been looking.

Late afternoon and though it's still September, there's a cloud of grey so thick it feels like nearly winter. There are girls coming home from the office who must've dressed this morning for summer, open-toed sandals tripping, skimpy tops all wet and clinging. Smallbone and Raff knock on more doors, but each face starts looking the same: narrowed, mistrustful eyes and sorry, shaking heads.

There's only one door that's different, and that wasn't locked in the first place: lock bust off and clacking in the damp, volatile wind. There's a mouldy, carpeted staircase that leads to some lightless, godless bedsit. Deserted, or so it looks. Socket for a phone, but no line or handset, couple of fuses blown, an empty, unloved kitchenette. There's sheets on the bed, though, ancient and rumpled and slept on, and a horrid old pack of condoms that makes Raff wrinkle his nose. Locals say the place is untenanted, maybe an occasional squat. Smallbone feels like he could weep. This just isn't getting anywhere.

– *Look again!*

The Guvnor bellows, and pushes his chair back. Raff's standing slightly apart in the grey and tawny office, in the space where the strips of light make the dust motes dance. The tiny flecks of dirt have made him start sneezing.

The Guvnor's so displeased his skin's gone a bit purple. Then again, maybe it's just his high blood pressure. He's given up smoking, and today there's not just the boiled sweets, but sticky tubes of liquorice and fingers of Kit Kat. Smallbone nods, doesn't say anything, steers Raff out of the office.

It's desk work this morning: gathering data, making phone calls. The killer's left no clues so far, so find out about the dead girl. At least there's some solid evidence, something beyond doubt. Papers certainly think they've got something to shout about. *Met in model murder dead end.* You can't say it looks good.

First off there's the ageing, celebrity boyfriend. Ex-boyfriend actually, even before the killing: years older with a beer gut, so that shouldn't surprise anybody. Music business and media mogul, so you have to go through five PAs to reach him, and even then they hedge, unsure of what the script is. It's only when Smallbone gets heavy about obstructing the course of justice that the line goes all buzzy and busy and the main man gets on the line.

   — Detective Sergeant Smallbone, sir. Metropolitan police. Investigating the suspected murder of Louisa Laverty. Model known as Sacha. We understand you were recently known to be . . . connected to her. Would you mind taking some time to answer a few questions?

There's some heavy, syncopated breathing.

   — I really can't tell you anything.

   —'Preciate that, sir, and that this must be upsetting for you. But maybe you can give us a few leads. Who were Sacha's — Louisa's — parents? Family, previous boyfriends?

The breather sounds like he's started spitting. Says he got the girl, not the entourage. And even the girl didn't last long. *And anyway, if you disapprove of me, officer, you should see some of the men she had before me.*

Smallbone gags at the thought of this childwoman already clocking up a lengthy sexual history. *Well, perhaps you could tell us a little more about that . . .*

   — Terrible boyfriend she had before me, says the big cheese, warming to his theme, and then he coughs, pulls himself up short, suddenly thinks better of it. *But I don't have anything to add. Anyway, I'm not under arrest myself, am I?*

Smallbone spits chewing gum at the wastebasket and puts down the handset, frustrated. Scribbles 'revisit' on a post-it note, but without much excitement.

Raff's been out doing legwork, and comes back in a little grey-faced. He's just been to the Stella modelling agency, where Sacha's starry pathway started. Apparently she turned up just days before her sixteenth birthday with an older man, her uncle – called himself John Laverty. Laverty got her on the books, started off as her chaperone, then she appeared to leave him behind as she got richer and more famous. Got professional minders and over-protective boyfriends besides. She kept her family out of the limelight. The modelling agency knows everything about her recent party-girl schedule, but when it comes to her past, they seem to know jackshit.

But Raff's got a contact number for John Laverty, and Smallbone lifts the phone and dials it. He gets through to a car parts shop, and puts down the receiver.

St Catherine's House next, looking for Louisa: born 5 May 1962. Eighteen-year-old model, hazy past, poor taste in sugar-daddies, beloved of the camera, chanteuse not-so-extraordi-naire. He goes along in person, walks the wide curve of the Aldwych. Steps into a hinter-room by appointment, submits a request slip, gets it fast-tracked.

– *Sorry, Detective, sir. No one with that name and date of birth. Maybe you should try again. Once you've double-checked your details.*

But Smallbone understands at once that there's been no mistake. This girl – Sacha, Louisa – gorgeous, glittery whoever-she-is, has left her past right behind. One cover after another, and now all the roots are well hidden. So if she sinks, it's without a trace, and he's as far away as ever.

5

The new house that Kit moved to was far from the shops and there didn't seem to be any neighbours. They rode a train to get there for what seemed like a hundred hours, and Kit watched the patchwork of trees and fields speed by in a blur. His mother buttered bread which she cut into triangles, and passed them over to him with paper-thin squares of cheese pressed between. He chewed peacefully and with a somewhat enjoyable curiosity, but when he glanced over at his mother her neck was bent forward and her hair covered her face, like a woman in mourning. She barely looked up when the man asked for their tickets, but fumbled loudly in her purse as though she were scared or angry.

After the best of the light had died, and after changing trains once, they alighted at a station with a tiny, wooden-fronted sweet shop. Very few people appeared to be using this stop, and those who did disappeared very quickly. He stood in the little crescent in front of the station house while Kit's mother paced up and down struggling with luggage and reading from a map.

They took a taxi to somewhere and the driver spoke in a thick-vowelled creak, throwing out words and sentences which mostly Kit couldn't understand. It was colder than where they'd come from and even after twilight the sky was a harder, brighter navy which had its own glare and shine. The road ribboned through meadows that had turned mono-chrome in the half-light. Kit heard the word 'north' a lot and supposed that was where they had come.

When the taxi finally stopped it was outside a little cottage, with grey stone walls and a slate roof, and chimneys like in picture books. There was a fireplace in the kitchen and a metal bucket for logs, and a broad rusty stove which gave off a smell like car fumes. The wooden door which swung into Kit's room was very much like the ones he imagined in stables. Kit's mother warmed milk on a gas ring and made hot chocolate and they sat and stared out of the window together. Transfixed by the endless expanse of the night, Kit licked the sugar between his teeth and relished the warm heaviness in his stomach. He started to let himself drift off into dreams. He heard his mother's breath grow heavier and more rhythmic beside him, then felt her soft fingers at the back of his neck. He cradled into the crook of her shoulder, thinking she – like him – must be enjoying the evening's peace, but when he stole a glance up at her, tears were glistening on her face.

In the slice of time that followed, days were both full and empty. Kit rose early each morning and sprang to the window, keen to watch the change of the light beyond the small square of tangled lawn. If he squinted his view took him to the fields of the neighbouring farm, and he could count distant grazing sheep and strain his ears for cocks crowing. When the morning reached its full brightness he'd dive back beneath the bedclothes, and watch the shapes of shadows playing till his mother called him to breakfast.

They had toast and cups of something hot at the same time each morning, and sat chewing and swallowing with some seriousness without saying much. Back in the old house, he'd had to dress and go to school, but the new grey-stone-cottage-life seemed to hold no place for such things. He asked his mother about it one day.

'Will I have to go to school?'

'Not just yet.'

'Why?'

'There's no room just yet.'

He didn't ask any more, seeing that she didn't look happy. She scraped her hand over her hair worriedly the way she did when she read certain letters – the sort that came on thin white sheets of paper sheathed in long brown envelopes. But he was pleased about the school being too small for him at the minute. It meant the days remained free so he could do really important things.

When the winter started to fade his mother let him play outside again. He could run the length of the garden and slip through the hole in the hedgerow, skipping and cavorting into the scratchy gorse in the meadow beyond. He learnt to tell the trees from each other by the colour and roughness of their bark; grew to understand the shapes of leaves from smooth elipses to fuzzy-fingered hands. He hoped one day to name the birds that cackled and called to each other.

One particular morning, he crawled out through the hedgerow and crouched down near the ground to trace the cries of a woodthrush. Against a wooden, five-barred gate a grown-up man was leaning, with a red, hairyish face and wearing green trousers and wellingtons. The man was smoking and gazing nowhere. Kit held his breath and crouched very still. A small green twig cracked sharply and the man turned and raised his eyebrows.

'Well, well, young man. I didn't see you there. You mustn't cower in that manner. There's nothing to be afraid of.'

Kit didn't hundred per cent understand the meaning of the man's sentence, although his shoulders stiffened with some remembered warning from his mother about strangers. He straightened and brushed his shorts with as much dignity as he could muster, and drew his eyebrows down his forehead so as to appear suitably suspicious. The man parted his lips to show yellow and grey teeth, and then opened his throat to let out a rough crack of laughter.

'There's nothing to be afraid of, see? What's your name, son?'

'Kit.' But he decided he wouldn't shake hands. The man chewed his teeth, and the air went a little colder and then downwind with the birds' calls Kit heard his mother shouting.

'Where *are you*, Kit? Come here, Kit.' Like the faintest, forlornest echo.

'That your mam, son? D'you think we'd better go find her?'

More worried cries filled the air and Kit pulled himself tall and stepped backwards. His foot hit something soft and slimy and he tumbled backwards on to the grass. A strip of something rubbery beneath the skin of his ankle felt like it had stretched and snapped into little needles of pain. He let out a high pitched howl. Over to his right he saw the man's mouth open again, the grey and black teeth a blur, his words incomprehensible.

'Kit! Where are you? Kit! Kit! Kit!'

His mother's searching screeches climbed an anguished arpeggio and then she tumbled through the hedgerow and found him lying in the wet grass.

'Kit! I've been looking everywhere! Where have you been?'

Her cheeks were flushed with heat and scalded with tiny diamond tears; her breath was whistling slightly. She looked all scared and angry and relieved. The grown man looked at her oddly with both eyebrows minutely raised, and took a step towards them, one nobbly, reddish hand extended.

Kit's mother raised her shoulders like a cat arching its back against danger and scooped him up into her arms so the pain jabbed even harder. She gave the briefest, angriest of nods towards the man.

'Very nice to meet you, sir, I'm sure.'

Then she half held Kit in her arms, and as though he were an overloaded suitcase, lugged him back towards the cottage.

As they sat together in the kitchen, a compress round his ankle and warm milk simmering on the stove, she placed a flat palm on his forehead and looked him gravely in the eyes.

'Kit. I want you to understand something. Never, never talk to strangers. Don't tell anyone who you are, not even if they ask your name.'

Kit nodded, but not understanding her, nor why the smooth whiteness of her forehead was suddenly covered in lines.

And later, when the evening was drawing in and he was supposed to be going to bed, he found her sitting at the little table by the latticed window in the front room. She was shuffling paper in front of her and there was very little light left, and the subdued glow of the one table lamp reminded him of candlelight. He walked up to her slowly and at first she didn't see him, and when she suddenly realized he was watching she gave a little start. Then she calmed herself, and pushed her hair behind her ears, and opened her arms for him, laughing.

'Kit, my darling. How would you like a new name?'

He frowned at such strangeness.

'I like Kit. My name's Kit.'

'Yes, you're still Kit. But our surname. We're starting a new life. If people ask you what your name is, don't tell them Kit Mallory, tell them Kit Laverty.'

'Why not Mallory, like before?'

'Laverty's a name I had when I was growing up. We're going to start using it again. It's going to make things a lot better.'

'Why not Kit Mallory?'

'Sometimes, for certain reasons, it's best to change and move on. I want us to have a fresh start out here, and put the old times behind us. And I want you to remember you're my son – Kit Laverty – I'm giving you the best possible upbringing and you mustn't let anyone tell you any different.'

She put her warm cheek on his and kissed the centre of his forehead. 'Now it's late. Time for bed. Go on, I'll come and tuck you up. I'll explain it all some other time.'

In those first months at the cottage Kit's mother remained solitary. He listened and waited for the erstwhile sprinkling of men who had used to visit and ruffle his hair, and drink in his mother's laughter. None came. There was a ginger-haired man with freckles who sometimes came in the morning, and brought big cardboard boxes of milk and eggs and butter. Sometimes he'd stare at her, with squinty grey eyes, and cock his head on one side as though something were troubling him. It wasn't at all the same look as the men who'd once come to have supper with them, but Kit couldn't say why not, nor was it his main concern.

The big treat, apart from the tree-leaves and the birdcalls, were the trips the two of them would make into the village. They took a bus which wound its way through a patchwork of farmland, driving past diamonds and squares of purple and tawny and green. They got off in front of a post office, with a police station opposite. In the village they would shop, which was something Kit loved, for often she bought him toys and other sorts of presents. His favourite gifts were little plastic models of animals, which he was collecting at home for his own private menagerie. The next favourite were books with pictures of animals and plants. One of these such books was particularly splendid. It had pages of drawings, some real and some cartoon-like, etched by a loving artist's hand. Each work represented a piece of flora or fauna in the neighbourhood, and below it a caption with its name, and a little story.

The letters danced like little black darts and would not settle on the page, so Kit couldn't make sense of either the names or the stories. But sometimes he'd get his mother to read to him, when she sat on the edge of his bed, just after she'd tucked him up, with only the aid of a night light. She read aloud names – *Birch, larch, red admiral* – and he'd repeat them just beneath his breath, then close his eyes and see the pictures. Sometimes he'd have to nag her to go through this little ritual: she might laugh, not understanding his peculiar preference. Sometimes she was bemused, or even a little frowny – resentful, perhaps, that he was less keen on regular stories. But he managed to be insistent, and she complied, and he listened intently, slowly building beneath his eyelids his own private, inner library.

Apart from the buying of gifts, there were two other main things which happened in the village: Tea-time and Enquiries. Enquiries involved his mother going to places like banks and post offices and dealing with lots of pieces of paper often with a creased-up, frowny look. The look started at a place between her eyebrows and worked its way outwards, reminding him of when she sat at the table in the front room also shuffling papers. Enquiries were time-consuming and rather boring and he had to sit in grown-up chairs swinging his feet, practising remembering the names of whatever it was he was learning. Adults might smile at him, or speak in a sort of cooing tone. But if he leaned towards them earnestly and said – for example – 'duck-billed platypus' or 'Monkeys are like people, but usually a lot nicer' – many would inexplicably pull away, especially the women. Some of the older ones made faces as though they were swallowing medicine.

The other of the staple activities – Tea-time – was by far the more pleasant. Sometimes he and his mother would spend unending hours shopping and enquiring, and eat very little lunch. Then Tea-time would turn into a sort of hybrid meal that was not quite lunch, or tea or supper. His mother called it High Tea, and now that the weather was warmer, High Tea might be a picnic, consisting of sandwiches and sometimes chicken legs and electric-coloured fizz. If the sun didn't favour them High Tea moved inwards, to the proud venue of Margaret's Tea Rooms.

The Tea Rooms had floor-length glass windows and chairs of red velvet which stood round polished glass tables. Waitresses in starched white aprons over black dresses wheeled silver cake trolleys which clanked along the carpet. Kit's mother said the place was really just a pastiche, an imitation of a more famous Tea Room in some far-off bigger, busier town. Kit didn't exactly understand the meaning of the word 'pastiche', but as pastries were of considerable prominence at Margaret's, he guessed it must be something to do with that.

He was looking forward to the Tea Rooms one nippy afternoon when he and his mother went into the village. Instead of going shopping, his mother had taken him to the library, and he was sitting happily in the zoology section, looking at pictures of ring-tailed lemurs. His mother stretched her palms towards him, motioning that they had to leave, but when he heard the word *enquiries* his heart sank. There was a lady with grey hair and spectacles who looked not unlike Miss Dickenson, and she was sitting on a low sofa reading a newspaper.

'Why don't you leave him with me, pet?' The woman appeared to be speaking to no one in particular, but on closer consideration it became apparent she was talking to them. Kit's mother raised her eyebrows, and then smiled with perfect teeth.

'Would you mind terribly? That's so very kind of you. I shan't be gone long. I've just got a few enquiries.'

Kit wanted to sit at the table and carry on with the lemurs, but the woman made him sit close to her and he smelled her stale-sweet, dried-powder smell. The newspaper she was reading was one of the smaller sized ones, and he noticed a picture of a woman with big teeth and few clothes. He wrinkled his nose, for he was rather repulsed by the show of bare flesh, especially the female variety.

He turned his attention instead to several wooden staffs on the low table. Rather fascinatingly, each held not one, but a collection of newspapers. The bundles of papers on their wooden sticks were more or less too heavy to lift, and the letters made little sense to him, dancing their usual chaotic dance. But the numbers were clearer and Kit studied them carefully, noticing each bundle of papers came from a different year. He saw the numbers were going backwards from this year – 1985 – into the past, all the way back to 1980. That was the year he had been born. He slid the bundle towards him.

Kit spread his hands flat on the table, kneeling beside it on the rough carpet. The paper smelt dusty, and conjured pictures of old people's wardrobes. Slowly, and with some importance, he began to turn the pages.

Because the words meant nothing – or at any rate very little – he spent second upon second looking only at the pictures. Most were of men in suits whose names he couldn't have told you, though he recognized one or two of them from the news he'd watched when they'd still had television. He recognized some of the Royal Family – Queen Elizabeth, Princess Di – and other assorted faces and figures who had floated in and out of the headlines.

Then, in one of the papers towards the end of the year, Kit found himself staring at a picture of a man. Next to him was a separate picture of a girl, who had bare shoulders and a wide smile and whose eyes looked all painted. Kit decided she had a nasty look, especially as she was wearing such skimpy clothing. But for reasons he couldn't understand, he found the man decidedly handsome. He had no idea what he might have done to merit being in the papers, but something inexplicable drew him inwards, pulling his whole body towards the picture. It wasn't very long before his small nose was as good as touching the newsprint. Somewhere behind and to the side the old lady's stale-sweet smell drew closer.

'Don't you go looking at that now. That's not something you should be worrying about at your age.' And then – more to herself than him – 'terrible business that was, and such a lovely, sweet lassie'.

Kit wanted to ask the woman what she meant, but there was the sensation of something sharp between his neck and his collar.

'*Whatever*, young man, do you think you are doing?'

His mother's eyes blazed and her tongue frothed with angry spittle. She sent darts of accusation first at Kit, then at the old lady.

'I thought you said you'd look after him, not just let him run wild!'

'He's hardly running wild, pet!' The old lady was so shocked her voice came out a quiet croak: she looked as though someone had hit her from behind, and her spectacles had gone slightly crooked. Kit's mother tugged him out by the wrist, her sharp nails close on his skin.

'That's the last time I ever leave you alone with strangers!'

Tears pricked and swelled at the back of his eyeballs. He was used to this sort of fierce reprimand when he ran away and got lost, or picked his nose in public or got his clothes unspeakably dirty. Simply looking at a newspaper, though, just didn't seem to warrant this.

He assumed, after that, that by way of continuing punishment he'd be deprived of High Tea. In fact, to the contrary, off they marched to Margaret's Tea Room, but in such a stark, frosty silence that it was more like extra punishment. Still,

Kit could not understand what his crime had been. He selected a chocolate éclair from the clanking, silver cake trolley, but was so scared of getting sticky he could barely allow himself to taste it.

Towards the end of the éclair, the lady with the spectacles wandered in, accompanied by another oldish ladyfriend, wearing a pink, turban-like hat. There was a rustling and lowering of voices, and the air turned very cold. Kit knew the women were staring and pointing at them: it felt like the Park Incident all over again, only twenty times worse. Kit's mother flung back the chair with such verve that their cutlery rattled, and whisked him out of the Tea Rooms with the force of a whirlwind.

For the remainder of the season, Kit noticed two things. When he and his mother went for walks in the village, there would be pointing and staring and his mother thrust her nose in the air. Sometimes he noticed her fingers trembling.

The other thing was that she began to close doors a lot more. She particularly didn't like it if he snuck up on her unawares while she sat at the table in the front room shifting her papers. She'd start, and flush, and get angry and upset, so he learned if he wanted to watch her properly he'd have to live among the shadows.

But as the summer drew to a close, and readied itself for the turn, Kit understood his life was to be filled with a newer challenge. One breakfast, when the sky was grey and the temperature distinctly cooler, she called him to sit on her knee.

'Kit, my dear love, I want you to get ready. Autumn is coming round and you'll be going back to school.'

6

Smallbone wakes in a sweat.

A nightmare face with razor-like teeth has been leering at him darkly. Now, with his eyes open, he sees it there still: hovering at the window, hunting and haunting him.

He jerks upright, flicks the bedside light on. Its dirty, almost shadowless yellow banishes any lingering sense of the surreal. A glass of water stands on the little bedside table: another jolt forward and he's swigging from it gutsily. Horrible taste – the glass has been standing too long, and the water's thickened uninvitingly with bubbles on the surface. But it's a necessary prop, to help pop a few Panadol, or banish the nightsweats on waking unexpectedly.

Liquid swills into his system, through his belly to his bladder. He's got to go for a pee now, like a schoolboy caught short. Embarrassing really, this process: standing listening to the hollow, fluting cascade on porcelain, not seeing his face, but guessing it to be all pasty. Odd, to feel so awkward, when there's only him here watching. But Margaret, the invisible angel, was an endless force for tolerance: it was so easy to be accepted by her affectionate inattention to detail. Only being alone spawns this bastard, hostile vigilance.

Too hard to get back to sleep now, so he drags on a bathrobe and pads out on to the landing. Downstairs, the open kitchen door gives on to a shadowscape of piled-high washing up and cardboard boxes. A house in chaos, without womenfolk. He hurries past into the living room.

Smallbone sits back on the sofa, tension battling with tiredness. The face floats again before him, staring sickly in the half-light. The teeth soften into slightly uneven canines and incisors; lips swell into the suggestion of a parting Cupid's bow. The eyes open, peer closely, grow wide and questioning: tiny frown lines tighten and hover over the bridge of the nose. The blunt nightmare features grow clearer and now he sees her once more.

Marianne.

Smallbone sighs. So many nights, since it happened, he has tried to forget, but succeeds only in persisting in a vague, nagging limbo. When he yields to the urge, lets her come, it's a relief. He loosens, slips back into memory. And looks at her.

She's not much past adolescence, he never found out her exact age. A dark fringe falling into her eyes giving her an on-and-off squint: snub nose, schoolgirl's pout. Pimped since her days in one of the those dirty, city children's homes; leapfrogged straight through the teenage years to become the tart with the heart.

— *I'm Marianne, fly me.*

Maybe her real name was Janet.

First time he met her, she was just another streetgirl. Brows drawn down resentfully, each time he came near her.

— *What's your name, sweetheart?*
— *Who wants to know, mister?*
— *Just trying to help you, love.*
— *Then why not leave me effing alone?*

Such sweet, sharp style, Marianne. Never used the full swearword.

Beginning of it all, she just didn't want to know. No favours for a police officer, least of all one like him. All salt-and-pepper hair and the beginnings of a second belly. They only got on to a different footing by accident, after the day she got knocked about by her old boyfriend. Called round and there she was: shirt torn, one eyelid purple. He'd only wanted information: not this broken, splintered girlchild.

– Lor, love, whatever happened?

She'd dissolved into puppy whimpers, and he pulled her into his chest, mussed her hair like a father would, like he was holding his own Julie. Then he felt her ribs beneath her skin, and the shallow place between her small breasts; wiped the snot from off her nose, touched her cracked, imperfect lips.

She'd looked up at him with fear and eagerness, soft-eyed as a rabbit.

– What d'you think you're doing, mister?

And he bent his face and kissed her.

Marianne was the useful contact, or at least so he told the Guvnor. Knew the wheelers and the dealers, was a kid who could name names. Skinny ribs from too much heroin and sniffles from the coke, but she had sweet lips and a sharp tongue and all the pimps and pushers pandered to her. The Guvnor wasn't stupid, could also see it. Smallbone got to see her every Thursday.

– Good detective work, Smallbone.

– Cheers, guv. I got my contacts.

Marianne. Timid and bold, stupid and wise. Never grown up, old before her time. She'd wanted to be a model – Christie Brinkley, Jerry Hall. Dress up as a mermaid, do a cover for Roxy Music. Not quite beautiful enough, though. Not really beautiful at all. Pretty, lithe, *gamine*. Beauty?

– It's an inner thing.

– But I wanna make it, mister. I wanna model. Be rich and famous. A starlet, a top girl.

And she pouted her lips and jutted her hip bones. Mouldy wallpaper with posters and glossy mags by the bedside. A hundred LPs and cigarettes instead of Elastoplast and groceries. Drawers of syringes. Dreams to line trash cans.

– You can't carry on like this, darling.

– Just you wait. I'm gonna be somebody. See if you can stop me.

*

55

Morning's coming through the windows and Smallbone's belly rumbles queasily. He holds a cushion to his torso, dreams the lips and ribs again. Hears a set of slow, remembered footsteps, sees a figure looming in the doorway. Still doesn't quite believe he never heard the key turn in the lock.

Day breaks in the garden, one dream blurs into another. A string of disappeared faces floating in the half-dark. Margaret, Julie, Marianne, and now this new one. Sacha. Another woman-child with no past and now without a future. All pimped up and packaged. Ready for the killing.

The guvnor's taken leave, something to do with personals. Mother-in-law's fallen ill, or somesuch similar nonsense. Just as well, all told, because this game's looking none too clever. It's coming up to October, nearly three weeks since the killing, and though the tabloids keep on whining there's precious little sign of a breakthrough. *999 Police* hasn't yielded anything, nor the boys at forensics. Loads of callers wanting their say, but no one telling them anything.

It's a dull, nothingish afternoon, which makes you just wish you could hibernate. The office – the carpet, the blind, the concrete – all boringly, mundanely grey. Raff's sitting skew-whiff at his desk, sorting memo cards and messages. He picks his teeth with the rump end of a lollipop, like he's playing at being Kojak.

– *Got anything for me, son?*

– *Bunch of nothing really. Jackshit.*

Raff says the words too poshly, like his mouth finds them too dirty. Like he's copying something he heard on some American TV cop show. Then goes on –

– *Just this, I suppose. Sounds slightly interesting. Two witnesses saying the same thing. Same time early hours, they heard a cry in the night. Looked out of their windows. Saw a small figure running.*

– *Distance?*

— Forty feet?

— Night-time? Good street lighting?

— Pretty hard to say, sir.

— And they'd recognize him again?

Raff's chin falls on to his chest. The afternoon ticks on.

Four-thirtyish, and they're taking a gloomy tea break. Guvnor phones in, leaves a message. Thankfully, Smallbone's otherwise engaged at the time. He pictures his moribund boss at his mother-in-law's bedside, gnashing his teeth at the sloth of his minions.

Still right where they started, a corpse without a killer. A hit man with no tracks, and a dead girl with no history. Sacha, Louisa Laverty. Who in fuck's name are you?

As evening draws in, the still air swells with stale tobacco. He looks across the room at Raff, who's sitting grimly with his feet up.

— Good God, son. When did you take up smoking?

— Sorry, sir.

— Don't apologize. But when did things get that bad?

They face each other gloomily. The telephone rings tinnily.

— Smallbone, CID.

— Incident Room, sir. Got a caller seen 999 Police. Wants to speak to you, sir. You're free to take the call?

— Put 'em through.

Smallbone raises a finger at Raff, mouths, *Gimme a second.* The line buzzes, he thinks he's lost the call, curses mildly but with feeling. And then a voice comes on the line.

— Hello? Hello?

— Detective Sergeant Smallbone, madam. Dealing with the Louise Laverty murder inquiry. I understand you said you knew something that could help us.

The voice coughs, hesitates, says nothing.

— You witnessed something perhaps?

— No, I haven't witnessed anything.

He feels his frown lines deepening.

– *Then what would you like to tell us? Perhaps you knew Miss Laverty?*

More silence, for several seconds, though he hears the caller breathing. Then the voice speaks sharply, with impatience, and there's a burst of bitter laughter.

– *Yes, I knew Miss Laverty. I practically brought her up.*

7

Miranda's body was changing, and she liked it. After many months at Hollybush she looked around at her peers and saw them bloom with some of the most vivid aberrations of adolescence. Yet the painful, pimply teenage years – of greasy, stringy hair and flesh stretching rebelliously – had never really afflicted her. Almost fifteen, she stared at her reflection, and hoped never more to alter, or at least not too much. She stretched her long fingers, watched the bones moving like slim straws beneath the skin, smoothed the auburn tresses away from the creamy slope of her cheeks Thank God – thank goodness – or whatever force it was, that had looked upon her so generously and made her the way she was.

Of course it could not be perfect every day. Inevitably, she might wake of a morning and see her eyes rheumy and bleary; notice, at an angle, the reddish-purple beginnings of a pustule. It happened today, as she stood before the glass, the light slanting on to the exposed place just above her ear. She felt the sore, reddish lump at first with her fingers, then turned sideways and swivelled her eyeballs and saw her whole face distorted. Warm, briny teardrops swelled beneath her eyelids, and in a rage of dissatisfaction she slapped her palm against the mirror. The blow was harder than she'd expected, and the soft underpads of her fingertips hit the the rough edge of the glass and came back hot and bleeding. She stared at her image, through the smear of blood and tears. Mark would be waiting for her. The bell went for breakfast.

'What's happened to you?' Mark looked at her critically as they queued up for cornflakes and weak tea. He was looking at the cut finger, now bloodying a strip of Elastoplast, but she thought he must mean the spot, and was sure he found her ugly. She brought a coil of auburn hair forward and flashed her eyes at him angrily.

'Nothing's the matter! What's up with *you*?'

He stepped back, head cocked, regarding her curiously. 'Ooh. Sorry I spoke.'

He walked off with his bowl of cereal, forgetting to add milk. At the breakfast table he sat next to Shauna, who smiled and batted her eyelids at him all through her toast munching. Miranda noticed that she opened her mouth at times which looked most unbecoming. She had protruding, horsy teeth, and she couldn't quite drink without slurping. Mark would never fancy her. She wasn't nearly pretty enough.

Miranda walked home at a distance from her schoolmates, who practised synchronized arm movements as they walked, which they would later try out at the disco. Back at Hollybush, most of the boys pretended to be hard, and preferred the Sex Pistols and the Stranglers, but Miranda liked classical better, though this was a fact she tended to keep well-hidden. Candy had a picture of John Travolta on her wall, but Miranda couldn't see what all the fuss was about. Still, she kept her views mostly to herself, wary of being bullied for snobbery.

It was nearly a week since the spot incident and her complexion had cleared, but Mark was looking at her guardedly and they had not spoken properly since. During a double chemistry lesson, she had stared vaguely at the flapping flame of the Bunsen burner, and felt a heavy, yearning absence in the pit of her stomach.

For five days they hadn't spoken by the time Friday came round. They breakfasted, packed lunch, and then went their separate ways.

The walls of Hollybush House became like the bars of a

prison cell to Miranda. Other girls howled at night, went to the bathroom and cut themselves, and spat nightmare stories of abuse as they gurgled in their sleep. Miranda shut herself in, separated even from herself. She could not understand how the smallest flicker of anger could put a distance between her and someone she loved so much. In the dorm, in the next bed to Candy, she curled tight into a corner and couldn't wait for lights out. Only in the dark, with the whole house softly snoring, did she finally relax into a fiercely tragic solitude. Her fingers travelled the slope of her belly and hip bones, and her flesh softened and tightened by turns as Mark's face swam beneath her eyelids.

One Friday evening, after supper, there was a surprise announcement. People were finishing their food, scraping cutlery across their plates, and Richard got up and cleared his throat and rang a little gong to catch everyone's attention. Sorry to disturb everyone's dinner, he began, and he really did sound apologetic as the low murmur continued. Boys swung backwards on their chairs and one of them – Elliot – fell right over, and there was a jeering and snickering. Someone chucked a mash potato pellet into the nowhere space by the doorway. Richard reddened a little – maybe from anger, or embarrassment. The noise showed no sign of abating so he started to speak anyway, and no one was really listening but Miranda strained to catch his words.

Some of the residents of Hollybush had to start thinking ahead, he said. Those who were sixteen would soon have to start fending for themselves. They couldn't stay there at Hollybush for ever, they'd have to think about their futures. On Monday someone would be coming in from the outside to advise on careers, and there would be leaflets and discussions about education and accommodation. The mashed potato pellets kept flying despite the announcement and in the face of such relentless nonchalance Richard gave up and sat down.

Miranda, however, experienced a lurch of despair. She bit her bottom lip hard. Prison-like as Hollybush was, she could not imagine a world beyond it. But more important was Mark, several months older than she was. By how much exactly she was unsure, but soon he must turn sixteen. He would be out and away in the adult world, and she would be left behind.

After supper, the young inhabitants of Hollybush went off to prepare for Friday night. The house became a frenzy of chewed up words and syncopated thuds, filtered and muffled through walls, floors and ceilings. Startled, lively creatures – neither children nor adults – emerged from their bedrooms in lurid, jagged clothing. Shauna wore a leather miniskirt fastened by a giant safety pin, her bare midriff exposed beneath a leopard print T-shirt. Many of the boys wore tight, plasticy trousers, which made drainpipes of their legs and clung unforgivingly to their crotches.

Miranda went and sat on the steps leading to the garden: the same place she'd sat all those months ago when Mark had first spoken to her. Soon it would be summer again: the evening sky suggested a faint indigo promise. She sat and stretched her legs in front of her, inhaled the minty smell of cut grass. The air was thick and alive with the click of nightbirds and crickets. Each time she heard footsteps, she turned, and then stopped herself: she kept hoping she'd find Mark behind her, but he showed no sign of appearing.

So she sat for longer than she could measure while the air chilled about her, and then not knowing the time, rose to traipse back to her room. She felt she must have been sitting alone on that step for ever. After the quiet of the evening, noise was re-filling the corridors, and there was the clack of door handles turning and a chatter of subdued thrills. On the landing where a handful of steps led up to Miranda's dorm, a random, half-drunken queue had formed outside the bathroom. She stared fixedly at the ground and bumped straight into Mark.

He looked down at her with wet eyes, smelling of stale, beery hiccoughs. Shauna stood beside him giggling, her skirt shorter than ever. Her bare legs were unexpectedly smooth, slim and brown. Miranda pushed sideways – 'Excuse me' – but he caught her by the elbow.

'Oi, Missy. Aintcha speaking to me no more?'

She raised her chin proudly. 'Sorry – excuse me – it's just that I have to . . .' She let the sentence trail unfinished as the bathroom door closed behind her, but when she emerged Mark was still there on the landing. He was half standing, half squatting, but rose to block her as she stepped out.

'Why aren't you speaking to me? Ain't I good enough no more?'

She lengthened her spine, meeting him at chin level.

'Moi? It's you who's not talking to me.'

He drew nearer, all sweat and beer, and a heavy, salty maleness; then bent and kissed her so savagely she could taste a thin string of blood.

The days lengthened into summer. At school, the classroom grew hotter and more airless and rank with the odour of adolescent sweating. The teachers got serious and started talking about O levels and CSE's. Miranda was among the clever ones; she would be doing 8 O levels next year. Mark was in the year above but he didn't go to school. He'd dropped out of the system altogether and was having home tutoring back at Hollybush. Some of the workers who tutored him whispered about him being difficult, and occasionally they'd leave his lessons sucking their teeth and frowning.

When they could, Miranda and Mark met up at the finish

of classes, and he'd walk her home from school, detouring along the tow path. Privacy was hard won at Hollybush, so they cherished those long evenings, especially when the way meandered into a camouflage of shadows and alcoves. Best of all was when Mark pushed her back on to the slope of long, wild grasses and slid his hand beneath her shirt where her chest cavity swelled and tightened. He traced the length of her body, its smooth curves and sharp angles, and pressed his fingertips into her flesh as though groping for the bones and organs beneath. When their hip bones and groins rubbed together and she felt her muscles slackening, she would hold her breath for as long as she could, and then let all her cares and fears out in a sigh.

Miranda could have spent her life like that, suspended in that summer, if only it hadn't been for the coming of the new girls. They arrived unannounced, two or three of them, one Saturday at tea-time, when all the doors in the hall were open so the breeze could blow through against the heat. Miranda, coming down the stairs on her way to the garden, saw them standing there all wearing the same shade of blue. Later she discovered they'd been shipped in from disparate foster homes, and been given identical blue bibs so their minders could identify them. But to her, at that moment, they looked like Victorian schoolgirls, refugees from something out of Dickens, or a half portion of the *Seven Little Australians*. Any moment now some harsh matron or stepfather might come and whisk them away to an unpalatable tea in the nursery. She stood for several seconds watching, and then someone started to play music too loudly, and it blared down the stairs cutting up the quiet in the hallway. She recognized the Sex Pistols in their tirade against the monarchy.

The record scratched, stuck in its groove in an abrasive, repeated staccato. The girlish figures in turquoise floated like

64

wraiths in the half light. The tallest, with long fair hair, stood with her back to Miranda. But as the record continued to stick and jump, she slowly turned and stared. Her fine fair hair fell forward on to her narrow, angular shoulders. Her breasts beneath the bib were small and high and hard, her legs were long with knobbly knees and thighs halfway between slender and skinny. She paused, as though questioning, like a traveller asking directions, and in a slow, protracted second looked straight at Miranda. Even in the shadows Miranda could make out that the other girl's eyes were a clear, corn-flower blue.

As summer reached its sweaty high point, Hollybush sim-mered and turned chaotic. Miranda stuck to her lessons, and attended school dutifully, but those who stayed behind for home tutoring grew increasingly restless. She returned home from school one afternoon wondering why Mark hadn't come to meet her, and immediately heard cries and a metallic clatter from the dining room. Through the half open door she glimpsed Mark smouldering behind an overturned table, the filthy detritus of lunchtime all strewn about and scattered. Mark was staring fiercely at Richard, who waved Miranda away – 'Go on, go to your room now' – and she turned and walked out. She didn't see Mark at all, not even later that evening, and afterwards discovered that he'd been hauled off to the police station. The matter never went any further, and Mark didn't have to go to court, but it was a long time since he'd slipped back into any kind of trouble.

The following afternoon, Miranda came to find him for one of their evening walks, but he was not at their usual place by the steps to the garden. She just caught sight of two lads and a girl – one of the new ones, she thought – snuggling and huddling together, snickering so hard they were grunting, the air around thick with a chemical stench. Miranda turned and left through the front door, and went by herself to the chip shop.

Next day, coming home from school, she was still unable to find Mark. She waited on the step and then hovered in the common room, and then went back to the step where her heel nervously, absently, turned something to ground glass, before she understood she was treading on a used syringe.

When it sank in that, yet again, Mark wasn't coming to find her, she no longer tried to battle with the tightening in her throat. She just sat there on the step with her knees bent before her face and held her head in her hands as an abundance of coloured dots floated beneath her closed eyelids. After the chaos had settled, she unfolded her body, and eventually went back into the hallway on soft, silent footsteps. But at the bottom of the staircase she saw something which startled her: stopping her mid-movement and freezing her to the spot.

Mark stood with his back to her, his shoulder blades tense and sensual beneath the thin fabric of his shirt. Beside him stood the Cornflower Girl, her profile turned up towards him. At first Miranda thought Mark would lean down to kiss the other girl, and her skin that had been laid bare to the evening began to goose-pimple into cold. She saw that Mark's cheeks were flushed, and could only guess at his desire.

But then she caught a familiar, unsettled grinding of his back teeth: he was bent forwards in anger, one hand clenched behind his back. His voice was concentrated and trembling.

'No,' he said, 'but you do it. Myself, I don't want to.'

His blonde companion lifted a delicate fingered palm towards his cheek, the fingertips straining at his cheekbones, tracing a sly, conciliatory arc. But Mark unclenched his fist and lashed the light fingers away, so that the manicured nails left a red spider-line across his skin. The Cornflower Girl gasped and swayed back on her heels. Mark turned abruptly and stared full-faced at Miranda.

A swell of secrecy and surprise, misplaced and mistimed, rose up between them. Mark's jaw had dropped and then snapped shut again, and now he leant forward towards her, as though about to explain himself, but she backed away angrily and flounced past, up the stairs.

Out of the corner of her eye she caught the Cornflower Girl smiling.

It was nearly end of term and Miranda was doing her exams. With a fierce, resentful ambition, she locked herself into her studies. Mark was in trouble again and had a date to appear at the juvenile court. He'd gone out with a local gang and snatched an old lady's handbag. Richard, exhausted and dispirited, had said goodbye to Hollybush, announcing his departure to despondent diners one supper time. His replacement was Karl, who had watery eyes and white blonde hair, and quickly acquired the nickname the Nazi. Mark started an almost instant hate affair with Karl the Nazi, who was strict, and imposed curfews, curtailing summer evening walks.

Now Miranda frequently found Mark brooding in the common room, smoking and rolling his eyes up into his skull. His feet would be stretched out absently in front of him, and often she would remark on a strange smell on his skin. Many nights he'd sit up late watching re-runs of *Starsky and Hutch* on a flickering, half-broken television screen. Even when she went and sat by him he might ignore her, though once as they lay there together in the flickering dark, she got up to leave him, but he pulled her back down, hard.

He grew less and less predictable. Though he would hover around the house, it grew harder and harder to find him. And every Friday evening, when the school week finally finished, and she would rush back to Hollybush, he was nowhere to be seen. Once she confronted him and he red-dened, shifting and staring at his shoes.

'There's things I've got to do,' he muttered, barely opening his lips. When she asked him, What things? he just carried on shuffling.

Once she heard him in the common room – traced a vague, simple recognition of the tone of his voice. As she reached the common room door, the air filled with a frantic flurrying, like the shuffling of many papers or the flap of giant bird's wings. When she stepped across the threshold, there was a rush of dying footsteps, and no one to be seen.

It was the last Saturday of term. Friday night had passed emptily. For Miranda a long two months of holiday lay ahead, and then in the autumn she would go back and study for her O levels. Mark would have to carry on his absurdly called 'remedial education', though to Miranda it didn't appear to offer any remedy whatsoever. Because he was a 'problem case' he might be kept for a while at the home while they worked out what to do with him, but she feared for the day when he entered a new world altogether. Worse still, these days there were things he'd simply stopped sharing with her.

She sat upright on waking, and blinked into the morning. In the narrow bed opposite, Candy was gently snoring. The window had been left ajar to air the room with the night breeze, and the curtain scraped and slapped the glass like a sail against the wind.

Mark must be somewhere in this house. She was deter-mined to go and find him. She would confront him, resolve the turmoil, make him say if he still loved her. Though her insides quaked at the thought of it, still somewhere within her she knew Mark was her soulmate and that he'd never leave her.

She slid sideways out of bed, and went quietly to the

landing. She was first into the bathroom, where she scrubbed her face vigorously, and washed her hair beneath the weak shower till it curled into damp, drying ringlets. Then she slid into a plain white T-shirt and a pair of khaki slacks, and, barefoot on the carpet, she went upstairs to find him.

Mark's dorm was on the landing just above Miranda's. She knocked softly, twice, and Todd the dorm-mate answered. His eyes were red-rimmed and rheumy but he gave a leery smile. 'Y'all right?'

'I'm looking for Mark.'

'He ain't here. Didn't come back last night. The Nazi's gonna slay 'im.'

Her insides gave a desperate twinge. She turned towards the staircase almost falling down headfirst. Candy was queuing for the bathroom; Miranda passed in hurried blindness, not knowing how to escape this terror. The only refuge she knew was the trusty concrete step: right now she wanted to dive face down into the scratchy, long, wild grasses.

But the step and the garden no longer offered any escape. For Miranda had to pass the Common Room, and there, scribbling, giggling and whispering, she found the last thing she wished for. Mark and the Cornflower Girl sat huddled close together. She couldn't tell what they were doing, except that they were bent forward, with pens and papers in front of them, as though diligently studying. The shock of this unexpected activity mattered less than their impossibly close shoulders, the slope of their necks.

Miranda coughed, broke the silence, and Mark and the other girl jolted upright. Her face was all sweetly sly pleasure; his discomposure, then feigned surprise.

'Miranda. Hello. Didn't expect to see you.'

'No, I bet you didn't.' The words came out sourer than she'd intended.

As she drew closer, she squinted to see what was in front

of them, and caught sight of an old black and white photograph of an intense, cropped-haired man. The Cornflower Girl was doodling on a blank sheet of paper, and there was a jagged grid and pencilled lines and names rather like a family tree. Miranda frowned distractedly; Mark's newer companion shielded her work like a secretive schoolgirl.

'This is all really boring, don't bother with this.'

'Don't be like that, Debs,' said Mark, his voice rising a little too high. 'Miranda, I've been helping Debs with some research, she's been looking into her family history, there's something we've been finding out.'

But Debs leapt upwards and cut him short, her lips nearly touching his shoulder.

'Miranda won't be interested. There's no need to bother her.'

Mark started to mouth dumbly, and Miranda gasped in disgust.

'Research, my arse,' she spat, and ran out into the hallway.

8

It's that time again – waiting for Julie. Never a punctual man in his youth, Smallbone can only laugh half-sadly: now it's a life ruled by clock-watching, an obsession with times and schedules. Who'd have dreamed fatherhood would be all about this? Showering before school prize evenings, planning birthday days out, waking to butterscotch sunlight and Father's Day breakfast-in-bed? He shakes his head silently – don't you flipping well believe it.

It's this: one in four weekends, hastily slotted between murder investigations; making sure the house is halfway tidy and worrying about mealtimes; huddling and shivering beneath the bus shelter because the car's conked out again.

He's early, of course, as he always is these days. He was late once or twice at the beginning of this access thing, and the sight of Julie's lost eyes, mouth scrunched against tears, was something he vowed never to cause again. Not to mention Margaret, needless to say. Her voice screeching so hard on the phone he had to stand back from the receiver.

– *Where in fuck's name were you, Jack? Your twelve-year-old daughter, waiting alone for more than ten minutes. Don't you fucking care about anything except your fucking self?*

See, you had to hand it to Margaret. Not always the angel. A woman of many parts she was, you couldn't take that from her.

So since then, it's been different: he won't let that happen again. He arrives well before time – sometimes fifteen, twenty minutes – and parks a little way from the school and rests, maybe listens to some music. Like as not, he'll light up before

71

Julie arrives, not liking to smoke too much when he's in front of her. Once it got pretty embarrassing: there he was, in his car, not too far from the school gates, and a policeman walked past and squinted at him sidelong. One of his own, no less, giving him the evil eye.

– *Anything I can do for you, sir?*

– *I'm waiting here for my daughter.*

– *Care to give me her name, sir? And verify your identity?*

Detective Sergeant Jack Smallbone, and you can piss right off out of here.

Today he's without a car, though, an experience sadly ever more frequent, so here beneath the bus shelter he looks just like any other poor sod waiting for public transport which only rarely obliges. Julie'll be disappointed, she so enjoys their drives together. Hopefully once she arrives it won't be too hard to grab a taxi.

Julie's just turned thirteen, getting to that awkward age. A pretty girl, got her mother's looks, thank Christ for that. Doesn't know too much about Marianne, long may it stay that way. Still lights up at the sight of him, but it can't stay like that for ever. She's not backward for her age, soon she'll have her first boyfriend; no doubt she'll go all clothes-and-make-up, start acting funny in his presence. Women, eh? Don'tcha love 'em? Shame they never had a son, could've gone to Saturday football.

Thinking about Julie makes him peculiarly nervous – it won't do to greet her like this, so he tries to take his mind off it with the newspaper, but that's all doom and gloom anyway. Thatcher talking about smashing the unions, and visions of a new consumer-led society. Suppose that's him out of the picture then. *What can I offer you, five robberies or three murders?* Talking of which, the only other thing that pops into his brain is the progress – or lack of it – in the Laverty murder hunt. Nothing's making too much sense in that department.

Guvnor's back in a few days, and still not much to show for it, save for this caller, who sounds a bit of a nutter.

– *Louisa Laverty? Knew her? I practically brought her up.*

A woman's voice – but not feminine – age indeterminate. Smidgen of cockney, a little bit butch and angry. Sort of woman he just knows Margaret would've hated. *These do-gooders, social workers, they've always got some axe to grind. Cares of the world on their shoulders, why can't they just relax?*

Not that he knows this woman is a social worker. But she's probably not too far from it, given all the circumstances.

– *Spent her life in foster care and children's homes, did our girl. Went from pillar to post, like a parcel no one wanted.*

She gave a raspy, phlegmy cough, so Smallbone knew she was a smoker.

– *So what else d'you know about Miss Laverty?*

A strange, hoarse burst of laughter.

– *What sort of thing d'you want to know?*

– *Anything. Just tell us. We'll decide if it's useful.*

A bit of wheezy breathing, voice sounding none too healthy.

– *Well, for starters, Laverty ain't her real name.*

He'd raised an eyebrow into the silence, listening out for more wheezing, mind ticking back to his fruitless foray into the world of birth certificates. So even the girl behind the cover was a cover for someone else. And to top it all, the dead body was in all that strange garb. Like the starry little nymph had some mania for disguises.

– *Look . . . Madam . . . I wonder if you wouldn't mind giving me your name?*

Another raspy pause, and the voice said flatly, Carol.

Sensing it wasn't right just then to probe further, he chose his words carefully.

– *Look, Carol, it sounds as though you might have some useful information. Perhaps we could talk in person, arrange a meeting at your convenience?*

— I'd have to see about that, said Carol, sounding more butch by the second. But she agreed, between cigarette puffs, to leave Smallbone a contact number. He pictured her as he scribbled it: a puckered, gnarled up smoker's mouth, pink lipstick round the butt end, dyed hair pulled back from her forehead.

There's a patter of light footsteps and a gathered raindrop splatters from the shelter's corner to his shoulder. Who could have predicted such nerves over his appearance on seeing his own daughter? He wipes his jacket shoulder dry, looks up, and there stands Julie. Like him she's a little rainsodden, and a little bizarrely dressed: that strange fashion for legwarmers all crumpled up around her ankles. *Is that really the best way of keeping your legs warm?* he wants to say, but knows she'll fly at him. And anyway, she's beautiful; his heart lifts on seeing her.

— *You dyed your hair, darling?*

There're blonde streaks among the mousy ones. She wrinkles her nose at him, as though warding off unvoiced criticism.

— *Not just me. Everyone's doing it. Don't you like it then?*

— *You know you always look lovely to me.*

— *That's not what I asked you.*

He places a hand round her shoulders and feels the small bones and muscles tensing.

— *Where's the car?*

— *Broke down again. I'll get us a taxi.*

And then the thunder claps overhead and it's bucketing down on them and suddenly — thankfully — they're managing to laugh about it.

He tried to telephone Carol twice without getting through to her. There was no other way of reaching her, and for a bit he grimly suspected he'd lost the lead altogether. Then, on the third attempt, someone picked up the receiver, and the hoarse, raspy breathing already sounded familiar.

Now he sits in his office and looks out at the morning. He can't help but feel an unusual optimism. Although the view is a totally uninspiring rectangle of concrete, a clear autumn sunlight has brightened things considerably. The week's been good-ish so far, starting off on the right foot, after his access weekend with Julie went off quite famously. They got back late on Sunday, and Margaret swore filthily, but he took that on the chin: after all, you can't have everything.

Carol left an address, which he's got scribbled in front of him: it's on a small square of card which he turns restlessly between his fingers. Plan was, he and Raff were going to see her together, but she sounded iffy, and mentioned privacy, so he's going alone this time. Check the lay of the land, and then take it from there.

There's a lightness in his stomach fuelled by real curiosity and he's hard-pressed to pinpoint the last time he felt this way. Guvnor's back next week and it gladdens his heart to think finally he might report that they've made a little progress. Besides, he's been in this business years now, and you do get a nose for things, and there's something about Carol with her butch rasp and smoker's cough. Something about her which tells him he might be on to something.

He's going to see her at home, somewhere beyond Acton way: he's checked it on the map and reckons on just under an hour's road time. He looks at his wristwatch, swallows a brew for the journey, then grabs his file and his car keys and heads on out westwards.

Traffic's light this morning, so the journey's quicker than it might have been. He cuts across Central London and on towards the Westway, then dovetails off the A-road into the dull maze of suburbia. Orange brick shoebox houses squat behind green oblongs of lawn, and at infrequent intervals there's a flash of autumn flowerbed. At least in the sunshine some of it looks almost pretty. He finds the address he's after, parks up and gets out.

There's a mystique about Carol that's been building in his mind, so he half expects a pale face to peer from behind net curtains. All creepy and mysterious, in the manner of TV detective shows. But after walking up the short path and rapping the letterbox he waits several seconds and there's no sign of life. He double-checks his wristwatch, then the address on the square of card, and flicks through his file to where he made a note of the appointment. All present and correct: she's bloody gone and blown him out.

He's so pissed off he takes a cigarette and lights up there and then, smoking fast before grinding the fag end with his heel into the doorstep. But just as he's about to go, there's a gust of wind and a creaking, and he turns to see the side gate swinging wide open.

He steps aside, nifty like, keeping close to the brick wall: quietly, this time, he edges into the back garden. No sign of an intruder, no trace of anyone running away, but the sash window by the kitchen sink is pushed up and half open. Beside it, a frosted glass door leads into the garden. He reaches in with one arm over a window box of herbs. The door opens easily and he makes his way inside.

The kitchen's tiny, but clean and tidy – neater than he'd have guessed. It's a small, cottagey house, probably two up, two down: across a little strip of hallway, he glimpses the front room, and then the street. The whole house stands in eerie silence, as though no one ever lived here: he can't quite pinpoint why, but it feels more than just empty. The open gate and window might suggest a recent burglary, but everything besides looks immaculate, undisturbed.

– *Carol? Anyone home? Jack Smallbone here to see you.*

He shouts into the silence, his heart beats a little faster. Nothing, no response, so he makes his way upstairs.

By the time he's at the top of the short flight of steps he's got this funny feeling in his stomach, like there's something bad about to happen. Both bedrooms doors are open to show beds all made up and comfy, but the bathroom door is closed and he doesn't want to open it. He stretches out his fingers, glad to see they're not yet shaking. The door swings at a touch and he steps back on to the landing.

It's as if all the chaos in this little house were tidied away and hidden, secreted in one place to burst free in this bathroom. There's a matching turquoise bathroom suite, and smart turquoise floor tiles, but the mirror above the basin is cracked, stained and smeared. Fuck knows what's happened here. All manner of liquid filth runs in the spaces between the floor tiles, the shower curtain's torn down and twisted, and draped halfway across the room. The print on it's a laughing dolphin, ripped cruelly in two. And there, skewed and crumpled, beneath the top half of the dolphin, lies a woman with dyed hair pulled back and a puckered, smoker's mouth. Maybe in her fifties, maybe older or younger: if this, indeed, is Carol, his earlier vision was uncannily prescient. But for Chrissake he never thought he'd find her like this.

Strangled by the shower curtain, spittle drying round her gnarled mouth, her skull askew on her thin neck: dead as a doornail.

9

Kit caught sight of her from some way off, waiting at the gates. Just then, he thought he saw her as other people saw her. But not just any people: grown-ups; and not just any grown-up: men. He understood at that moment that his mother was a precious thing – fragile and special, infinitely breakable.

The startling red of her hair against the whiteness of skin drew him in towards refuge from a cruel and jeering world. Hearing and vision played tricks with the moment: the playground gates came forward, all giant and gaping; the noise of others receded, like watery echoes at the swimming pool.

She blinked vigorously on seeing him with wide, moist eyes, and then he forgot everything as she caught him up and he smelt her safe, friendly smell. One of the other boys passed by, and his echo voice got clear and close, and Kit didn't hear words but caught the sing-song tone of cruelty. His mother's fingers pressed his scalp, rubbing away the hurt and bullying.

Every time he stepped away, out through the playground gates, Kit felt sharp, sweet relief and never wanted to go back. Next day, when morning came, unfailingly he attempted to feign insurmountable illness. Sometimes it worked, and his mother would smile down on him, and smooth the warm, crumpled counterpane with her white, straw-like fingers. She might bring strips of soft toast to eat propped up in bed, or they would sit by the television watching coloured, gurgling puppets. He might hear her talking on the telephone to someone teacherly at school, and then when he was better she would give him a note.

But other times she was harsher with him, and would jut her sharp chin forward, her jawline strong and threatening in a way that made her look less pretty. He might pout and widen his eyes, imploring without words, but she would set her heart against him and insist he went to school.

Either way, whether he got a day in bed or not, sooner or later the same cold morning came round. It always felt too early when she pulled back the covers and smoothed his hair from his forehead with sad, smiling indulgence. She helped him dress, and clean his teeth, and they walked together to the bus stop, and in the early, chilly winter days he breathed with purposeful venom. He watched the lace patterns form in the air, and then the ghost vapours dispersed, and the further they went from home the more his stomach skipped with nervousness.

It all started one innocent afternoon with reading lessons. Kit was nearly six now, and many of his classmates could actually read whole stories, their words carefully announcing the adventures of brothers and sisters, pets and parents. Kit hated the mythical, too-perfect families, preferring to let his mind wander to animals and plants, but he envied as well as scorned those slick, picture-book worlds. Today the class had to take it in turns to read out loud in sections from the board. As usual there was a girl, a boy, and a fat stripy cat. None were doing anything very much more sophisticated than sitting, eating or running, and there were pictures on the board which gave pretty good clues as to the words. But when Kit's turn came to read a sick giddiness came over him. Sound stuck in his throat as though big biscuit crumbs were lodged down there, and a horrible grinding noise came out like an engine not starting. Not knowing quite why, Kit stumbled to his feet, and saw Mrs Berg's greying eyebrows drawn into a beetlish frown. His vision went blurry as though he'd eaten something bad and he lurched forward on to the desktop, just narrowly avoiding being sick.

A blend of breathy gasps and snickers rose up into the classroom. Mrs Berg came forward and asked Kit if he was all right, but from her freezing, gingerly touch he knew she was slightly disgusted. She asked two of the other boys to take him to the lavatory and he went with Alan and Gerard to relieve himself and wash his face. In the cold air of the corridor he began to feel better, but when he came out of the cubicle the two other boys were staring at him. Their unnaturally wide grins made their lips look stuck on to their faces. He ran the tap, his shaking fingers sifting water, and then felt sharp pain in his neck, his skull and face crushed forward. Water was dripping from his eyebrows, the length of his upside-down cheeks, and through his coughs he heard laughter, but could not decipher words. When he went back into the classroom his hair was matted and dripping. Mrs Berg looked at him strangely, but didn't bother to say anything.

From that day onwards Kit sat alone at the front of the class, the rest of the class's eyes needling from behind. Sometimes Mrs Berg fixed her gaze on him, and gestured grandly at the whiteboard, as though it were tiny and invisible though it took up half the wall. Kit found this ridiculous as he could see perfectly well. She had a smile he found repulsive, it looked like such an effort, and it showed up her smeared lipstick and the fine grey down on her upper lip.

Maths lessons, it turned out, were no better than reading, and Kit never got asked to say the answers to sums. For reasons which were confusing even to himself, the numbers made him even angrier than the words. He felt as though the mysteries of addition and division ought to come more easily, without the pain of stories. But there were puzzles to solve that were worded so stupidly, he could find no way to pause, understand and unravel. *Jane, Sally and Susan are out buying fruit.*

Jane buys three apples, Sally buys two and Susan doesn't buy any. How many apples do they have altogether? The prospect of such an unholy trio as Jane, Sally and Susan out shopping was so immediately repugnant Kit could not bear to work the sum out. He pictured three unbearably self-righteous children, mirroring their smug namesakes among his classmates, and found himself absorbed by the fervent hope that they would drop all their apples and finish up with no fruit at all.

But at other times numbers carved themselves into his brain with a clarity that burned. Like the time Mrs Berg read out a puzzle about a watchmaker: her sour anodyne voice droned and Kit watched the page before him dancing. At the bottom of a paragraph were a series of clock faces, etched prettily in pencil, times digitally inscribed beneath. Eight faces in all, which Mrs Berg drew to their attention, all the while scratching at her furry upper lip.

'Now all turn your books over, class. And I'm going to ask you some questions. It's about the watchmaker and the times on the eight different clock faces.'

Kit blinked briefly with the book face down on the desktop and saw the clocks clear in front of him, their times written beneath. Mrs Berg's gaze flitted over him in a way that could only irritate, and he spoke out unhesitatingly and clearly, reciting from left clock to right:

'3.45; 4.15; 1.25; 12.05; 11.35; 9.02; 8.32; 5.55.'

It wasn't the answer to any question, indeed no question had been asked, but there was a quiet that fell over the other children and the room turned slightly colder. Mrs Berg cocked her head weirdly and said, Very good, Kit, but it wasn't nearly the same as when she said those words to the other children. Just to add icing to the cake, she went on, 'But I haven't asked anything yet', and there was a smile on her face which looked strangely, definitely unhappy.

'Clever dick, know-it-all,' hissed Alan and Gerard. They

were outside at breaktime, and they stood near to the chestnut tree, speaking in almost identical voices. Kit stood at a distance, loving the shelter of the tree, concentrating on the shiny brown conkers and the huge, fingered leaves. Alan and Gerard's voices got nearer. Kit held a fingered leaf in front of him, but it was replaced by human boys' fingers. Small grubby hands were pulling his face forward, squashing him breathless, pressing him down into the earth. So many seconds passed before the hands at last loosened that his chest tightened in pain and terror and Kit believed he would die. Nobody intervened but there was the sound of a distant bell ringing and then Kit fell forward abruptly as a trail of cackles receded.

The horse chestnut tree incident became just one more in a long line, but something Kit hadn't quite bargained for was the disapproval of mothers. He had begun to expect what he must from louts like Alan and Gerard, but it felt as though grown-ups should know better. Yet when Alan stood pointing at the school gates, beside his mother, Alan's mother forced the hand down but stared lingeringly herself. Kit felt his cheeks burn and stared back abrasively. Then, as he looked longer, he realized something peculiar: Alan's mother wasn't staring at him, but at his own mother. He looked up, as though for explanation, and she pressed his face to her body, shielding him from the glances and walking him briskly away.

'It's terribly rude to point, Kit,' said his mother in her clearest voice, a little louder than necessary, like rich important people on telly. 'Just you remember that. Don't you ever do it yourself.'

Fortunately, the pattern of learning did change with the weeks. Kit no longer had to sit with the class through every single lesson, but was taken outside to a little room some way down the corridor. A woman with long, side-parted chestnut hair was sitting there waiting; at times for Kit alone, occasionally for other children also. The woman's name was Miss Cracknell, and she was a special kind of teacher. She had full, glossy lips and when she smiled, her eyes crinkled and lit up. Up close her skin smelt sweet, like the wet perfume of flowers: she wasn't as pretty as Kit's mother, of course, but a distinct improvement on Mrs Berg.

The others who sometimes came to the class with Kit were Daisy who had pale hair and a cotton wool eyepatch, and Darren, who stuttered and swung around in his chair a lot. Both could read and write a little and do some basic arithmetic, but they had very poor memories and knew no tree or animal names. Kit watched them and felt himself thoroughly superior.

One day, the three of them had a double lesson with Miss Cracknell. They started off with boring word games but as the minutes ticked over, the weak winter sunshine scratched insistently at the windows. A sweetly faint smile played at the corners of Miss Cracknell's mouth.

'Class,' she said grandly, even though there were just three of them, 'I mentioned this morning that the teachers had a treat for you. After our reading, we planned to go out into the playground and talk for a while about nature around us. I told Mrs Berg we'd wait, but as you've all done so well, I don't see why you three shouldn't go outside a little early.'

Shivering with delight, Kit stepped outside with the other two children. The playground was empty as it wasn't yet break-time, the wind a magnified whoosh between the trees' naked branches.

Miss Cracknell asked questions, her smile always constant. *Do you know the name of this tree, that bird, this butterfly?*

Sycamore, said Kit. *Chaffinch, cabbage white.*

Miss Cracknell looked down with an expression of

surprised pleasure. Kit sensed a distant, warm stirring in the pit of his stomach.

'That is excellent,' said Miss Cracknell. 'Kit, you must receive a star. Now, class, do any of you know how trees grow?'

The boring, non-remedials were now coming out to join them, filing into the playground in crocodile and ranging round Kit, Daisy and Darren.

'Seeds, Miss,' said one voice.

'Oaks grow from acorns.'

Miss Cracknell's smile floated in front of Kit, her glossy lips parted, and he straightened his back and started to speak.

'Where there are trees which have flowers, the flowers have seeds which fly on the wind and then plant and grow. When trees have cones, the seeds for the new trees come from cones. You can have male and female flowers and male and female cones. So trees are like people, only better, beautiful not ugly.'

The rest of the children had gone completely quiet. Kit had been concentrating so hard, he hardly knew what he was looking at, but now he set his gaze on Miss Cracknell and she was shaking her head slowly. Her lips no longer smiled, though the jaw hung a little open, but as she took steps towards him he saw she was pleased.

'Kit,' she said at last, a soft burr above the silence, 'that is absolutely excellent. How do you know that?'

'My mother read it me from a book. The book had animals as well.'

'And why is it you think trees are better than people?'

'Trees are good and they help you. Only people hurt you.'

'You may very well be right. Class, I hope you all heard that. Good work this afternoon. You'll get three stars in your exercise book.'

Kit kept his eyes on the ground, but even his shoes went

all blurry. For several long, blissful minutes he thought just of Miss Cracknell, until the lesson ebbed away and the bell trilled through the playground. Only then did the pupils disperse, and Alan and Gerard came up to him, and he saw them near and sharp and mean-looking.

'Oooh, hello there, nancy boy. Who loves ya, baby?'

'Mummy's boy. Divvy. Who's your father, Sissy?'

Kit didn't understand why they were being so horrid just then, but their faces were so close he could smell their foul breath. They honed in below eye level, and he realized for the first time how much taller he was than they were, saw them flimsy and breakable. They ringed their eyes with their fingers, blinking and squinting owlishly, poking fun, he knew, at his different coloured eyes.

'Nancy boy. Divvy. Who's your father, Sissy?'

The sing-song words drummed as blood pulsed in his skull. Their faces were far too near, their owl-ring eyes ugly. Kit raised his head and managed to see right over Alan's. He lifted his arm, saw its thickness and the length of his fingers. He let his tendons relax, loosen: first wrist, then shoulder, elbow.

Thwack! went his palm, open fingers on Alan's cheek.

Thud, went his fist into the socket of Gerard's eyeball.

He heard children's cries around him, the blurred squalls of pain and terror, but too much giddy strength rushed through his limbs for him to concentrate or care. He just stood there, still and smiling, the blood tingling in his cheeks, while a slow, happy groaning started to gather in his throat. He didn't realize until later that the groaning was laughter.

Lots of teachers started rushing out, creased, grave faces full of crossness. They pulled Alan and Gerard away and embraced them like their own sons. Kit got sent home for the rest of the school day. At first his whole heart sang with joy, but then he heard his mother sobbing.

*

The next day Kit played ill and scrambled beneath the covers. His mother sighed and made a funny blowing movement up over her face, so that stray strands of hair flew up and outward like sparks. She didn't struggle with him, or try to make him go: but she didn't smile either, and there were no fingers of toast.

Later, he stood at the hall doorway and overheard her talking. 'Yes, we'll meet with Mrs Berg. Yes, that is a good idea.' When she turned from the telephone her face was strange and scrunched up. He was so near, she had to see him, but she looked all blind and glassy.

Kit tiptoed round for two days, and she didn't force him to get better. When he thought of going back to class, his stomach did sick somersaults, but he began to be scared, in a different way, of staying at home. His mother wandered round, distractedly, and on the second day she didn't get dressed. She hadn't washed her hair that day, and it looked raggedy and ropey. She didn't bother to give him breakfast, and didn't appear to eat herself.

By the time lunch had come and gone and he'd still eaten nothing, Kit stood at the kitchen door watching and waiting. His mother stood with her back to him, still in her dressing gown. He wanted to approach her, but she appeared lost in thought, so for many long minutes he kept a cold, fearful distance. Eventually, though, when his stomach growled too painfully, he took a tentative step forward and cleared his throat.

'Mummy. Can we eat? I'm hungry.'

Her shoulders moved only slightly and she didn't turn round at all so he spoke a little louder and reached out and touched her. Then she wheeled round abruptly, her eyes wide, wet and fierce.

'I'm preparing lunch. Can't you see? What do you want to do, rush me?'

He saw she'd been chopping vegetables and still held the silver-bladed knife, a slivered ring of spring onion glistening on its tip. He stepped back, and away from her, but she laid a hand on his shoulder, the blade alarmingly near.

'Don't you rush me, OK, Kit? Don't you think you've caused enough trouble.'

His eyes widened uncontrollably, started to hurt in their sockets, he tipped backwards, away from her, and slipped out of balance. She was above him, arms waving madly, as tears bubbled up out of him, and he lay there, skewed and snivelling, before her face at last softened.

'Oh, Kit, darling. I'm sorry. I didn't mean anything. You're not hurt, darling, are you?'

She helped him to his feet, pulled him close, and he could smell the scent of onions. She patted his hair gently and then went back to chopping vegetables.

On Friday, they both went back to school for the meeting. Mrs Berg was there, and the headmaster, whose name was Mr Evans. Kit kept hoping Miss Cracknell would come, but unfortunately she didn't.

The talk seemed very serious, but Kit didn't really listen. His mother sounded upset and Mrs Berg looked cross, and Mr Evans just spent the whole time smiling wetly at his mother. By the end of the meeting, Kit wondered if he could leave school, but Mr Evans stared at him, and grinned stupidly.

'Well, then, young gentleman. Back to business as usual, then?'

Outside it was home time for the rest of the children. Kit noticed now it was not the children, but the mothers pointing. Their faces turned towards him like shop window dummies, and a blanket of whispers iced over the playground. A demon voice pierced the dullness at the corner of Kit's brain, and the ugly face of Gerard swam into focus.

'Recognize this, Kit? Remind you of anyone?'

He appeared to be waving a small newspaper cutting. Gerard's mother shook her head but she didn't try to do anything. Kit's mother's arm swung round him and she swept him off the ground.

'You silly little bully,' she hissed at Gerard as they left, her voice shrill amongst the whispers, and a couple of the other mothers gasped, open-mouthed. 'Just go back to your fucking games and leave my son alone.'

Sometimes they hurried home, but this afternoon they flew. She didn't put him back on the ground till they'd reached the front door.

For the next week, after all, Kit didn't go back to school: his mother told them he had flu, and would take several days to get better. She fed him, and smiled at him, though sometimes from a bit of a distance, and he began to form the impression that the rest of the world had disappeared. Then one day he came downstairs and from the landing he heard voices.

'No,' said his mother. 'I told you. No. Never.'

The other voice was deep, a man's voice, speaking carefully like a foreigner.

'Say it,' said the man. 'Say it. Go on. You know it.'

This dialogue went on with little major variation, Kit hiding behind the banisters, knowing it was best not to be seen. The two voices were having a battle, and his mother's voice was winning. Eventually the man went, closing the door loudly behind him.

Something about the stranger was familiar, but Kit was not quite sure what. He concentrated hard, squeezing his eyes shut so tight that tiny dots of dark purple floated beneath his eyelids. Then he saw the old house from before, and he was standing at the garden gate, with Miss Dickenson's hand on his shoulders gently pushing him up the path. Through the window he saw his mother with a tall, straight-backed stranger, and when she had finally shut him out, the whole house had trembled.

He knew the man who'd just left was the same, unwelcome visitor.

IO

Smallbone checks his watch, scratches his cheek, and lets out a big, groaning yawn. It's the Guvnor's first day back, there's a meeting in an hour. He should be preparing his progress report, or at least his excuses. But (perhaps not surprisingly), like a student running from cramming, he's doing everything humanly possible to distract himself from the task.

He's had three cups of tea, answered a pile of non-urgent mail, and now – will you look at him? – he's reading a woman's magazine. Not even one for women, really, but for girls: left behind by Julie, after she'd sat here in this room, flicking away disconsolately waiting for a lift over to her gran's. A favour to Margaret that one, for being so late last Sunday: he did it gladly anyway, but, just like a real cabbie, wasn't allowed inside the house.

The magazine's so vacuous he despairs at up-and-coming youth – which is not, as a rule, a hobby he much indulges in. Page upon page of quizzes about boys, slimming and menstruation; singers and film stars in fuck-me photos, only so saccharin it doesn't look like they could. All the boys look like girls and all the girls look like boys. At least Julie, with her long hair and short skirts, hasn't gone down that route yet.

He thinks back to his own wild younger days – minis, Beatles, revolution. Same old blurred androgyny, different sort of politics. But this girl advertising cleanser, she's got that sixties look: big smoky eyes, starved cheekbones, lips like she's got frost-bite. Gamine, you'd call it. She looks a lot like Marianne. Prettier, but not so pretty. More perfect but less comforting.

There's so much reminds him of Marianne it hurts. You'd think, with lovers like that, the wreckers of marriages, once it's over you forget them. You're supposed to realize your mistake, and then it's the lost wives who really matter. And it's partly true – Margaret does matter: her absence is all about him. He misses calling home mid-morning, the thought of her sitting with her feet tucked under her on the sofa. His chest twinges in panic thinking of the empty kitchen at supper time.

But it's the memory of Marianne that has real sharp, sweet poignance. He feels vaguely fond of the desk because she sat right here once, opposite him: he likes to walk past the park bench where they fed the pigeons. He can conjure the texture of her tongue, the touch of her fingers on his back: thinks if he concentrates hard enough he can re-sense each separate fingernail.

Day after day he tries to unravel this craziness. How this urchin, this streetgirl, has sneaked so far beneath his skin, whereas Margaret's squandered, steadfast, long love inspires only a nervous, vague regret. Will it change with time, grow lyrical: will the pain finally disappear? Or will his heart be scarred for ever just because of how it ended?

Raff's coughing at the door and Smallbone's suddenly embarrassed: what must it look like, him all lost and glassy-eyed, sitting not doing any work with this teeny mag in front of him? Raff looks a little awkward – just how long has he stood there?

– *Come on. He says he's ready for us. Once more into the breach.*

Watching the Guvnor getting angry is like watching someone off a sub-standard, seventies sitcom: a face contorted in cartoonish fury and disbelief. But there's no real mirth in this comedy – it's just painful and embarrassing. Smallbone hears the words spewing out, but tries hard not to listen.

– *What do you MEAN? All this TIME? No FURTHER forward.*

Smallbone thinks of the pasty, fleshy man by his mother-in-law's bedside, arms round his wife, a stalwart in difficult times. *You must have been through a lot*, he wants to say. *Your first day back and all. Take things easy. Wasn't there a death in the family? Or at least a terrible illness. How important can this case be, compared to all that?*

But the Guvnor doesn't look like he wants to take it easy. He's coughing and spluttering like he'll be next up in hospital.

– *All this TIME I've been AWAY and you've achieved precisely NOTHING. And the one witness who could have been helpful has ended up . . .*

Smallbone waits for the last (literally) fateful words to spring out, a little explosion of ire, but instead there's more spluttering. Raff finishes the sentence, with that one missing syllable, and says it so soft and deadpan Smallbone can't catch his eye. He thinks the two of them would crack up, despite all this grimness, because Raff's an all right kid really, give or take a few plummy vowels. In fact, now he comes to think of it, Smallbone feels the chuckle rise in his throat. He has to do a couple of fake coughs to both stifle and hide it. Guvnor's spluttering so much he probably doesn't notice, but when he's calmed down his eyes bulge at them, nastily. He doesn't need to say the words – *So, where do we go from here?* – but Raff shuffles about awkwardly, like he's trying to be invisible. Like he's saying, I'm the junior here, this isn't my fault.

Smallbone clears his throat, redundantly.

– *We could look at this in a positive light, sir. The witness being dead. We have to turn a setback to our advantage.*

You wouldn't have thought it possible, but the Guvnor's

eyes bulge out even further: if he opens them any wider, surely the balls'll spring from their sockets. Amazing as it may seem, Smallbone finds the sight almost sexual: the visible swelling of the organs, the almost tangible response. Sensual, but grotesque. The Guvnor cleans his teeth with his tongue.

– *Would you care, perchance, to expand a little?*

– *Another murder, sir. Stands to reason the same killer. Wanted to kill off a main witness. There'll be common strands to track down. More tracks is easier tracks.*

As soon as he's said it, he realizes his mistake. The sentence babbled out of him, incontinently, announcing its stupidity. Who in fuck's name gets more optimistic at *another* dead body. Even Raff shakes his head wonderingly. But the Guvnor doesn't react like he expected.

– *What*, says the Guvnor, still rolling that tongue around – *what gives you the impression that your witness was murdered?*

Smallbone's upper body stiffens, as though he's been winded. He did the crime report, got the SOCO people, they treated the scene as suspicious. He filed all the relevant papers. They agreed with him, he thought. He pictures the box house, west of Acton, with its orange brick walls, sees again the neat window box, the clean kitchen, tiny hallway. And then that bright turquoise bathroom, with its torn, dolphin shower curtain, Carol's face inert and crumpled, the neck luridly twisted. How could it . . . how else . . .

– *Your witness was a bit of a goer, apparently. Used to be a social worker, that's how she knew our pretty Miss Laverty. Visited poor distressed kiddies in their foster placements, just to make sure they were all right, only you see, she had to give it up, because she wasn't all right herself. Drink, medication. Sufferer from depression. Had several domestic incidents in the past, prone to the odd seizure. Plus her volatile behaviour leads us to suspect her as a suicide risk. As far as this incident goes, there was no breaking and entering, no witnesses to anything suspicious. Old lush in domestic accident, probably half what she wished for.*

– But

Smallbone doesn't even let himself finish the sentence. This is just too surreal, it has the logic of nightmare. The smeared filth on floor tiles, the side gate squeaking in the wind. The sinister, timely coincidence of it, just before his appointment.

– Don't look at me like that, Smallbone. What do you suggest? We devote energy and resources to a case that's going nowhere? We can retain an open file, an open mind. But you concentrate on the real job.

– How do you know all this, sir? About Carol, the witness?

– A couple of your . . . colleagues . . . checked out the neighbours. There were some GP records, as well, plus we got some info from the Local Authority. Oh, and somebody came in to see us.

Smallbone doesn't understand: how did the enquiry roll on without him? He shoots a sharp look at Raff, feels like the carpet's sliding beneath him. Someone, somewhere's got tabs on him, mistrusting, condescending. Is it all because of what happened before, because of Marianne?

– A friend of Carol's also turned up, a young man, apparently. Saw one of your colleagues. Confirmed Carol's history.

– Someone turned up? Just like that? How do you know he was telling the truth? Who is he?

– Carlos Someone. German looking.

– Carlos is a Spanish name.

– Perhaps Karl, then. Look, I don't have the details, Smallbone. The point is, he was co-operative, and everything he said fitted with what we already know.

– But he might have had a motive for lying. Coming forward, alibi-ing himself.

The Guvnor glares. The eyes bulge once more, dangerously.

– He was responding to our plea for information, just like a good

citizen. The way people usually lamentably fail to do, or perhaps you've forgotten? He answered all questions put to him, co-operatively and thoroughly. What, you want him arrested, do you? Without reasonable suspicion?

Smallbone doesn't listen much for the rest of the meeting. He understands that his status in this investigation is in jeopardy: he recalls fragments of the past, and knows how much might be at stake. His earlier, yearning, self-pitying, the whole Margaret/Marianne melancholy, has suddenly dissolved, or at least been superseded. In its place is a sharp heart-thumping, a pulsing of the blood in the ears. That light-stomached nervousness when you know something's going wrong. He doesn't know which is worse, but this second mood's more frightening.

Despite the pressure, Smallbone takes a long lunch, goes to a caff that's just about far enough away to feel distant. He knows he's got to speak to Raff, but he'll put it off for a little while; he doesn't want to get angry or apprehensive, will have to choose words judiciously. At least he's still thinking clearly.

At the grubby caff table, he smokes more than he cares to count, at one point lighting up accidentally between forkfuls, then noticing there's still more on his plate. This morning's nostalgia is beginning to seem like indulgence, like the luxury of drinking scotch alone, listening to sad music. He tries to tell himself love's all that matters, to believe that all this work stress is trivial. And then it all becomes too crazy, a ghastly see-saw of misery and every which way is down.

He drinks tea so slowly and absently that by the time he's finished it's cold, and stumbling back to the station he's feeling quite sick.

– *You feeling all right, sir? You look awful.* It's that blonde WPC. And here's that young gun from Robbery.

– *Cheer up, sir. Might not happen.*

95

He passes by Raff's office and sees Raff rise and come towards him, but he staggers on, nauseated, thinking it's not yet the right time.

— *Sir.* Raff's voice is urgent, unwelcome.

— *Not now. Give me a moment.*

— *But, sir, it's important.*

So's my stomach, thinks Smallbone. And the fact I might puke on you. But Raff persists, undeterred.

— *There's someone here to talk to you. Looks like we might be on to something. Some good news at last.*

Candy had been crimping her hair. She used a machine like a sandwich toaster which gave off the same burnt, foody smell, and her hair came out of it looking not unlike crinkle chips. Singed tresses flying, she pranced round the room, caterwauling at the top of her voice and pretending to be Kate Bush and yearning for Heathcliff.

Miranda felt a deep, superior sorrow for her peers, that none of them appeared aware that Heathcliff was originally the creation not of some halfway eccentric pop princess, but of Emily Brontë. The book had long been one of her favourites, and though she was trying to read Iris Murdoch's *The Sea, The Sea* for a taste of something more contemporary, she found the older classics invariably offered a more thorough and rewarding escape. It was so easy to imagine oneself as Cathy, at home on the desolate moorland, the winds buffeting her bedroom windows as she dreamed of her lost love.

Granted, few may have observed as keenly as Miranda the similarities between an isolated homestead like Wuthering Heights, and a north-west London children's home such as Hollybush House. But for Miranda, Mark was every bit as elemental as Heathcliff, their love no less mystical and overwrought, especially after the disturbing episode in the Common Room.

Then, after she had surprised him with the Cornflower Girl, he had come running after her, his Adam's apple bobbing nervously. He had apologized, begged her to believe him, said he and Debs were just working on a project together.

When she remarked with a snort that it seemed to taking up an awful lot of time, he made her feel good and bad at once by saying not everyone was as clever as she was. Besides, Debs was trying to find out more about her personal history, and her ex-social worker said it would be good for 'self-development'. Miranda thought the Cornflower Girl didn't need too much help in that department, but this was a thought which, for the moment, she kept to herself.

So in the end, she believed him, because she wanted to so badly. Later she would berate herself with a clarity beyond her years: idiot, fool, you just hear what you want to. An act of wilful self-delusion, was what she accused herself of, no better than any other weak female in love. Yet it was a sad, simple obstacle she couldn't quite step beyond. Oh – and yes, there was a postscript: she melted when he fucked her.

They argued a lot about the Cornflower Girl, and it was always better after arguments. Like the rainy Saturday afternoons when Mark's dorm was otherwise empty, and they lay across his and Todd's beds amidst a scattering of exercise books.

'Is it because of her? D'you like studying because of her?'

'Come on, Miranda.'

'*You* come on. Tell me.'

He sighed and set aside his papers with a rustle, his torso sliding tightly into his skinny teenage stomach. When he leaned closer, she could see the shaving rash and stubble; then he rolled on to his side and tried to sneak his hand beneath her sweater. She stiffened with reproach.

'You're so full of bullshit.'

But he had made it under the sweater sleeve, and was tickling her armpit. Her cold-edged scorn faltered, a hiccoughed suggestion of laughter. Now the other big hand was curled round her small body, drawing her inwards, turning her toward him. She rolled with movement, turned belly upwards.

'Mark, you fucking – ', but he placed a palm over her mouth, then slid a finger between her lips, past her teeth on to her tongue. She rolled the softness of her mouth round him, sucking, frowning, laughing. He pulled her sweater up and stared at her, as though seeing her for the first time, sucking on each nipple till it was blood-rouged and hardened. Now he pulled away for a second to look at her, as though admiring his handiwork, and she raised her face and body towards him but he pushed her back downwards. The tips of his fingers travelled the slopes of her thighs, while his mouth worked its way moistly down to her belly.

He always stayed clothed until she herself was naked, had slid free of each last garment, and then he'd spend long moments staring. By the time he slid into her he'd be pulsing to feel her, and would rock inside with a blessed and giddy relief. Afterwards they breathed deeply in the jagged aftermath of pleasure.

Miranda thought of the scrofulous Holden Caulfield in *The Catcher in the Rye*, telling tales of messy adolescent sex that was all tentative, unfinished fumbling. But she was convinced this wasn't it: surely adults did it no better? Salinger might have written about uncertain, straying children, but the love she shared with Mark was strong and shaped by destiny.

Sex, dreams and schoolwork, and tending to her own beauty, were enough for the most part to take up Miranda's time. Those rare minutes that remained unclaimed usually got used up thinking about the future. Miranda thought perhaps she would like to be a writer – if not a novelist, then a journalist. Whatever it was, it should be important and serious.

'You're a clever girl, Miranda,' said her form teacher, Miss Byers, not adding the unspoken obvious *especially since you're from Hollybush.* 'Use your brain wisely. Don't squander your talents.'

Mark, meanwhile, remained at Hollybush as one of the oldest residents. Various social workers and serious types from a place called Juvenile Justice would occasionally hold meetings with him and talk about work placements and further education and accommodation 'in the community'. Miranda thought the bit about further education particularly absurd; if Mark were to be educated, he would have to start right from the beginning. Mark assured her they would wait for him to sort himself for at least another year, that having lost so many months from his schooling he had effectively stolen extra time. But Miranda found herself waking, breathless, from occasional, anxious, meandering dreams, jolting into a panic over whether he was about to leave her.

'Do you ever wonder,' she asked him, as they walked the canal tow path, 'what you might do with yourself when we're grown up?'

She breathed deeply, almost gagging on the stench of gathered rubbish. As the year headed towards winter, it had started to accumulate in rotting piles, which lay oozing and uncollected as the city stewed about them. Adults were forever talking of looming discontent, as though the very turn of the seasons was hindered by the detritus. Miranda thought some cataclysm were needed to cleanse the filth away, and then she could leap headlong into the future dragging Mark into adult territory.

Yet her question came out stupidly, like the musings of infants, and Mark looked at her oddly before giving a half smile.

'We are grown up, Miranda. We're not little kids any more.'

'Oh, Mark. Don't be stupid. You know what I mean.'

He just bent towards her face and drew a palm across her buttocks.

*

She did wonder, sometimes, whether he'd love her if her looks faded: if she were scarred in some accident, or even on simply growing older. At only fifteen, the threat was, admittedly, a distant one, but it swam into focus one afternoon as she sat in the common room. She had been reading *Lolita*, and it was getting somewhat intense, especially the sad bit near the end where Lolita's ankles got all fat. So she set it aside and instead flipped through a glossy magazine, a suitable diversion containing lots of appropriately beautiful girl-women. But then she reached a two-page spread which made her pause and reconsider; eight women sprawling for the camera and the words *Fabulous at Forty*.

Women far too old to be preening and posing across these pages, limbs and torsos curled round captions which gave clues as to who, they were. 'Lynn, commercial director' 'Diana, doctor' 'Jessica, former model'. But their bodies bulged and dimpled in all the wrong places, the skin at their necks was lined and folded, their thighs lax and listless. Motherless for as far back as she could remember, Miranda had no real, close-up notion of what time did to women's bodies. There had only really been Mrs Davis, and she was a creature apart anyway. But if these were the fabulous forty year olds, what about the average or ugly ones? Unconsciously, the heel of her palm pressed her flank, digging into the hard crevice between hipbone and waist.

Jessica, the ex-model, was particularly brazen; as though determined to show her heyday was not truly over, she curved bare-stomached for the camera in black lacy underwear. To Miranda, this looked like a pathetic attempt at the feline. But a cruel scar snaked a divide across her lower belly. Miranda imagined its roughness, like a rope cord pulling the flesh taut.

'Caesarian,' said a soft voice over her shoulder. 'I never want to have children. What it must do to your body.' As if conjured from the ether, the Cornflower Girl sat down opposite, kicking her endless legs up over the arm of the worn sofa. She sucked a spherical lollipop which rouged her lips like an infant's. She had faded jeans which rode low across bony, boyish hips, and a tiny cropped T-shirt which exposed a honeyed midriff. Miranda stared without wishing to and knowingly, as if on cue, the girl's long-fingered palm patted her stomach. It was a gesture of satisfaction, as though she'd swallowed something tasty. She returned Miranda's gaze and curved her lips into a smile. The blue of her eyes startled all over again.

'You're Miranda. Mark's friend. We've never really chatted before.'

For the first time in her life, Miranda felt a strange discomfort. She found herself stretching her limbs in front of her to mirror the long-bodied girl opposite, yet each muscle and sinew appeared to rebel and curl inward. The girl had a jagged, bony face which Miranda found rather horsy, and big teeth to boot, which completed the effect. But her eyes sparkled effortlessly, and with her elongated physique, she drew the room inwards like the mid-point of a painting.

'I'm Debs, of course,' said the girl, 'as if you needed telling. I'm changing my name though. This week I'm trying Tasha.'

Miranda raised her eyebrows. 'You have a different name each week?' She wanted to ask, *which one does Mark call you?* but the words stuck in her throat and her cheeks were growing hotter.

'Just trying them out,' said Debs-cum-Tasha. 'Debbie Burke's so *ugly*. I can't be that for ever.'

'But it's your name,' reasoned Miranda.

The other girl tossed her pale fringe aside meaningfully. 'It's all right for some. How would you like it if you had an ugly name? I wish I was called Miranda. Besides, I've got to think of my future career.'

She spoke tinnily, and her vowels were slightly nasal, and

Miranda heard her own voice, by comparison, come out strait-laced and madame-ish.

'What d'you want to do then?'

'Me? I wanna make it as a model.'

As though to stress the point she slid her buttocks down into the basin of the sofa, giving the impression that her legs stretched out even further. Miranda closed the magazine and picked up her book again.

'What about you, Miranda? What do you wanna do? You're really pretty too, you know. Someone must have told you that.'

Miranda smarted with the faint praise, but pretended not to notice. She opened her book and shrugged and didn't look at the Cornflower Girl.

'Dunno. Have to wait and see. I wanna go to college. Then maybe be a journalist. Do something useful.'

'What, like a music journalist? I love the *NME*.'

'Not really, no. More politics. Arts.'

'Ooh, you're really brainy, ain'tcha? Mark always says you're so clever.'

Miranda breathed heavily into a short, crisp silence. There were muffled thuds as the Cornflower Girl kicked off her shoes. She picked up another magazine, and turned the pages noisily.

'Now she's really great. I'd love to be like her.' The magazine spread open at a picture of Blondie. 'That's something else I'd like to try out: a singing career.' And the girl warbled thinly, but not altogether tunelessly, picking out one of the songs of her peroxide-haired idol.

'Nice,' said Miranda, with what she hoped was suitable terseness.

'Can *you* sing, Miranda? Is that something you'd like to do?'

Miranda could sing, quite sweetly, but chose not to answer.

'I want to do something . . . serious,' was all she would offer.

'*I'm* serious,' said the other, and her voice suddenly hardened. 'I'm gonna go out there and get what I want. Just watch me.'

Miranda did just that, and as an experienced watcher, she recognized in the Cornflower Girl another one of a kind. There she'd be at breakfast, all of a sudden opposite, chewing her damp cornflakes, milk dribbling between fat lips. Or lying in the common room in her school-less afternoons, talking about Miranda's O levels and painting her nails.

'I bet you'll do well,' she said, stretching her long, decorated fingers, as Miranda inhaled the scent of oily, synthetic banana.

'I notice,' said Miranda, 'that you and Mark still go off studying. He's told me about your project, but it does seem to take up a lot of time. Just because you're remedial, does that mean you don't get holidays?'

The other girl tossed her head coltishly and laughed a loud laugh.

'It's not just *studying* Mark and I do. I mean there's all that family tree stuff we do together. But there's a lot more to it than that. Let's call it self-discovery.'

The Cornflower Girl never tired of praising Miranda's cleverness, but her own cunning was quite clearly equal to her prettiness.

'Have you seen Mark?' asked Miranda, as they stood by the garden steps. 'He's supposed to be meeting me. Wasn't he just here with you?'

'I don't know where Mark is.' She batted her eyelids. 'Men. Isn't it terrible? They're a law unto themselves.'

Miranda shifted uncomfortably, pretended to look at her watch. A thin film of sweat was prickling beneath her T-shirt.

'I wouldn't wait, love. You just let Mark be. You know what he's like. When he's ready, he'll find you.'

*

Now the Cornflower Girl's laugh echoed everywhere through Hollybush. Sometimes it mingled with Mark's familiar low gruffness, and she rushed downstairs and through corridors to see if she could catch them together. Somehow, though, whatever she found, it was never exactly what she feared or expected. The Cornflower Girl might not be there – it could be Shauna or Candy – or Mark might not be there: had he escaped her already? Or Miranda's steps led her nowhere: she'd be stumbling into emptiness.

Then again, there were times when she'd get it just right, and there they were on the sofa together, or hunkered down on the garden steps. But there'd always be study cards, and exercise books, as though to strengthen the alibi. And though their faces might be close, there was always distance between them. Seeing them like that, catching smiles of apparent innocence, Miranda never quite knew if she felt relief or disappointment.

But today – still and dull and after lunch – apprehension floated round Miranda like a huge, malignant butterfly. She was thinking ahead to the turn of the year, and her stomach was light with queasiness. The future lay before her, with all its uncertainty, and she craved reassurance, but she couldn't find Mark.

She sat on the landing stairs outside her dorm, a book resting beside her, but found she couldn't read. She laid her head on her hands, felt blood rush against the skull. And then, wafting up the stairs, came the Cornflower Girl's laughter.

The weighty drowsiness at Miranda's temples had melted in moments, and she found herself, instead, stiffly cold and awake. This laughter wasn't lazy and arch like it normally was, but more high-pitched and hurried, and something else besides. What was it, that syncopation, that arhythmic breathlessness? Miranda wondered, then understood. It was laughter mixed with fear.

Miranda raised herself from her sitting position and trod softly downwards. She'd only been listening to the laugh for several seconds when she heard what she least wanted to: a gruff male response. The male laughed, too, but cruelly, and the girl with him gasped. Her voice came out high, in a strangled blend of pleasure-pain. Miranda guessed she was with Mark, though he sounded different, too, but then the chaos of grunts and groans was distorting everything.

Making her way into the hall, Miranda swallowed mouthfuls of air. A sticky nausea seeped through her and bloated her stomach. If she blinked even for a second ghastly dreamscapes rose before her. Mark and the Cornflower Girl, face to face, chest to chest. As she stepped closer to the common room the girlish squeals got more urgent.

The common room door was pulled to, but it hadn't been lodged shut: it swung inwards at the lightest touch of a fingertip, Miranda stood by the doorway, wanting to hide, to see round corners: but she managed to slide back and look in at an angle which half-hid her. What she saw through the doorway made her temperature surge.

Her arch rival stared outwards, her blue eyes wide open. Her gaze was glassily blind, maybe pleasure, or terror. Her arms were round a man's back, and she was pressed against the wall; his head was buried in her shoulders while his torso heaved wildly. Both were fully clothed, though the man's hands scrabbled frantically. But the most surprising thing of all was the man wasn't Mark.

There, doing it in the common room, with the Cornflower Girl, was Karl the Nazi.

First off, Smallbone thinks, this isn't quite right. It feels a little too weird, how things can turn around in an instant. The way Raff stood there, acting all awkward, he thought someone was being funny.

– Someone's here. Wants to talk to us. About the Laverty case, sir.

There was a boy stood at the counter – he really was just a boy – and he didn't want to say anything until he was dealing with Smallbone.

– You are the officer dealing with this, aren't you? There's no one else I need be seeing?

He kept asking it over again, like he'd been rehearsing this for ever, and now the big day had come he just had to get it all right. Well built lad, this one, a little bit skinny, but tall, with good shoulders. And savagely handsome – even Smallbone could tell that. OK, so his hair was almost ginger, but he had these glaring green eyes. Stand out a mile, they would: you wouldn't miss this one in a crowd. And clean looking too: not like your average con. Birds of his age must be falling right over theirselves.

Anyway, there he is, stood there, so Smallbone answers his questions.

– Yes, I'm Detective Sergeant Jack Smallbone. I'm the officer dealing.

– My name's Mallory. Mark Mallory. I want to speak to you in private. And at that point Smallbone notices how badly the boy's shaking.

They go through to one of the side rooms, and Smallbone closes the door beside him, and when he motions that they should sit down, the boy's polite: he says, Thank you. Only he doesn't so much say it, it comes out more like a whisper – all wobbly and squeaky, like his voice hasn't long since broken. But that couldn't be right, could it, because this lad's past that stage: maybe seventeen or eighteen. Must be pure nerves.

Smallbone sits opposite the boy and steeples his fingers. He leans inward gently and offers him a drink. Lad shakes his head, his jaw tightened as though in pain.

– *So, son. Mr Mallory. The Laverty murder case. What is it you're itching so badly to tell me?*

The boy looks right at him – briefly – his green eyes full of terror. Then looks down and away, his fingers winding and weaving.

– *I did it. I killed her.*

There. Just like that. No preamble. No messing. No trumpets, no thunderclap. Biggest case of Smallbone's career, his whole future hanging on it; tabloids champing at the bit, and the Guvnor's eyes bulging. No clues in a five-mile radius, no witnesses, no leads.

And then suddenly this.

Smallbone shifts in his seat: it's the reprieve he's been waiting for. So why does everything about this moment feel so . . . wrong? He coughs, searching for the right words. Sweat gleams on Mallory's high, handsome forehead. There's something gets him about this youth, his skin unpitted by acne scars. And those wide, scared green eyes. He looks somehow – the word comes to him – somehow so *innocent*.

– *Well*, Smallbone says, when the pause becomes just too awkward. *Well*, he says again, *you're quite sure about this, are you?*

The anticlimax, the absurdity, it almost makes him want to laugh. Here he is, nailing his villain, and he's talking more like a bloody bank manager. If not for the poor lad sure as bricking it this would just be a comedy. Smallbone's starting to feel it's like some sort of sodding Monty Python sketch.

But there's nothing else for it. It has to be done.

— *Well, son, on that basis, I'm going to have to arrest you. You don't have to say anything, but anything you do say may be given in evidence.*

Smallbone takes his charge through to the custody suite, gets his details for the custody record before popping him into a cell. Turns out the lad's just turned eighteen, would have been seventeen when he did this, barely past being a juvenile in the eyes of the law. Around the station, the whispering and winking seems to start of its own accord. Like Smallbone's showed up with some flash bird, and they're all eyeing her up. He gives the lad tea in a plastic cup and sees his hands are still shaking.

— *We're gonna have to interview you, son. Get your story down formally. You might wanna get a brief in to help you.*

Smallbone thinks then, as he has done before, of his very first murder case: the nineteen-year-old smackhead who stabbed his elderly neighbour. How his confession spilled out of him just like the old girl's blood. He'd felt all sad and sorry, and he supposed it was always like that: if your prey came to you easily, you had more time for sympathy.

And that's how it feels now, with this lad here in front of him. True, they've waited for weeks for this, no clues but shit to follow, a game of blind man's buff and no tunnel's end in sight. But now this boy's come forward, he's making it easy. And it's sad, he doesn't look the type, so young and so . . . clean looking.

At first, Raff's going to come into the interview with him. But they've shipped in someone senior, DCI Dean. Heavy mob for this one. What really makes it so important, Smallbone can't help wondering. Just because the girl was famous and pretty. Went to parties, wore flash clothes.

Anyway, as it turns out, they don't need to do much questioning. Boy does it all for them, chucking it out like nobody's business. Like he's been storing up the guilt for weeks, and now wants to get rid of it all. Goes full steam ahead and each time he reaches a sticking point, they only have to wait a while then it all starts over again.

Brief doesn't help matters, keeps holding things up. Keeps asking for breaks for further consultation and the like. Female, as it happens, – which sends a little ripple through the charge room – and dead hard, you could see that: inside and out. Kind of good looking, with good legs in sharp shoes, but not really pretty, too steely to be feminine. Smallbone and Dean and Raff stand outside fagging while she's talking to her client, and whenever they go back in she keeps trying to shut him up. *You have the right to remain silent*, she says, like he might have forgotten already. Much good it does her. The lad clearly wants to speak.

– *I did it*, he keeps saying. *Debs and me. We grew up in the same children's home.*

Known each other for two years. Really had something going. But I had another girl – I was so scared. Debs was going to tell her. It all got out of hand. I didn't want no one to find out.

And then he breaks down, all shuddering, and they have to take one of those moments.

The story's a simple one – they've all heard it before – but Smallbone keeps thinking back to the girl on the pavement. The dowdy clothes, the wig, and the ghastly facial scars. It still doesn't feel right.

But the boy's got plenty of answers, seems determined to give them.

– *It was a secret, me and her. Don't you understand, everything was hidden?*

He looks at Smallbone directly and his eyes are so strong and green that Smallbone starts to believe him.

Still there's a lot, when it comes down to it, that the boy doesn't want to say. They ask him about his background, about the other girl, and he gets all sulky and silent. Just mutters, No comment, or nothing at all. Well, who can blame him really? He's saying he's guilty anyway. He's hardly getting any brownie points just for telling a prettier story.

After several hours of going back and forth, countless breaks for tea and tears, they can't go on much further and they decide to call it a day. The boy looks up expectantly, suddenly seeming even younger than his tender years. It's written all over his face: what on earth will happen now? Smallbone thinks of the tabloids, the public baying for revenge. Rotten eggs and filth thrown at the dark windows of the prison van. The stink of Feltham, Scrubbs or Wandsworth. Does he know what lies ahead of him?

— *We'll be back in the morning, son. Have to ask just one or two more questions. Put you down for the night.*

The brief clicks out in her sharp shoes, after re-doing her lipstick. Later, just before leaving the charge room, down the corridor from the cells, Smallbone hears someone weeping.

There's a drink up in the pub, just to wind down after a long day, and a bit of mutual back slapping, not to mention relief. But Smallbone gets a six-pack and a takeaway and goes home early, alone.

Collapsing on the sofa, the aftertaste of spice on his tongue, he thinks over the day's work, see the boy's face in front of him. Thing is, after all this, why doesn't he feel better? He tugs at the ring pull of one more beer can, leans away as it spits open. Kids all of them, kids. His mind winds back the weeks.

There's the girl on the pavement, her skinny, stained body, her beautiful face all cut up. Breasts sliced up by mania. His detective's gut feels bad now, like he's eaten something rotten. He thinks of Julie, instead: what they'll do this weekend. And he realizes with satisfaction that it's nearly two days since he's thought of Marianne.

Next day's grey and misty: he has no trouble waking. All night he's drifted in and out of light, fitful dozes. It's almost a relief to be sitting, exhausted at his desk. He makes his way upstairs to do some paperwork before going back down to custody. Raff looks in on his way past and raises an eyebrow.

– *Early start, sir?*

– *Still got that boy down there. Can't afford to waste time.*

– *By the way, Guvnor's looking for you. Said he wanted a quick word.*

– *Blimey. That's all I need.*

Raff looks half-concerned.

– *I don't think he meant that at all. He was saying how well you'd done.*

Coming out in Raff's posh vowels, the comment washes over him, and Smallbone screws up a ball of paper and aims for the wastebasket. But a few moments later, it happens. The unthinkable.

– *Ah, Smallbone. Hoped I'd find you. Just wanted to say, Keep it up.*

There he is in the doorway. The Guvnor congratulating him.

The words – the scene – the sense of it – all take Smallbone aback, and he has to work a bit to stop his mind and body reeling. He steadies his elbows on his desk, starts to realize just how tired he is.

– *Smallbone. Ready to go again? Ready to go back down for the kill?*

Maybe it's those words . . . the kill . . . that does it to him. Reconjures the girl's body, and the young lad downstairs crying.

– *Smallbone?* The Guvnor's voice is so surprisingly gentle

it could be coming from knowledge of past favours. But also real concern. *Anything wrong, man?*

Smallbone looks up at his Guvnor, his gaze tired and direct. Too weary for pretence.

— *I'm not sure he did it, Guv. Something just doesn't feel right.*

But those ugly eyes are bulging, and the frost descends once more.

— *Nonsense. He's confessed, hasn't he? And, Smallbone, he's your only suspect. Now get down there and nail him. We're sending this one down.*

PART TWO

2001

13

The light had nearly faded before Kit let himself breathe properly. In the grainy monochrome of evening he had felt oddly exposed: stripes of grey poking through the windows picking at the outline of his blanketed body. And the funnelling of air as he exhaled and inhaled was too rude and too loud, as was his heartbeat.

But now darkness had fallen and everything was safer. He might turn in the narrow bed so the springs squeaked and creaked, but they became no more than the unnamed whispers that exploded with the night. Just as owls' cries and tyres screeching might be the howling of ghosts, noises were peculiar and detached and caused wonder rather than embarrassment.

Kit flexed his muscles, felt his body stiff and constricted. Yet even in the tiny bed the sense of freedom was magnificent. It had been so long since he'd lain like this, in a room with curtains and a bedside lamp. And his mother breathing deeply in her sleep just next door. The sensation was so fresh, yet so confusing, he could weep with sheer joy.

These past years he'd seen his mother less and less and then, of course, for eighteen months hardly at all. The boys' homes didn't let him have too much contact, while the Unit had discouraged something they called 'family dependence'. Then of course, once you were inside, no one saw anyone very much.

Kit had never been to secondary school, but he knew lots of social workers. He liked Errol, from the Special School, who bought Swiss chocolate and played guitar, but most –

like Ron and Elsa – he could frankly take or leave. They used to frown when they spoke to him, and treat him as though he were stupid, and talked about his mother being unable to control him. Kit found the idea of his supposed wildness utterly ridiculous, though adolescence did make him broad-shouldered and shamblingly lanky.

He was thirteen and a half when he had to go away to the Unit. By now Kit and his mother had moved to somewhere far nearer to a town, because his mother spoke of something called 'access to special services'. Kit didn't know what that was, and his mother didn't explain, but for a reason he could not pinpoint he knew the specialness of it was to do with him.

To tell the truth, he had wanted a change for some time. Home life was not as sweet as it had once been, and in fact for some months now he had noticed a strange coldness settling about the house. In part, the reason for this was quite simple: during the long winter season his mother had hardly put on the heating. If she caught him huddled and shivering by a silent, lifeless radiator, she would throw him an extra jumper and tut a little unkindly. Also there was far less chocolate than there used to be, and she no longer brought him special treats when he was unhappy.

If he asked her why this was, she didn't answer properly, but made nonsensical comments about tightening belts, and about something called Recession. Understanding this was important, Kit resolved to follow the television news, in the hope this might offer a clue as to when he could eat chocolate again.

When he started the fire at the Sports Centre it had been only a small thing. An evening out with the Special School with Ron and Errol and others, and a chance to play football beneath the bluish, urban floodlights.

'Choose teams,' cried Errol, chewing gum and cracking

his knuckles. The boys divided into two teams. No one included Kit.

'Sit down there,' Errol had said, 'we'll get you on after half time.' Kit didn't much care, and wandered off by himself. The cries of the football boys grew distant like the squawking of monkeys. The sports centre was open, and he made his way into the changing rooms. A cleaner said hello to him, and Kit smelt the sharpness of turpentine, and both of them ended up scrunching his nose at the other. Then the cleaner passed and Kit was alone in the dull, strip-lit corridor.

He found the matches in an empty locker and the place was full of cast-aside newspapers, pictures of footballers, and politicians, and huge-breasted half-clothed women. Kit watched the flame for a long time, transfixed by its blueness and orange, and when he lit the naked woman he enjoyed the warm papery smell. He threw the paper on to the shiny floor and the smell thickened with a slick oiliness.

As the air got too heavy Kit ran out and down the corridor. He didn't look behind him and as he reached the glass swing doors the only thing he really noticed was Errol's wide eyes and open mouth. Errol's throat started jolting because he'd swallowed his chewing gum. Kit never understood why they all took the fire so seriously. No one got hurt and there was barely any damage.

Afterwards, his mother started off on his side, but then a little while passed and even she appeared to shift. She took him to see lots of special doctors, including a woman called Dr Rosen, who wore very thick glasses and reminded him horribly of Mrs Berg. Dr Rosen would spend about an hour with him asking stupid questions, like what he thought of messy pictures, and how he got on with his mother. She talked in whispers to his mother and said things like 'syndrome', 'closed' and 'Tistic'.

Kit could see that, with all this, his mother was growing

angrier. One day, she sat him down and spoke very softly and sadly. She said something which, looking back, he could still hardly believe. That regretfully, reluctantly, she was letting him go away.

The last night they spent together they sat in the kitchen of the small house. Kit could not remember the quiet being as deep or as heavy. She had prepared a big meal for them with soup beforehand and pudding after. Neither of them ate much but the room was full of warm, rich smells. She had peeled the label off a wine bottle so it looked like a fancy vase and filled it with water and tulips cut at the stem. She sat eating with her head bent and each time she flicked her hair back she had to blink her eyes hard as though there were grit and dirt lodged there.

It seemed to Kit, from his memory bank, that he'd spent a small eternity in the Unit. His mother dropped him there by daylight and kissed him goodbye without coming inside. He stepped across the threshold and was met by another female, faceless social worker. Immediately he noticed the smell, and the wandering, mindless crazies. Mad people, not like him. There were no bedrooms, he discovered, just dormitories, and lots of rooms with garish carpets. The dining room had long tables and they served lots of horrid, sloppy food. Eating in the place bothered him, you never knew what they might give you. He'd pick at crusts of bread to remove offensive-looking caraway seeds. When he'd done this at the Special School, many of the others had laughed at him. But here, in the Unit, he saw others did it too. Andrew, who had a braying laugh like a donkey's, would cut up his food for hours then eat only several forks-full.

The Unit was near London, and he pleaded with his mother to move nearer, so she could visit more often. Once they were sitting in the crescent-shaped sun lounge with the pink carpet and frilly curtains, and he asked her when it was that she might be moving closer. Her eyes got very big, the dilated pupils merging into the rims of dark blue iris, so the overall impression was of angry, shiny blackness. A glare of harsh, white light flooded through the curved glass, and for a second – for the first time – he saw the faintest spider's web of lines around her eyes. Her teeth were set and her jaw trembled. A blue vein stood out on the back of one hand.

'Kit. You know I can't come any closer. I can't discuss this any more. You're going to have to forget about it.'

'Mummy. I miss you. Why can't you move nearer?'

'Don't ask me such questions, Kit. You'll just have to accept it.'

She slammed a hand on to the coffee table and an unvarnished nail broke. They sat for some moments in the still-trembling silence. Then she leaned forward and kissed him and he breathed that soft, flowery smell of hers. She held him for a moment, then turned and was gone.

From the other side of the sun lounge Kit heard a cruel, shrill wolf-whistle.

'Mummy, I miss you so bad,' bleated Thomas, in girl's falsetto. And then, changing tenor, in a growling fake American accent, 'Don't yo Mama love you no more?' He was an orphaned thief and a drug user, and an established Unit bully. As Kit turned to look at him he collapsed into snorting, nasal laughter, joined by groups of boys who sat around him. Andrew sat with them, his laugh higher and less controlled. His wide, pale lips were putty-like, his forehead all shiny. Kit clenched his fingers behind his back and strode towards them.

'What you laughing at?'

Kit's voice came out high and low, like a recorder played badly. Andrew jabbed the air with an ill-controlled finger, as though pointing at some secret he was unable to reveal. Thomas just slouched and snickered, one eyebrow raised.

'Don't you get nasty now. Your mama won't like it.'

A desperate hostile curiosity burned at Kit's temples. He loomed tall above the others. 'Tell me what you're laughing at.'

Thomas snorted up at him. 'Steady, freak-eyes. Steady.'

Kit would have slapped him had not one of the residential social workers walked into the sun lounge and shouted, 'Calm it down, boys.'

But Andrew carried on braying his stupid, donkey laughter. 'I know what he's laughing at,' he breathed between hee-haws.

His wide lips shone repulsively. Kit burned up to share that malicious, sneering secret.

Kit had known, of course, that there was a secret ever since earliest boyhood. The locked door of his mother's bedroom was enough to tell him that. But it disturbed him that Thomas might know it, and clearly would not disclose it: that even idiotic, braying Andrew knew something he didn't. And of course Rhys, the very social worker who'd told the boys to calm it down, was probably the one who knew the most of all.

Every so often, after, for example, education sessions, Kit had to sit with Rhys in a room and have a chat. Rhys occupied a role referred to slightly pompously as 'key worker', a phrase which never made sense to Kit, but which he sensed Rhys thought important. There appeared, in fact, nothing key about Rhys, who scratched his head and stammered and gave off an air of vagueness. Typical questions in these sessions included 'How are you getting on?' and 'Why is it, do you think, you have such problems with the other boys?'

Frequently the questions appeared to Kit to be so blatantly absurd that he simply declined to dignify them with an answer. This meant minutes would pass in a silence that was palpably sulky, causing Rhys much animated scratching of the head.

Now and again he'd further intensify the stupidity with comments like 'You don't want to talk about this, then?' or 'I can see that you're obviously finding this hard.'

It went through Kit's mind that there were really better things to talk about – like the two boys, younger than he was, being tried for the murder of a toddler in a shopping centre. Their trial was to be at the end of the year, which was immensely exciting, and Kit very much wished he could go and watch. He wanted to meet the boys himself, for he felt sure they were as misunderstood as he was. But as Rhys blabbered on a little meaninglessly, Kit usually remained silent.

One afternoon, though, he looked Rhys in the eyes.

'I'm not getting on well and I have problems with the other boys because I don't want to be here. I want to go back to my mother.'

Rhys looked awkward, and yet triumphant, and ran his fingers through his hair.

'Ah, now, Kit, I'm afraid that's something you just can't do.'

The words came out to Kit's ears weighted with a peculiar significance. And Kit knew, at that moment, that Rhys also knew the secret. And as one in authority, he must surely know the most. Almost fourteen and still growing, Kit felt his body trembling. Memories of the sun lounge bullying started to replay in his mind. He stood from his chair and swayed, towering over Rhys.

'Why can't I go home? Why not? Tell me why.'

'It's just . . . not . . . possible,' stammered Rhys, avoiding a direct response, and thus confirming the suspicion that there must be some more complex, hidden truth. If he wasn't prepared to talk he would have to have it shaken out of him.

Kit bent towards his prey and lifted him by the shoulders.

Rhys came unstuck from the chair and rose limply, like a label peeled from a can.

'Honestly, there's nothing . . .' he kept spluttering and stuttering, each denial a further emphasis of his deceit. The lies, the duplicity all around here, were too much for Kit, and he placed a hand over Rhys's lips and stuffed two fingers in his mouth. The absurdly titled key-worker choked and flushed up, and little bubbles of spittle foamed out around his mouth. His voice came out in grunts, his tongue now literally tied, and Kit saw with a thrill that he could no longer breathe. He might have pressed him further, just to see what it was like, but other boys' key-workers arrived just in time, and pulled Kit away roughly, before cradling Rhys like a baby.

Kit stayed for another eighteen months, growing to like Rhys no better, and then someone invisible in authority decided to move him to another Unit. They felt a change of scenery might help Kit to change himself, though Kit couldn't see why this was necessary. Actually, the new place wasn't very far, and inside everything was extremely similar, and Kit knew it was really just another branch of the same place, like an outlet of WH Smith in a different part of town. Apart from the move, nothing happened as such. But just for a while, before he left, the key-workers looked at him oddly. They whispered in low voices in the corridor, as though letting him know there were things they hadn't forgotten.

He spent over four years at the next branch of the Unit, and by now his mother was visiting less and less. This was a mixed place – boys and girls – and sometimes pairs of them snuck off together, with beer cans and cigarettes and fingers tightly entwined. Sometimes huddles of boys sat in clammy circles and whispered about the girls, but Kit was never included or party to this whispering. He understood his contemporaries were changing, growing ever more distant from him, but found their adult swaggering distasteful and couldn't see what they had to boast about. He himself was interested in other kinds of development: in both the cities and countryside, in wildlife and politics. He spent hours avidly listening to radio and television, making notes for special landmarks, like new peace initiatives in Northern Ireland, Labour winning the election, or even a new panda arriving at London zoo. And he wandered outside as well, always alert and remembering, keeping fresh his catalogue of bird and tree names. Books were a great fascination to him for he hungered for knowledge, but he had to select volumes judiciously because words remained largely mysterious. If he saw patterns of letters repeatedly he grew to recognize them, and attach them to their meanings. If they appeared alongside photographs, so much the better.

But this struggle to extract the meaning from things was a constant reminder of his own buried past. And as others could read and make sense of sentences long before he could, so he balked at the knowledge that there were more personal truths hidden from him.

Hence his set-to with Paul, who like the hapless Rhys before him was a key-worker with an unhealthy interest in Kit's childhood.

'How are you feeling today, Kit? You're not looking too happy.'

Kit, in fact, had for some time realized that he had long ceased being truly happy. Not since about the age of four, when he and his mother had left the first house. After that, though he'd experienced varying degrees of contentment, the sense of a niggling, missing jigsaw piece had interfered with true bliss. Though this particular jigsaw piece related to a personal puzzle, Kit was quite sure everyone else also had their own secrets. He couldn't understand why they seemed so lax in this pursuit. As a result, he regarded happy people with some condescension: they must be lazy, or ignorant, or hadn't quite cottoned on to something.

So when Paul told Kit he wasn't looking too happy, he immediately went into the bad books. Kit did what he always did when wishing to convey disdain: he bent his head over his knees and refused to say anything. He was forever hopeful that whoever had offended him would get the message to shut up, yet it was astounding how many chose to soldier on regardless. Paul, on this occasion, just would not let the subject drop.

'I know your mother's not been to see you much of late. I understand how you must miss her.'

This really was excessive. Not only did Paul have the audacity to talk about his mother, but also to pretend he understood complex, private feelings. Plus this was a personal intrusion surely too much for anyone to stomach. When Paul responded to Kit's silence by digging even further, the re-emergence of so many demons became all too inevitable.

'I know,' said Paul, stupidly, administering the fatal blow, 'that there are things about your family you must find difficult to talk about.'

If there was anything to anger Kit, it was this presumption of false knowledge. Like so many before him, Paul had to suffer Kit's fists.

This time fellow key-workers didn't arrive quite so quickly. Paul got a chipped tooth, but worse, Kit's fingers went into his eyes, and he had to be rushed off to casualty, while two of his colleagues stood by ashen-faced, looking perilously close to retching. Kit later discovered he lost the sight of one eye, and never fully regained use of the other one. Plus, the old files came up with the memoed attack against Rhys, not to mention the danger Andrew had been in, and countless other minor incidents. There was clearly something wrong with Kit, but people were starting to lose sympathy. He might be slightly unbalanced, but that didn't make him criminally insane. Kit's lawyer hired a doctor, but the Judge wasn't having any of it. It was time he was taught a lesson, except this was learning things the hard way. Three years, said the Judge, of which he'd serve half if he was good.

Which was how Kit ended up in the Young Offenders' Institute.

Having lived for so much of his adolescence in one Unit or another, the process of incarceration did not, of itself, feel novel. But there were other things besides which marked Kit's new life out as different. Astoundingly the food was significantly worse than before. Formal meal times consisted merely of different coloured runny stuff, and heaven knows what foreign bodies might be lurking within. Kit, with his complete phobia of even the innocent caraway seed, found it necessary to devote considerable energy to vetting what he ate.

But a change for the better, Kit noted, was that here he was no longer bullied. On the contrary, those who'd heard of his crime and the injury he'd done to a social worker – a professional, adult male – looked at him with wary admiration. Sometimes, on nodding to him, inmates vaguely muttered, *Respect*. He kept them at a distance, but a more comfortable one than previously. There were no girls here, and the fact that Kit encountered women only in dreams was by now the norm rather than some freakish mark of an outsider.

His mother's visits grew sparser and he longed for her constantly. When she came, they talked little, but he would sit and study her closely. There was a harshness to her smile and to the patterns round her eyes which was no longer obvious only when the sun burst from the clouds. But for the most part she was absent, and his brain held her image as she always had been.

There was one respect in which life for Kit in prison was much improved. For it was here that he first truly began to develop his encyclopaedic knowledge of crime. Other inmates, too, perhaps not surprisingly, exchanged nuggets of information they had gleaned about notorious villains. Kit listened endlessly to the radio he was allowed to keep in his cell and if there were ever items about criminals he made careful mental notes. He engaged with concentrated gravity in debates about police reform, and parliamentary questions about capital punishment. Using his usual technique of recognizing words and studying pictures he took books from the library about the Kray Twins and Peter Sutcliffe.

For all that pastimes such as these made prison life more bearable, Kit still longed to move freely amongst the animals and trees. He spoke regularly to a visiting doctor, Dr Geoffreys, whom he understood to be more of a healer of minds and souls than bodies. Dr Geoffreys squinted often and used phrases like 'long-term care'. Kit had visions of being returned to a world of pink carpets and frilly curtains. He knew once he was released he must formulate a plan.

The day he came out Kit's mother met him at the gates. In the hard light of winter her orange hair had dulled to red-brown, and when she turned her head in greeting he saw several skinny streaks of grey. But she smiled and held her hands out and then he placed his arms about her, and the thin bones beneath her skin were small and fragile as a girl's. They turned and walked towards the station; men still turned and paused for thought.

The train ride back to the house was packed with childish excitement. Kit's mother had even made him sandwiches, just like a train ride long ago. On arrival, she made supper and they sat together in the kitchen. The night air blew in through the window and Kit breathed its gentle sweetness.

But as the evening drew in closer his mother started to look distracted. She fidgeted a lot with her hair, forever tucking it behind her ears.

'I spoke to Dr Geoffreys,' she said, with a vague wave of her fork. She was going to say more, but instead took a sip of wine, and then appeared not to have gathered sufficient energy to speak further.

Not that it mattered. Kit knew what he knew. If his mother had spoken to the doctor, it meant only one thing. Plans were afoot; designs which he alone could foil. Dr Geoffreys might not wish to sentence Kit to a life in prison, but those perfumed locked wards could, frankly, be much worse. And his mother the doctor's ally! Now he had to move swiftly.

And this was why, lying here in the dark which was now dense and velvety, Kit worked more and more detail into his plan. He had pushed his brain so hard he could almost hear it ticking. Escape was a big part of it all: that much was clear. He must acquire independence and head out for the city. It mattered little to him that he had never thus far turned on a gas ring, much less boiled an egg or made toast spread with marmite. Food was of secondary importance and he was convinced he would last miles without sustenance. If he had no money for transport he would walk tireless to his destination.

But the other part of the plan was all to do with the secret. The secret Rhys knew, and Paul; that Thomas had sneered at and Andrew brayed about. And before that Alan and Gerard, and even Robbie and Danny. All the whispering, pointing mothers and their giggling, bug-eyed offspring. All the way back to the Park Incident, there had always been something.

Kit knew with a certainty deep down in his stomach that the world was fatefully closed to him while the secret remained hidden. It was as though he must watch everything through a smeared pane of glass, and if he leaned closer, to see clearly, he would bump his nose painfully. Moreover, the secret started here, with his mother in this house. It was she who had kept things from him, right from the start. Of course he had loved her more than any other creature, and if she wanted to maintain a distance might have been inclined to respect this. But then she had stopped visiting, and had mentioned Dr Geoffreys. There came a time when even she who was adored must be disobeyed.

Kit had watched and listened carefully during the evening, all the while sitting on the sofa in front of the television, watching a programme about serial killers and pretending to make notes. (This was a favourite activity of his, and quite unspoilt by his ongoing confrontations with spelling and the alphabet in general.) His mother occasionally ruffled his hair but did not attempt conversation, and thinking he was absorbed, wandered freely round the house. But Kit wasn't making notes about serial killers at all. Not that that, in itself, was a worthless pursuit: far from it, in usual circumstances it might have engaged him thoroughly. The point was, on this occasion, he was listening to and watching his mother, trying to work out where in this house she was keeping the secret.

He remembered the bedroom of the first house, her keening fury when he'd burst in on her. Here, in this home-stead, must be some similar sanctuary. She might have thought he wasn't looking, but he'd spotted it after supper: the little side-room downstairs, just opposite the kitchen. She'd gone in there after washing-up, with Kit sat on the sofa; stayed inside a little while, and locked it with a key.

Now, in the sprawling night-house, Kit slid from the bed. The thrill of cold on his bare skin stiffened his bones and muscles, and he had to flex his toes singly before sliding them into slippers. There was a creak or two of floorboards, but it sounded similar to the clank of pipes. Beyond the bedroom door and the landing, the stairs winding downwards were wild and dark with possibility. Kit trod softly outward.

His breathing arrested, momentarily, when he saw his mother's door open, and in a crazed panic he wondered if she'd heard him, and risen from bed too. Then he spotted the extremity of her white form poking from beneath the blankets, her head sideways on the pillow, her jutting shoulders and her forearm. He stood for a moment watching her, as she must have so often watched him, and then with an odd loosening of his chest muscles he tore himself away.

Slowly and lightly, he reached the bottom of the stairs. He placed nervous fingers round the handle of the door to the side room. Just as he'd suspected, it rattled locked in the door frame. This could only mean one thing: he was getting nearer to the secret. His mother surely had the key, probably ensconced beneath her pillow. Fortunately this posed little problem for Kit, who had developed a wealth of handy skills whilst inside. On a little table by the telephone he discovered his mother's wallet, which contained a modest but adequate selection of bank cards. He slid an oblong of plastic between the door's edge and its jamb. The lock uncaught, the door opened, and he slid inside the room.

There was an uncurtained window which gave out on to the tiny front garden, so the room was lighter than elsewhere even before Kit flicked on the desk lamp. Now, with the benefit of a dull glow and flickering shadows, he observed a small table and chair, a bookcase and an old vase. The vase held pampas grass and dried flowers, and the air was damp and smelt musty so that the whole room gave the impression of being older than the rest of the house. It was somewhat akin to a spartan hideout of a study.

Kit didn't have to search long before he found what he was looking for. On the desk by the window was a little box carved intricately, with the marbled surface of walnut and a froth of silver edging the lock. This time, however, the key was behind it on the window sill. It announced its presence blatantly. Kit opened up the box.

By now his fingers were shaking, not with the fear of discovery, but with the vivid shock of memory, of his mother hiding this very box. At first he was disappointed, because the inside gaped open to reveal apparently nothing more than an abundance of pleated paper. These were letters – sprawling, inky handwriting – which he could never decipher. But there were newspaper cuttings, too, some stiffened and yellow with age, and there were words he could recognize among the big, black, blocked letters.

GIRL . . . DEAD . . . BEAUTY . . . MURDER. A pattern was forming, and there was a cluster he knew well by now, *HMP WANDSWORTH.*

But when he came to the photographs, the tiny square face looking up at him, it started to fall into place and he thought he understood. Even in the half-light, smudged by the vagueness of old newsprint, the handsome features stared at him with bold and startling clarity. He squinted at the words beneath, and recognized at least one of them. An old word, from his boyhood; a name word; *MALLORY.*

14

Looks like it's shaping up to be a funny old summer.

The winter's vacillated between a clammy mildness followed by all that catastrophic flooding. And then there was the
dull, elongated spring that never truly blossomed. Smallbone
thought about the year ahead, and worried it would all be
like that: too humid and wishy-washy for a true holiday feel.

But today it's all change. Sweat and heat gathers in his
armpits before he's even properly awake. He props himself
upright, elbows on pillows. He'll have a quick cup of coffee
and then it's time for a shower.

Blimey. Old age. How it creeps up on you. Though he's
not really old, of course – late fifties, you'd call it middle age.
Middle of what, though? He's blowed if he's set up to last till
110. Much rather pop off by seventy or so, still young enough
to enjoy a pint. Which makes him . . . what? . . . three-quarter
aged? It all starts to get silly.

Smallbone peers into the bathroom mirror, tries to blink
back the years. Recalls as vividly as yesterday the self-critical,
almost forty year old. How decrepit he'd felt, pitifully
watching his youth slip over the horizon. The remembered
melodrama makes him snort. For crazily, there was nothing
then that couldn't have been solved: by a good haircut, for
instance, or a few less beers and curry. A bit of getting out
of the old motor, using his feet and getting fresh air.

Not any more, though. Then he could hold a fragile
schoolgirl in his arms and be quite the handsome father
figure. Now he'd be nothing but a dirty old man. The things
you don't realize till you've passed too far on to appreciate

them. Doesn't matter, though, because that's all behind him. The restless daydreams, and the yearning; the unceasing pulse of flesh. He looks back on his youth, and even the middle years, and through the bowed lens of nostalgia there's a regular Casanova. He thought he was just a lech, mouth-watering at the sight of candy: now hindsight tells him it was more subtle, but he's too far gone to care.

A new man, that's what he is. Clean living, no smoking, just the odd glass of wine with supper. Maybe some time soon he'll find some elegant older woman with handsome, lined features and a pleasing rasp to her voice. Together they can settle into the whole slippers and cocoa era. For now, this is enough. Good food, good books. Margaret ringing at Easter and Christmas and occasionally other times: she and Smallbone now too distant and civil to collapse into cat-calls. And beautiful, brainy, brave adult Julie. So long as she's well, nothing else much can matter.

Smallbone makes his way into the streamlined, cream-and-blue fitted kitchen. His bachelor pad, Julie calls this, with her irresistible grin: that lopsided tilt of the lips he so loves, the childish wrinkling of her nose. It's largely down to her that it's all in such good order. She's responsible for the sofa bed and wicker chairs, the slatted blinds in the bedroom. How she dragged him to all the huge warehouse stores around London, her patience angelic, her enthusiasm unending. If it had just been up to him he'd have had a three-piece suite and curtains. Still, young people these days. You've got to admire their style.

He flicks open a cupboard, whips out the coffee and cafetière. Can't even remember the last time he had Gold Blend. He was going to give up caffeine, but you've got to keep some vices. Heat's melted his appetite, so he doesn't bother with cereal, but gulps tap water thirstily while the kettle shudders and hums.

Thinking the papers must have arrived now, Smallbone goes to the door to collect them, and bends to pick the rest of the bumph and junk off the door mat. So much paper, it's a wonder it can fit through the door. He gathers up the bounty, and retreats to the kitchen.

All the different bits of newspaper are bound by clear plastic, and setting his nails to prize it open is a little like opening gifts at Christmas. As soon as the sheath's discarded, the glossy magazine bit slides free, leaving behind a welter of black-and-white grown up newsprint.

An actress who went to a film premiere wearing very little. A footballer caught *in flagrante* with an ageing rock star's wife. A minor member of royalty all drugs-bust and bankrupt, while one of his more prominent cousins went to a formal do in a baseball cap. All highly important. Some things don't change then.

On the more serious front, they're talking about the next election. Blair all up for the presidency, now the foot-and-mouth crisis is receding, he says, although you wouldn't exactly think it to judge from all those pictures of culled sheep. Who the fuck cares anyway these days? He battles the familiar malaise and goes back to the breakfast bar.

Semi-skimmed milk simmers in a saucepan, and Small-bone adds it to his coffee. Hand shaking a bit as he pours, so he gets a nice layer of coffee froth. *Cor, Dad,* said Julie, when he first did it for her. *You've come over all cappuccino.* All these skills you acquire once you're single and semi-retired.

Money's not too tight, these days. He did a bit of speculating some years back, bit of buying and selling property. Made a nice little nest-egg, could afford to cut back his hours. He'll stop work altogether soon, develop his hobbies. He's a real beneficiary of Cool Britannia: a success of Blair's Britain. Pity he's not a bit younger, then he could go wild and enjoy it all.

Or older, with grandchildren. And then there'd be some point to it.

He never speaks to Margaret about that, because they've become so careful with each other. And with Julie in her thirties, it's not as if there's any arguing over access. So meetings are rare, and polite, and the only time he really feels grown up. Like just recently, when they started *liaising* over a special present for Julie. She's just been promoted at her law firm, and will soon be based in New York. They want to give her something really special, something expensive and indulgent for the flat, perhaps, or tickets for a fancy weekend away. Went for dinner over in Upper Street, to talk it over and catch up.

It was odd, sitting there opposite Margaret, as though they were strangers. They kept doing the sort of things that people do when they don't know each other, like shifting unnecessarily in their seats, and starting sentences together. Then they'd look at each other and laugh – but without real amusement – and say politely, exaggeratedly, *No. Go on. You first.*

Time, he thought then, had changed Margaret irrevocably. It wasn't a physical ageing, for she was still robustly handsome: in fact with her big bones and full bosom she'd rather grown into her womanliness. No, something less tangible had altered. There was no brittle spark of excitement. No awkward memory of intimacy, of the delicious stumbling of early love; no hint of the fiery, dissatisfied woman who'd left him, but who'd still loved him.

And he, for his part, felt a complete absence of tension. Margaret was turned out in a matching skirt and top of shot, navy velvet: smart, not too loud. Her thick, subtly silvered hair was pulled back from her face, showing off her taut skin and cheekbones and clear, gentle eyes. He knew her pinkish, fresh-soaped skin, the full curves beneath the velvet, but felt no twinge of that old closeness, no nostalgia for lost passion. Just a rational comprehension that she was a calm, kind, strong woman, and the smell of her just-cleansed body was a thing of the past. Was this finally, he wondered, what it meant to grow old?

Amazing, when you thought about it, what it took to grow up. In his case, a failed marriage, a string of affairs, sailing too close to the career winds, and a successful, adult daughter. Julie, of course, is busy *not* growing up. Still reed-slender like a teenager, and a different man each month. Or it sometimes seems like that anyway. He loves her too much to dictate, having learnt from past mistakes. But he wishes she would settle, calm that bold and restless spirit.

Smallbone finishes his coffee and heads for the shower. By now the heat's really thickened, and he can smell the sweaty sheen on his skin. The harsh jets of water, pummelling flesh, bring a purgatory relief. He dresses quickly, in real cotton, one eye on the brittle, bright outside. Not a moment to be wasted. Time for a morning constitutional.

He may have slimmed down since five years ago, and yes, he's given up smoking, but still there're some depths to which Smallbone will not sink. You'll not find him wearing poncy sweatpants and one of those stupid bandanas to become a sixty-year-old jogger panting round Regent's Park. A brisk walk's quite enough.

Smallbone exits the modern mansion block and turns left on the narrow pavement, and after about a hundred paces he's reached the main drag. All at once, in a nano second, it's like a different world. The concourse crowds with a slow-moving soup of young people. The ones in black leather make you sweat just to look at them. Kebab stalls on the corner send out heavy smells of cooking, mingling with the stale beer and meths that cloud over the beggars at the tube station. Smallbone holds his breath till he makes it through, over the road and up towards the park, where the crowds start to thin and it gets a bit nice again. Down here, it's like a teeming zoo. Keep all your wits about you and a hand on your wallet.

And it's not before time that he wakes up to this last thought. Because he's no sooner past the tube than he feels a rough tugging, and someone brushing his backside in the humid crush of the crowd. A mild panic pulses beneath the skin of his forehead, but his fingers grope his back pocket and the wallet's still there. His other hand reaches instinctively for the opposite pocket, feeling for a mobile or pager, but it's all right – his mind works furiously – he remembers leaving them at home.

Smallbone pushes on hurriedly, distaste gathering on his tongue. Keeps the hand protectively cupped over the back pocket in question. But there's some sort of unpleasant closeness, a presence hovering at his elbow. Like the would-be thief's hanging on, just waiting his chance. Smallbone twists his neck, irritably, trying to find the offender. Years of detective work would usually help pick him out quickly. But the density of the crowd makes it impossible to turn, and all around there're just droves of these odd, bug-eyed youths.

He presses forward, trying not to inhale when the kebab smell gets stronger. Pictures the wider pavements up ahead, and the decorous curved green of the park. But there's a rhythm behind him, literally breathing down his neck. Sod it, could it be some pervert? He's getting really uncomfortable.

Smallbone reaches the pavement's edge, and just catches the 'Cross now' green man. Trots his way clear of the traffic and reaches the other side. He's walking up by the cinema, and the crowds have got thinner, and he breathes a sigh of relief, his shirt sticky on his skin. But as he turns up towards the park he hears the footsteps behind him. Mimicking his, step for step, stopping, slowing, just as he does. When he turns behind him to look a figure slips into a newsagent, but when he re-starts his way forward the nagging presence is still there. Maybe he's being paranoid, but this doesn't feel imagined. Smallbone wipes a hand across his brow.

Looks like someone's following him.

15

Miranda clasped her long white fingers tight behind her head. Then she unclasped them and let one hand stray free, travelling sidelong down her body, feeling the firm, pale flesh. Though she rarely failed to be startled by the passage of time and the constant newness of things, as she reached her late thirties, she was relieved by her body's apparent resilience. Her skin was still firm enough to announce the boned outline beneath; the flat plane of her stomach, the hard jutting of pelvis.

With her other hand still trapped beneath the base of her skull, she played loosely with the matted hair that splayed on the pillow. She touched the apex of skull and spine and reached for the roots of her tresses; let a thumb travel and nudge at the very topmost vertebra.

But all the while, she was telling herself that these hands, these fingers and this caress, were not hers; this wasn't some sad and lonesome self-indulgence. In her mind they were Mark's hands, his touches and his tenderness; and his eyes were half-closed to a low, intent murmuring.

Such sweet, crazy solitude! How fantastic it was to breathe free once more, after having her privacy invaded. She knew she should be nervous, the way events had unfolded recently, and the alarming manner in which she had found herself home alone again. But things had been so strange, perhaps it was only to be expected.

The morning was bright and the air hot and sticky. Miranda's dreamy wanderings took her back in time, to the tow path by the canal and the steeply sloping banks. She recalled the grasses, wild and scratchy, and felt Mark's hand creeping slyly up the pale slope of her thigh, groping beneath her knickers, searching out the folds of skin beneath. Her eyes grew a little wet, her breathing quickened, and the muscles between her ribs tightened and convulsed. Then a sweet fatigue washed over her and she let out a long, low sigh. The sun was strong at the window and from the next-door neighbour's lawn there was the smell of fresh cut grass.

But Miranda was still nervous, and not only because of these last few days of strangeness. There was also the abiding anxiety, at once vague and sharp, over starting afresh and the passage of time. She had visited Mark on and off over the years, but in such limited constrained circumstances that it almost prevented them from seeing each other properly: the occasions were so intense, that Miranda felt embarrassed to scrutinize Mark too closely, as one avoids looking at freaks. And Mark himself – he had found the meetings so awkward that latterly he had requested she didn't visit him at all. The absences of weeks and months had multiplied into – what? It must be years now. Of course, Miranda told herself, he had not wanted to see her because he loved her too much, it was too painful to have her company for only snatched, sporadic hours. Once he was coming out for good she would be the very first thing on his mind. But it was impossible to say how they would greet each other now: standing up, face to face, in the blazing light of day.

From the savage confidence of adolescence Miranda had grown up, and had known what it was like no longer to feel beautiful. She had had her belly swollen and stretched by childbirth; seen the skin beneath her eyes pucker and hair dulled through times of strain. Yet her waistspan was still narrow, the planes of her cheeks chiselled and smooth. She was equal, she thought – just about – to the challenge of reunion with Mark.

Now, thinking all this, and looking inwards and back, Miranda wound back the clock two decades to Hollybush.

In 1979, the year she'd done her O levels, the winter and spring months had hurtled by like choppy fields beyond the glass of a railway carriage. Exams came and went in a dry-mouthed, stomach cramping frenzy, and before she could blink, Miranda was waiting for the results. Mark, amazingly, had been given that much extra grace that he still haunted the common room and the dining table at Hollybush. Because of his 'learning difficulties' they had not – just yet – cast him out, and neither had she stopped loving him. She decided not to dwell on the brittleness of their intimacy, throwing herself instead with vigour into exams and dreams of a glorious future.

As for the Cornflower Girl, she still hovered, but was elusive. Miranda heard her name connected in half-jealous rumours with words like 'stage school' and 'talent scouts'. But she kept her nose in her books and thought how, once she was properly educated, she would become a famous writer or a politician and far outshine the other girl. That one probably spent her Saturday mornings learning to tap-dance or sing tunelessly, like the poor starstruck waifs you saw in movies who were much better off getting real jobs.

There had been only one moment, one slice of a long, lonely afternoon, when Miranda was shaken from her concentration and her focus on exams. It was a few days before her first paper, which was English literature, and she was beginning to think that if she learned any more quotes from *Macbeth* then the whole play would stuff and numb her brain cells and she wouldn't be able to think at all. Deciding she would benefit from a break, she headed for Mark's dorm. At this time of day, she only half-expected to find him, but it was worth trying.

Approaching Mark's landing she saw his dorm door was open. She would have quickened her pace, as good as skipped through it, had not the voices warned her first that perhaps she wouldn't be welcome. Nearing the room itself, she saw Mark with the Cornflower Girl: both wore light summer jackets, and the Cornflower Girl carried a small bag, so they looked like a couple readying to go out, or else just returned from somewhere. Miranda made no attempt to hide herself, but remained effortlessly unnoticed. Mark and the other girl were intent upon each other.

'I know this is difficult,' she was saying, 'but you can't just pretend it hasn't happened. Things are more certain now. You're going to have to tell her.'

Miranda's heart would have frozen and she might have openly wept, but for the unexpectedness of Mark's swift and strong response.

'Don't you go telling me what I can and can't do.' He moved towards the girl, his voice a vibrato of anger. 'This is none of your business. Why can't you stay out of it?'

'I think it is my business, don't you?' Then her tone changed, she grew wheedling, her voice insidious, treacly. She placed a hand on Mark's neck. 'Besides, I sort of started this. I do feel somehow responsible.'

Mark's fingers flew to the space just below his hairline where she had touched him. He cast her hand aside so heavily that the whole arm arced, high and clumsy.

'Ouch,' she said, 'that hurt.'

And Mark replied, 'Good.'

The Cornflower Girl flounced from the room, her eyes and cheeks stinging. She must surely have seen Miranda but paused not a split second for acknowledgement. Miranda waited, almost breathless, for Mark to turn and spot her. But when he did, he just smiled weakly, with a sort of exhausted embarrassment.

'I didn't see you there,' he offered, as though he weren't himself at all. And then he walked past her, at a slight distance, touching her arm with an oddly formal pat.

Miranda was disconcerted, but put it down to the strain of making choices. It appeared, on the evidence, that Mark had clearly made the right one.

The day the exam results were due Miranda woke early. She counted the impossible hours before the post arrived. When it was properly time to rise, she jerked upright out of a half-dream and went to jostle with the other residents to collect the morning mail. Her stomach was hollow and tight as she picked up the plain brown envelope.

She unpeeled the flap and pulled out the sheet of paper. Letters and numbers blurred, brightened and focused on the white sheet in front of her. Then she swallowed air in pleasure. Five As and three Bs. All dreams, in that moment, seemed half-way to being realized. Her path would be out of a fairy tale, and she would prove a worthy heroine: the brainy, beautiful, changeling, battling poverty and rootlessness, rising to a glorious career with fame and fortune following. Anything was possible, in this brave new dawn of opportunity – there was, after all, for the first time, a newly elected woman prime minister: girls could do it all now, and Miranda would be one of them. And always, it went without saying, she would have her trusted handsome beloved at her side. The future sparkled in front of her. She ran to find Mark.

But Mark's reaction to her news was to gaze out of the window. As so often they had before, they were lying across his bed. Miranda's sweatshirt sleeve was tugged downwards to reveal a pallid, bony shoulder, the exposure and dishevelment of their usual fumblings.

'Think what we can do, Mark,' Miranda was babbling. 'I'll go on to sixth-form college, and from there on to university.

Get qualifications and a good job. Start building for our future.'

Mark steadied her hand where it rubbed his chest in a frenzy. He turned towards her with contempt in his glassy green eyes.

'Miranda, I've got to go. There's things I've got to do.'

'But you can't go just yet,' she babbled, 'there's things we've got to talk about.'

'I've got to go. I told you. Now get out of my way.'

He shook her off his arm with such strength that she tilted backwards, heavily, her spine and ribs jarring. She was half-sitting, half-lying in an ungainly, side-strewn heap, the beginnings of a bruise on her chin and her breath jarring her ribs. Mark was out of the room, the door slammed hard behind him. Her head spun in disbelief. She wiped her mouth with a handkerchief.

In the days that followed the summer snaked in and out of heatwave. One morning Miranda would wake and be so sticky that the thin viscose sheets would cling to her skin in patches. Other mornings there'd be smears of purple and grey sky shielding pathetically weak sunlight, and a chill in the air. There was a kind of cloying, anti-climax which hung in the atmosphere like damp. She had waited so long for this time: for the holidays, and then for the exam results. But now that both had arrived, the future was heavy with uncertainty.

Fortunately, she already had her place at sixth-form college – a large, converted Victorian house on the edge of North Finchley. She had visited during term time for a mutual assessment of suitability. She was to go there to do her A levels, which would certainly include English and History, and it looked as though the staff might help her find accommodation. But Mark's future was far vaguer, his behaviour increasingly unpredictable, and still, through it all, she could not bear the thought of their parting.

It was as if they had reached the threshold of adulthood with alarming speed, and were ill-equipped to deal with the pitfalls ahead. His voice was deeper and his face coarsened with young bristle; her legs had grown longer and her curves more pronounced. They had learnt the responses of their bodies more intricately, encountered unfamiliar, volatile feelings, but for all practical intents and purposes they were floundering children still.

During one of the last of her days at Hollybush, Miranda sat alone in the common room. She hadn't bothered to eat breakfast, and didn't know whether or not she'd missed lunch. She had an aching inside, a heaviness, which she could no longer ignore. She hadn't seen Mark for days and had no idea where he was. If he wasn't mooning around oafishly, he'd be wasting his life down the arcades playing Space Invaders. She pictured herself as a Shakespearean heroine – Ophelia, Desdemona – hopelessly lost and misguided in love. The purplish-brown patch of skin beneath her chin pulsed with a light but lingering pain. And there was a sickness in her stomach which was another thing entirely.

The clitter clatter of shoes on the staircase interrupted Miranda's reverie. She sat straight and waited to see who might turn the corner. The sharp quickness of the footsteps marked them out as female. Miranda wasn't wrong: it was none other than the Cornflower Girl.

But how she looked today! She came in and sat on an armchair opposite Miranda, and kicked up her high-heeled shoes, crossing her legs. Miranda caught the blur of cerise-varnished toenails. Her already blonde hair had been further bleached and streaked into chunks of light and dark gold, and scrunched into bunches with a spiky, wild-child fringe.

Her eyes were darkened round the edges with a navy blue kohl, her lips glossed and parted wetly, her perfect skin slightly rouged. The effect was quite unreal, and disturbingly harlotish, like a child dressed as a woman, or a dummy passed off as human. She wore a tight shirt and jeans which hugged her elongated skinniness. She was a ballerina on a music box, a miniature maid in a souvenir shop. The effect could have been grotesque, but surely out on the pavement, not a single head would fail to turn. Miranda shrank from the light, her bruise pulsing slightly harder.

The Cornflower Girl sighed with exaggerated high-pitched girliness. In a second, Karl was at her side, planting down a well-filled suitcase. The girl fluttered up at him.

'Will my taxi soon be here?'

Karl said nothing; perhaps he replied with his face, but Miranda could see only his back. There was the merest movement of his shoulders and then he had gone. Miranda took in the painted girl and her suitcase.

'Are you going somewhere?'

The Cornflower Girl smiled and flexed her varnished toes.

'I'm leaving Hollybush. I'm off into the big wide world.' Her voice came out clipped and strained, as though she were trying to sound posher. Eliza Doolittle, thought Miranda: she probably practises in front of a mirror.

'Where are you going? What are you going to do?' Too sharp a curiosity made Miranda's voice desperate. The other, by contrast, was the acme of nonchalance.

'Oh – ' she turned her head, 'I've got myself a modelling contract. Karl's going to look after me for the first part of my career, and I'm going to stay with one of my old social workers till I get a flat sorted out. They say there's lots of money to be made in modelling these days, but you've got to be careful. I've already done one or two assignments. Here. Look at this.'

She flipped a copy of *Sixteen* onto the low table in front of her. It was folded onto a page headed **Drive him wild, girls** followed by ten top tips on how to get the hottest schoolboys salivating. This imparted wisdom was illustrated, as ever, by a photograph: this one of two teenage lovelies with clean hair and bright teeth. One of them had long legs and jeans cut low across her midriff: she had bright blonde hair and painted eyes, wet lips and big teeth.

It wasn't, Miranda was later to think, that this image was one of beauty: each component was near-perfect, but the whole was unremarkable. Nor was it that anyone would particularly want to appear in *Sixteen*. But for the first time in her life Miranda felt things pass her by. Here was the Cornflower Girl, with her suitcase, waiting for her taxi heading out into a city where she would be feted and fending for herself. She was hard and ambitious so without doubt in no time she'd find her feet. In a second the Victorian converted college in North Finchley became absurdly parochial.

'Well, good luck,' said Miranda, for want of anything better. Maybe the Cornflower Girl said, Thank you, but a car horn drowned her words. Karl came back in the room and picked up the suitcase.

'Taxi's here,' he muttered, 'and someone's here to see you.'

A squawky, older woman's voice, was calling down the corridor. A caricature of welcome, papery with cigarettes.

'Where is she, my beauty? I'm coming to find 'er.' And once again, a foreign figure appeared in the doorway.

'Debs, my sweet. Ready to make your way out into the big, bad world?'

The woman was thin, with a bony face and narrow, muscular calves. From a distance you might think she was young, until you noticed the looseness of her skin which was as papery as the voice. Almost a drag queen's voice, and a drag queen's bouffant hair. Maybe dyed to hide the grey. She was smoking with some energy.

'Hello,' said the Cornflower Girl, giving the older woman a kiss. 'This is Miranda, one of my friends here at Hollybush.'

Miranda gave a silent nod, which the older woman briefly acknowledged.

'All right, my love?' – and then – 'You ready to go, Debs?'

The Cornflower Girl wrinkled her nose as though a rotten smell had filled the room. 'You know, I'm changing my name now I'm going into modelling. Debs is much too ordinary. Please call me Louisa.'

Miranda raised her eyebrows. 'I thought you were going to be Tasha.'

'There's already a Natasha on the agency's books. I thought I'd be different. I wanna be unique.'

'If I were you, love, I'd worry more about your surname. Natasha, Louisa, all very pretty, but a Burke remains a Burke.' The drag queen cackled like a parrot, but her young charge paused for thought.

'I shall choose a different surname at some point. What's your surname, Miranda?'

Miranda said 'Laverty' quietly and then wished she hadn't told her.

The Cornflower Girl smiled oddly. 'I thought – oh, never mind.' Then she straightened up, adjusted her hair, as Karl came back and picked up her suitcase. 'Laverty's a nice name. And it starts with L. Maybe I'll have that name. We can be like sisters.'

The older woman clicked her tongue against the roof of her mouth and rolled her eyes. 'Come on, now. Let's get you home first in one piece, then you can have as many names as you like.' She nodded across at Miranda. 'You gonna leave a number so yer friend can reach you?'

A coldness gathered in Miranda's guts as the other girl

hesitated, and for almost the first time in her life she felt the queasiness of being slighted. But then the other made her mind up, scribbling something on a piece of paper, and handing it over with tinny enthusiasm. 'Of course, we *must* keep in touch. Miranda, this is where you can reach me. And, before I forget, the most exciting thing of all. I might be releasing a single – please listen out for it. You will buy hundreds of copies, won't you?'

She flashed a smile, and then vanished, like the genie from the lamp. Miranda would have torn the piece of paper up, and scattered its fragments to the winds, but for the fact that she wanted to appear nonchalant even to herself.

Miranda didn't know how long she remained seated in the common room. The air cooled about her, and late summer clouds were gathering, so the outline of the dowdy furniture started to blur. Now and then she shivered, and knew she ought to fetch a jumper, but she could not will herself to move, so she simply rubbed her goose pimples. The pain beneath her chin grew sharper, then dulled again. There was something she had to discuss with Mark, but how to find the words to tell him? When she looked up and saw him standing beside her, she had no idea how long he'd been there.

Mark sat down by Miranda after flicking on a side light. The room remained dimly lit; like Christmas, or a power cut, instead of a late summer's evening. Mark was either very tired, or had suddenly grown up: or perhaps it was Miranda's mood which made him appear so worn. The copy of *Sixteen* remained where it had been cast onto the low table. Miranda picked it up and flicked through it ostentatiously, stopping at the page with the Cornflower Girl.

'She's gone, you know,' said Miranda, without further explication. Mark put his crossed feet onto the table and stared straight ahead of him. She studied him for reaction.

'She told me she's got this modelling contract, and she might even be making a single. She's headed for the big time.' Mark didn't turn to look at her.

'Do you know the Cornflower Girl's got something going with the Nazi? She says he's going to be her manager, but I know there's something more. I caught them at it the other day, in full view in this very room.'

'For fuck's sake,' Mark's trainered feet swept the magazine from the table, 'do you think I care what some poncy model girl is doing with some pervy cunt? Shut it, Miranda. I've got stuff on my mind.'

Miranda had no time to activate any defences. She stared at Mark in a trance of misery and horror. He sucked air inwards and straightened, his body stiffened and his hand raised. The whites of his eyes showed, like those of a frightened horse. At first it was all she could do to stop herself from crying out and running. But she stilled her shallow breathing, though the effort made her ribs ache. His hand flapped the air in exasperation, but she caught his wrist in her fingers, pressing down against the bone.

'Don't be this way, Mark. I've got something to tell you . . .'

She had spread his palm flat against her belly and waited for his face to change.

Now, lying here in the summer bedroom, she wondered how he might look at her today.

16

It's been days now.

Smallbone lets his fingertips creep across the top of the varnished deal coffee table. The packet of cigarettes lies there, top invitingly ajar. The slim white and brown cylinders are ranged within evenly. They remind him of liquorice, something sweet and inviting. He edges closer to the packet, claws at it; then flings it aside in self-disgust.

What the fuck does he think he's doing, giving in after all this time?

He's been off the fags for years now, can remember with horror the hollow, phlegm-streaked coughs which woke him in the night. Started to view himself as contemptuously as the smack- and crack-heads he interrogated. No use without a prop, shaking without a fix. Pale, sweaty and helpless if called upon to cope without the drug of choice.

And then the pleasure, the exhilaration, when he realized he could do it. The joy of waking up and breathing deeply and not having it hurt. Of being able to skip – yes, *skip*, like in nursery rhymes – down the stairs to the pavement, and not having to crouch down, wheezing, or even stand aside and vomit. The first time he went for a long country walk with Julie – that weekend they spent in Uplyme – and rejoiced because the twinge in his lungs wasn't breathless, blocked agony, but the thrill of cold autumn air, hitting the spot.

So what's all this edginess that's pushing him back to the brink?

It must be Julie really, mustn't it? She's all that really matters. Not that, as far as she's concerned, there's anything wrong.

She was round here only the other night, looking better than ever: all slim and fresh in some posh designer label, straight out of some — what did she call it? — urban spa, if you please. God knows what they get up to, with all these massages and facials. But she was full of the joys and all. Can't keep a good woman down.

But you know how the old cliché goes — it's not her, it's him. She's looking forward to the future, licking her lips and ready to go, geared up and revving for that job in New York. And he's gonna miss her like crazy, can't go on without her. Why is it every sentiment comes out in the corniness of some song line?

Smallbone parks himself right on the outer edge of the sofa. His breathing's heavy, he's outstaring the fag packet, like some fucked-up, addicted matador. He thinks of Julie gone, and the loneliness: then tells himself it's not so bad really, there's time and money now, he'll visit. Doesn't seem to make it better, though. Must be something else still bothering him.

Smallbone lifts a cigarette and lights it, then grinds it brutally to a butt. Temperature's soared since this morning, after several days of gloom. He rinses a glass noisily, enjoying the roar of the tap. Too sweaty by half. Better let some air in.

He slides over to the far side of the broad, light living room. The big picture window that looks down onto the pavement is the only one with a net, the one throwback to the old style. Julie hates net curtains, declared them outlawed and outdated. But this window's so blatant, she allowed it: a single concession to modesty.

His hand reaches up beneath the net to unfasten the window catch. As always, when he does this, he feels oddly indecent, like he's reaching up beneath a woman's blouse and unclasping her bra. But today the indecency is all strange and different, making him feel funny the way he's been feeling since this first started happening.

He looks down, at an angle, his body shrinking instinctively. Just as he expected. The boy's right there, where he thought he'd be. He stands against a lamp-post, his back at a stiff, awkward angle. So false, so contrived, you could hardly call it leaning. It's as though he's seen this pose in a movie, or perhaps a hundred movies, but when it comes to reproducing it he's too bloody uptight. But you've got to hand it to him, this kid. His antennae are switched on. As the curtain twitches, his head tilts: looks straight at Smallbone's window. He knows he's being looked at. Bloody sixth sense or what.

Smallbone feels like he's been a prisoner of this watchfulness for months. In fact, he has to remind himself, it's only been days. That first time, walking through Camden and going up to the park, he sensed it then: the footsteps, the presence at his elbow. Kept turning round to catch someone, and there'd be this shadowy figure: infuriating, evasive, disappearing just in time.

And then he was convinced it was the same boy who was following him next morning. He was popping out for milk, that clichéd morning expedition, and he got a look at him then, though not really at close quarters. A tall, thin, shambling youth, but strong-looking, broad-shouldered. Hard to tell his age, anything from nineteen upwards. Browny hair that shone with auburn tints in direct sunlight. Face too far for a good reccy, but something about him not-quite-handsome. Too awkward, even clumsy, long thin movements uncontrolled. Like the separate pieces of him were all right, but stuck together all wrong. Smallbone could've sworn he trailed him to the corner shop, but when he came out the boy'd gone.

But he was there the next day, and the next. Not always first thing. Sometimes afternoon, or evening. Right old fright, it gave him, when he came out from the underground car park, brushing the dust down off his trousers, then looked up and found him staring. *What the fuck* . . . started to form at the back of Smallbone's throat, half-whispered, half-thought, not quite spoken out loud. The boy just stumbled and said, Sorry, in this startlingly sweet and quiet voice. Then scuttled off, like some scared, surprised animal.

It's crossed Smallbone's mind a hundred times what he might be able to do about this. Take it to the boys, report a stalker. What else is the Protection from Harassment Act for? And then he has to laugh and shake his head as the irony hits home. What it feels like, after all, when the boot's on the other foot. All those conversations past, dismissals of complaints, come back to haunt him now like he's Mr Scrooge at Christmas.

— *I'm sorry, Mrs So-and-so. But what d'you expect me to do about this? The lad's done nothing wrong. It's not a crime to walk down the street.*

— *Are you trying to tell me, officer, you can't help me until it's too late?*

— *Bring me some solid evidence, ma'am, and we'll see what we can do about it.*

— *You disgust me, officer. The state of justice today. No wonder this country's going to ruin.*

Et cetera, et cetera.

Well, OK, so he needs evidence. He'll bloody go and get it.

Smallbone steps back from the window, retreats into the bedroom. A strange resolve prickles beneath his skin. Everything seems connected these days: the regret at Julie going overseas; his need to rein in his ageing body; the haunted-looking, stalking youth; this unsettling, sticky heat. As though one imbalance were running seamlessly into the next, so that by solving one he might at least start to address the others. He puts a thin T-shirt over his bare torso and dons a pair of cotton slacks. Before he's got time to regret it, he's shimming down the stairwell.

Out on the pavement, the sun's rays are much hotter. His

eyes crinkle uncomfortably, balk against the brightness. The heat bounces off the paving slabs, creates a blurred, filmic effect. The boy's still leaning against the lamp-post, and now he knows his prey has come to meet him. Smallbone takes several steps forwards. His heart knocks beneath his skin. Now he's just a foot away. The boy swivels his fixed profile. They stand there, staring, eye to eye. The boy's lips part, perhaps a smile.

— *I've been following you, you know.*

Smallbone swallows, knocked back by the youth's unexpected candour. He'd like to be clever, insouciant — *Yes, I'd noticed, as it happens.* But he just stands there, speechless, not yet understanding.

— *You're Detective Smallbone, aren't you. I was wondering when we'd meet.*

It's like a simultaneous thrill and chill; the sweat goes cold on Smallbone's skin. The boy speaks slowly, with a forced, over-careful precision. As though he's reciting his lines from some period drama. And he's put together all wrong: head too big for his body, or is it the other way around? Most of all though — fuck knows, his eyes are seriously creepy. One green and one blue. When he talks it's like they're looking in different directions.

— *Why are you following me?* At last the words come, and the anger. *What the hell do you want from me? Don't you know stalking's against the law?*

The boy curls his lips: there's that half-smile again. Despite the physical clumsiness, he doesn't seem afraid or embarrassed.

— *Ah, you appear to be angry. Please don't be. I've waited for so long to meet you. Perhaps we could talk in your flat.*

The splutter comes out involuntarily. *No, we bloody well cannot. I'm not some lunatic, or idiot. Now tell me what it is you want.*

The boy pauses, straightens up, beyond the gauze of soft focus heat.

– *What I want to say to you is quite simple.* There's a few seconds silence, with those damned spooky eyes staring. And then he continues softly, clearly. *Mark Mallory is innocent.*

It's like one of those moments in films where they start to play far-off haunting music. Smallbone knows he's going to look back on this later and remember it. At first the name – Mark Mallory – means nothing to him, but for a vague, nagging familiarity. And then as the seconds slip by the nagging dissolves into clarity. A case from two decades back: a frightened, bright-eyed youth confessing. A beautiful skinny girl hideously twisted and cut up. The dirty solitude of his old flat and the space in the bed left by Margaret. The sleepless nights torn by misery and the memory of Marianne.

The boy's eyes fix him intently with a strange, quiet triumph. Now he looks familiar, too, as though they met in some former life. Smallbone steps away, wanting distance; he puts his wrist against his brow.

– *Mark Mallory. The Laverty murder case. That was twenty years ago.*

– *But you were the officer in the case, weren't you? You got the wrong man.*

– *But he came to us. He confessed. And anyway . . .* Smallbone's mouthing dumbly, helplessly. How did it come to this, him floundering in front of some stranger? *What the hell is it to you?*

The boy doesn't answer. His head rocks back on his neck. He's looking down his nose now, all superior, from a height.

– *I'd like to talk to you properly. I'd like to come up to your flat.* He doesn't seem to have any idea of how inappropriate his suggestion is. Smallbone shakes his head, incredulous.

– *No, no. That's just not possible.*

– *But I want to talk properly.*

— Well, you can't. Not here. Not now. You'll have to find me in the office.

Smallbone turns away from the boy and slams back inside the mansion block. Why the fuck did he say that instead of *Piss off and don't come my way again*. Like when those cold callers catch you, and you want to swear at them but you just say, *It's not convenient*.

Back in his living room, Smallbone sits hunched into thought. He tries to pinpoint what unsettles him most about this odd exchange. The fright, the jolt of being followed, of having a stranger know his name? Or the recall of past memories he'd much rather have buried? There's an uncomfortable truth, which only the passage of time has blunted.

When Mark Mallory confessed, he really did think they had the wrong man.

They never had any forensics, and they never got any eyewitnesses. There'd been the 'accidental' death of his witness, snuffed out before he could reach her. And the confession was unprompted, but there had always been something odd about it. Such haphazard motivation for such calculated cruelty. So many details missing – or to Smallbone's ears at least.

He even recalls, halfway through court proceedings, there'd been whisperings of a withdrawal of plea, starting everything off again. The whispers never came to anything – who knew if there was any truth to it? – but the whole department got nervous, the Guvnor looming ghoulish as ever.

— Don't let me down on this one, Smallbone. Remember how I've supported you in the past.

It simply wasn't the right time for him to explore his inner doubts.

Sometimes, even now, with so much water under the bridge, Smallbone looks back down the years and feels he made a pact with the Devil. He let the Guvnor protect him, and then he owed him one for ever. So maybe he let the wrong man get convicted and the whole cycle could've started again. Now, just when he'd almost forgotten it, all the wrong ghosts are returning.

Twilight smudges over the front garden he once shared with Margaret, he pushes the gate ajar too late, trying to rub a woman's scent off his skin. His mouth is dry as he climbs into bed, his skin prickly with misplaced desire; his fingers yearn for Margaret's buttocks but she shuts him out, turning aside. Julie frowns at him at breakfast, her nose set towards her cornflakes. The corridors at work are thick with murmurings; he dozes between jobs and dreams of whisky.

— *Don't let me down*, the Guvnor whispers, as Marianne's white, phantom face lies screaming.

He snaps a match into flame and lights up: sits back and inhales, savagely.

17

Kit had started out on the first day of his journey just after dawn. Utterly confident of his own stamina, he had wanted to walk for as many hours as the sun shone. He prepared carefully, like Dick Whittington, of whom his mother had long ago read to him. His insides fluttered with a heady mixture of nervousness and pleasure. He did feel slightly bad about taking all the bread and chocolate from the fridge, and searching in the hallway so he could empty his mother's wallet. A muscle in the back of his throat twitched and he rolled his eyes skyward for he had no wish to plunge her into either hunger or poverty.

He wanted to leave her a note, to express his competing feelings, but his limited writing skills made subtlety impossible. He wrote on a scrap of notepaper 'Se you very sone', accessorized with three shaky crosses, and closed the door softly.

Kit had been sure once he reached London he'd have no trouble finding his way. The city had always fascinated him, and in his strangely kaleidoscoped world, maps and A-Zs had long since been among his favourite reading matter. He learnt to recognize district and road names even if he could not spell them without copying. If he closed his eyes he could picture whole pages of the London Street Finder, the white criss-cross maze of streets trellised against a background of pink. He knew where tube lines crossed the borders of zones and which postal districts were neighbours. He knew that the Central Criminal Court was in the Old Bailey EC4 and could have walked his way blind towards New Scotland Yard.

The city was to be a friend to him, and he looked forward to meeting it in person; but getting there, though exciting, was an altogether different proposition.

Kit did not entirely understand his mother's penchant for moving, but certainly this latest place she'd settled in was in an area unfamiliar to him. Frankly it appeared quite dull: the narrow street lined with blunt-edged cars, and the low brick houses with brown-red roofs, lacking architectural age or character. It all reminded him of the house they'd left when he'd been only four, but without the significant local shops and park, or the exciting proximity of Town.

But on his way here from the YOI, he'd seen the big motorway, and the large signs with white writing and arrows marked 'London'. If he followed the road into the city, he'd be bound to get there in the end. The walk might take him days, but he had no especial deadline. He toyed with the idea of taking the train, but did not wish to use up all his money. And if he wandered by the road's edge he might be able to hitch a lift.

Kit began his odyssey by counting the plane trees that lined the road his mother lived on. It gave him a sense of comfort and control to be able to label and contain the world by numbers. On that road, there were sixteen in all, and he saw how, as he headed on and outwards and the streets got bigger, louder and dirtier, the trees got more and more spaced out until they disappeared altogether. Then he had a momentary sense of disorientation, and went into a news-agent's just to make sure of the direction to the motorway.

Moving towards the counter, he bumped into a woman with a big basket. She looked him up and down with a tight mouth before exiting swiftly. The shopkeeper cocked his head on one side and narrowed his eyes.

'Can I help you, son?'

'I'm trying to get to the motorway.'

The man drew down his eyebrows. 'The motorway? Where are you headed?'

'I'm trying to get to London.'

'You're driving then?'

'Oh, no.'

The man shook his head, not understanding. 'Aren't you better off going to the station?'

Kit's stomach lightened oddly. 'Please, I just want to follow the road.'

The man spoke slowly, in a manner which reminded Kit of a documentary about circus trainers he'd once seen, the way people spoke when addressing wild, dangerous creatures. 'You turn right at the lights, and follow the road right up to the roundabout. But you do know how far it is to London, do you? And you can't walk along the motorway.'

A short, unattractive woman had joined him at the counter, and as Kit turned his back he heard receding, muffled whispers. On his way out he bumped into another shopping-laden woman. Her basket tilted, and she drew a sharp breath, and looked at him with alarm.

'I'm terribly sorry,' said Kit, meaning it, though he wouldn't have had it in him to straighten the basket. But he spoke with a steady, clear precision, that he'd learnt years ago from his mother. The woman looked at him and smiled, instantly comforted.

Kit felt better back outside and found the roundabout easily. The thick, fast traffic frightened him at first: he wasn't accustomed to cities or main thoroughfares. He tried to cross the road at a rather unsuitable point, and a driver rolled down his window and spat out the word *Cunt*. But he was pleased to see that there were others who were following the motorway. A huddle of young people stood at one of the roundabout's exits with cylinders of luggage and large cardboard signs. There was a girl with a pierced, bejewelled navel off which the sunlight glanced archly, and a boy with her whose feet played incessantly with a line of empty beer cans. They had big slabs of cardboard with writing in felt tip pen; beyond them stood another similar couple, and beyond them a single male. Kit didn't pause to make out all the signs but on one he did see 'London'. This reassured him immeasurably, and also made him excited. He walked briskly along the grass verge past the straggling hitchers. The male of the first couple belched loudly as he brushed past him. He was probably a few years older than Kit, but for some reason struck him as a typical careless youth.

Kit shadowed the hard shoulder for as long as he could manage. When the ribbon of tarmac dipped or rose out of reach, he skirted down the border slope, careful to keep the traffic within earshot. If the road rejoined his path, allowing him to bend and move with it, he was careful to read signs whenever he had the opportunity. It wasn't until hours later that he saw one saying 'services'.

Kit read the word out loud, haltingly, rehearsing the syllables in solitude. The knife and fork motif helped him, and he guessed there must be a restaurant soon. He crossed a car park and entered a building through high glass, automated doors. A chilly current hit him in the face, making him shudder after the still, warm air outside. He caught his image in a long mirror and saw dark stains under his armpits; his body felt tired, sticky and empty and a lady with a pushchair veered away, frowning. He bought some chocolate and some soap and headed gratefully for the washroom.

Afterwards Kit sat in the shiny, curved corridor that ran between a fast-food cafe, a convenience store, and a buzzing amusement arcade. He wondered at this technicolor world he'd never truly lived in. He'd been penned inside one or other institution for so long that these surroundings seemed peculiarly and savagely new. He was face to face with things he knew existed, but had never previously experienced. He hadn't wandered freely, by himself, since learning plant names in childhood.

Now he sat and watched young men in tight jeans rolling down the corridor, looking pleased as punch talking loudly to themselves. It took a while to understand they were having mobile telephone conversations. But they appeared to babble into thin air, utterly wrapped up in themselves. Likewise those who sat on benches gravely entranced by tiny computers. Their universes were cordoned off; invisible barriers were everywhere.

Feeling less self-conscious than usual Kit prepared to stretch his limbs and sleep. But by now the light was fading and a brown man with a matching cap and shirt approached him with mop and bucket, his head shaking from side to side.

'Mate, you can't stay here all night.'

Kit heaved himself upright and left, wandered back towards the roadside. As the stars filled up the sky he lay down in the grass and slept.

The journey had continued like this for days. Kit often had trouble following the road, and would find himself stumbling through grass and concrete to the edges of nondescript villages. He could not guess by how much this lengthened his journey. But he didn't mind for it made him feel like some grand explorer, like the wildlife experts he watched on telly. He subsisted on chocolate bars and the rotting provisions he'd brought from his mother's kitchen. He always looked forward to washing at the service stations.

Despite his fondness for counting, Kit couldn't have told anyone exactly how long it took to reach the city. He knew that his clothes were darker and patchworked with stains, and his skin had turned uneven and bristly. His belly yowled frequently for he had run out of provisions and the scent of his body was rising off his skin. Strangers, on passing, often wrinkled their noses. He didn't quite understand why, but he had a sense of his own strangeness.

And then, all of a sudden, everything changed. He passed a huge roundabout at the end of the road – like the one from which he'd started but much bigger, blacker and louder. Again, people in sandals without socks straggled at the roadside, holding up slabs of cardboard with writing on. He followed the road round and it remained broad but much slower, with wide, shop-lined pavements and people wandering along. There were bike shops and cafes and stores selling hardware, and all of them appeared to have huge dirty windows. Not a single passer-by paused or turned their heads to stare at him. He might have stopped someone and asked, Is this London? Am I here? But then he spotted a street sign, and recognized a postal district. His stomach thrilled lightly. This was the gateway to the city.

As Kit made his way inwards, he realized he was no longer alone or an outsider. There were hundreds like him, with stained armpits, solitary and wandering. People who walked warbling and muttering, their eyeballs rolled heavenwards. If he rested briefly at the roadside, he would spot someone else doing the same. Never before had he felt a sense of such community.

Kit spent one further night on the pavements before arriving at Centrepoint. From the back alleys of Cricklewood to the gardens of Regents Park, he had started to love this city. He prickled with excitement on thinking of visiting Parliament or the Old Bailey. Growing nearer to the heart of things, he asked others on the pavements where he might stay, and they guided him towards the city's central shelter. Here he found an exhilarating ingathering of misfits and exiles. In a large open room that made him think of an underground shelter, dozens of streetfolk milled and mingled, or sat resting their tired limbs. True, many were smoking while he preferred to eat chocolate, but they did not turn and look at him with wide or sneering eyes. Official-seeming types stood at the edges of huddles shouting.

'Who're you then?' asked a small man with a ginger beard.

'I'm Kit. How do you do?'

'You're posh aintcha?'

Kit glowed with pride. 'I don't believe I've had the pleasure of learning your name.'

Ginger Beard looked at him oddly, his neck pulling backwards. But before he had time to respond there was a voice behind Kit's shoulder. Kit heard a wolfish howl which made him think of a football crowd hooligan.

'Olay – Olay, ginger, you raving poufter. Making new friends again? Who's your nice new friend.'

The newcomer to the conversation was preceded by a strong, dank smell. Shortly following the putrid fumes, a huge broad figure stumbled forward. Ginger Beard looked as though he were going to be sick: next to his red beard, his skin glowed a strange dull green. The newcomer leaned over him:

'Aintcha going to introduce us to your new friend?'

Ginger Beard shrank into himself, speechless and shaking gently. After years of experience, Kit clocked the bully and his victim. Smelly Breath was leaning close, all leering and contorted:

''Coz if you don't want to tell us, might have to do something ourselves.'

Kit didn't know what unhappy history lay between these two enemies, but Ginger Beard had called him posh, and had been friendly and polite. This new arrival appeared nothing but a thug and a drunk.

He said, 'Leave my friend alone, please.'

'Ooooh,' said Smelly Breath, all camp surprise, his voice

coming out high with the mockery usually used on women. 'What have we here then?'

The thug swayed towards him, but Kit wasn't afraid. He was dimly aware of the surrounding buzz hushing to an attentive quiet. Smelly Breath leaned inwards, one big dirty hand raised. The weight of the man swayed forwards, but Kit was too quick this time. He raised his own hand pre-emptively, caught the thug on the face; saw the unshaven cheek swivel and the looming weight of him flop. Before he could hit back, two men in T-shirts had arrived.

'Oi – oi. We'll have no trouble in here.' A clean man turned to Kit. 'You – I've not seen you before. Any violence like that and you'll be right back where you came from.'

'It's not his fault,' said Ginger Beard. 'He was protecting me. Bomber's pissed again.' And there were murmurs and nods of agreement from several surrounding. One of the T-shirted men gave Bomber a look of disgust. Ginger Beard turned to Kit.

'Ray, mate. Useful right hook you've got there. Very pleased to meet yer.'

Ray, despite appearances, was only thirty-eight. In a matter of the next few minutes he had given Kit a potted version of his life history. 'Ex-law clerk, me. You've got to see the funny side. Had a family, the works. Smashing wife and kids.' The funny side being the fact of it all falling apart as a result of a mixture of booze, adultery and joblessness. This did not actually make Kit laugh, but then he often found humour mysterious.

'And what is it you do, er . . .'

'Kit,' assisted Kit. 'I'm a criminologist. I research into the history of crime. I have a very wide knowledge of the subject, almost encyclopaedic in fact. And I'm very much looking forward to visiting the Old Bailey EC4.'

Ray showed no sign of surprise at the extravagance of Kit's

introduction, which encouraged Kit in his belief that the two of them might become friends. In fact, Ray gave Kit a hearty thump on the shoulder. 'Good on you then. You can't knock education.'

Kit looked at him thoughtfully. A plan was forming in his mind.

'The thing is. I am highly intelligent. Don't get me wrong. But I have a certain . . . shall we call it, a condition? I believe Einstein and other geniuses might have suffered from it.'

'Say no more, mate,' said Ray, with good-natured incredulity.

'But you see,' Kit persisted, 'I think you might be able to assist me. Do you mind if I tell you a little about my project?'

Ray looked for a second as though he might laugh, and Kit had a flashback to the playground. But Ray was kind, and as an ex-law clerk, he'd be bound to be just right. 'A favour for a favour, mate,' he said, and it was at that point that Kit had explained about the quest.

Next day, Ray took Kit to help sell some copies of the Centrepoint Chronicle, and introduced him to some other people he knew on the streets. By the afternoon they had more than enough for a bus fare to Colindale. They made an odd couple, certainly, shuffling towards north west London, Kit with his gawky body and Ray with his brash colouring. But few turned to take notice, and Kit daydreamed with satisfaction. His fingers dug deep in his pockets and curled round the special sealed envelope. It was his own private parcel, the cuttings he'd taken from his mother's secret box. He'd always known newspapers were of enormous significance. He remembered Alan and Gerard at primary school, and the local library near Margaret's Tea Rooms. And now they were going to the National Newspaper Library.

Ray, in fact, was familiar with the place, from his previous life as a person with a job and home to go to. Kit was grateful for the leadership as they headed inside the building. They went past a desk where you had to have your bags checked, only they didn't have any bags, and then proceeded into a vast room with an air of quiet, slow study. People sat at desks, tapping on computers or flicking through large ring-binders. Kit and Ray stood dumbfounded for a moment, and a library assistant approached. Ray put on his best voice and told her about their research, that they were students finding out everything they could about a murder case from back in the eighties: victim, Louise Laverty, defendant, Mark Mallory. The library assistant spoke in a slow whisper as though they were children with learning difficulties. She showed them how to look things up on the computer and also check the records manually. With old cases, you never knew. At one point she leant right over one of the computer keyboards, and Kit noted, with some distaste, how Ray moved his nose close to her breasts.

But they were making progress, that much was sure, and Kit asked Ray to scribble notes. By the time they had finished Kit knew almost the whole history of the Laverty murder case, the date of conviction and the sentence, and the date of birth of the guilty man, and the fact that on sentence he'd been given life in Wandsworth. He knew the name of the crime team that had dealt with the case, and of the officer in charge: Jack Smallbone. Later, as an addendum, looking through phone directories and street maps, he got Ray to find out the officer's home address and the street where he lived.

On the way back to Centrepoint Kit thanked his new friend profusely.

'Like I said, a favour for a favour, mate. Whatever you need it for.'

Kit thought of all the photographs in amongst the news-print. It was a wonder Ray hadn't guessed.

As his search gathered momentum, Kit obtained some information with ease. He found time to visit the old police station which had dealt with the Laverty murder case, and to discover that the serious crime squad had dismantled and relocated elsewhere. Also that Jack Smallbone was no longer working there.

'Jack Smallbone?' said the boy behind the counter, 'works up Holborn or Albany Street.'

Not that it mattered. Ray had confirmed there was only one J. Smallbone in the phone book. It wasn't your everyday name. Kit knew he would find the man somehow, but for the moment he had other priorities.

'You've reached Her Majesty's Prison Wandsworth,' said the automated voice on the other end of the line. 'If you have a touchtone telephone, and know the extension you require, please dial it now.'

Kit recoiled with the welter of information the message provided, and almost panicked and gave up, bewildered by the hybrid of human and machine. But he did manage finally to talk to someone by ringing the number for Social Visits, which, however, sadly took him little further.

'I'd like to make an appointment to see Mark Mallory, please.'

'Remand or convicted?'

'I beg your pardon?' Kit was struggling like a non-swimmer way out of his depth.

'Has he been convicted? After trial?' The voice was stiff and impatient; Kit imagined an uncouth woman with dyed hair and chipped nail varnish.

'Convicted,' he stammered. 'About twenty years ago.'

'Right,' said the voice. Perhaps she was winking at a

colleague, mouthing, *Right joker we've got here.* Kit guessed from the voice that she was like one of those secretaries on telly sitcoms, particularly, perhaps, the old-fashioned ones he'd once watched with his mother. Out loud she explained, 'Well, in that case you'll need a visiting order.'

'How do I get one of those?'

The woman's voice rolled upwards. 'The prisoner will send you one. Or write to him and ask.'

Kit wondered for a minute if this were a realistic proposition. He had a vision of sitting by candlelight and dictating a letter to Ray.

Dear Mark Mallory, it started, for to use another form of address at this point would surely be too shocking. But whatever would he say?

An unhappy anxiety, bordering on panic, was bubbling inside him like a bad, queasy stomach. He'd come so close, these were the last steps of his project. The final discovery of the missing jigsaw piece which he'd always deep down known about. Now this cheap and snipey female was standing in his way.

'How do I write in?' he blurted. 'Do I need to know anything in particular?'

'Well, the name of the inmate,' said the voice nastily, 'and of course the address. And the prison number helps.'

'Can you tell me the prison number?'

The girl sighed, and Kit was reminded of shop girls who said things like, Don't waste my time. But amazingly, for once, she was going to be helpful. 'Tell me the inmate's date of birth and I'll see if I can find it for you.'

Here, at last, was something Kit did know. He told the girl what she wanted and he heard her rattling a keyboard.

'You want GF,' she intoned, '8472. But I might wait a bit if I was you.'

'I beg your pardon,' said Kit.

'He's being released,' said the girl. 'Next Tuesday morning. By the time you've sorted your visit he'll be back on the outside.'

Kit had slept on the common near the prison right from Monday, just to be on the safe side. The crows there were huge, almost as big as small dogs. Their glossy black presences hovered around the park bench where he slept, and the soft beating of their wings made him think of creatures from the underworld.

Tuesday dawned light and clear, and Kit was dizzy from lack of food. For days he'd been unable to swallow more than scraps. Although he styled himself as an explorer with a professorial bent, snapshots of the past jostled within him causing his heart and blood to race. He veered between memories of warmth and those of loss and rejection, and tried not to think too hard what this newest of meetings might bring.

He parked himself outside the prison gates and waited. It was far too early, at first, for anything to happen, and by the time the morning had fully gathered he was already beginning to feel conspicuous. One time a woman even came out from one of the pretty, cottage-like houses just across from the prison and asked if anything was wrong. He shook his head vigorously and she made a funny pinching motion with her mouth. Later, he saw a figure from across the street twitch a curtain and peer out.

A shiny car blaring thumping music screeched by and pulled up. Two men in jeans and denim jackets leapt out yelling loudly. At first Kit thought they might be angry or frightened. But then he looked behind and saw a third youth with a large, sausage-shaped shoulder bag. The three leapt together, punching the air in a footballers' huddle. At that moment Kit guessed this was a prisoner released. He looked anxiously ahead, to see if any more were coming.

The car receded with its music and once more a dull quiet descended. An old man shuffled out and away without being met by anyone. Kit heard him curse and spit and he stopped to roll a thimbleful of tobacco. He waited a little longer and then, just as he was beginning to worry, it happened.

He knew him from a distance because the auburn tints in his hair shone like metal in the sunlight. He was tall and broad-shouldered – not unlike Kit, naturally. Kit strained to see him more clearly, even as his heart thudded. He was still a young man from a distance, shabby in jeans and a tattered jacket, but with the look of hard flesh and loose limbs. It was immeasurably comforting to Kit that he was not a withered old man, though as he drew closer he could spots flecks of grey hair.

He walked slowly, taking two or three steps and then stopping, looking about him. Despite the strong-looking body his movements were shaky, uncertain; as though everything were new and strange to him and he did not know how to react.

Kit walked right up to the man's shoulder before making his presence felt. He had time to take in the crow's feet and a faint scar below the left cheekbone. He felt such an intense rush of homecoming that at first he could not speak. The man noticed him and looked at him. They stood still and stared.

Kit remained silent, and the distant burr of traffic faded. The man raised his eyebrows as one about to ask a question, then started to shake his head uncontrollably from side to side. Kit looked at the bones, the set of the jaw, the green eyes, like one of his own. He felt like someone was giving him back a missing piece of himself. But neither touched the other, nor did they smile.

Eventually Kit said, 'I'm Kit. I've found out all about you.'

It seemed utterly unnecessary to introduce himself more

formally, for his quiet presence standing here was enough to tell all. But the older man was staring now, lifting a hand towards Kit's face without actually connecting, like a blind man trying wildly to brace himself for a meeting. He stepped forward, then back, then forward again, frowning. He said, 'Kit,' and added, 'how . . .' but his voice trailed away helplessly.

Kit said simply, 'I'm so pleased to meet you,' delighted at his words' careful politeness. The older man looked as though he might be about to fall over.

'Pleased to meet me?' said Mark Mallory. 'Your old man, a convicted killer.'

Kit rose to the occasion, drawing on all his encyclopaedic knowledge.

'Even if you're convicted, doesn't mean you're guilty.'

The older man carried on staring, his incredulity tangible. Again he made as if to touch Kit, again he thought better of it.

'No,' he finally agreed. 'Not necessarily, no.'

And suddenly Kit understood, as though some higher purpose had sent him here. Mark Mallory was kind and good and it had all been a mistake. This was his mission now: to uncover the truth.

A drop of moisture gathered at the corner of one of the older man's eyes. His voice came out slowly.

'We've all made mistakes. Back when we were younger, your mother and I . . .'

At the mention of his mother, all Kit's muscles contracted. A surge of new excitement rushed through his tired body. His father was free and she would surely see sense again now, and stop saying those offensive things about whatever Dr Geoffreys was on about.

'You must come back to see her. My mother needs to see you.'

But Mark Mallory stepped backwards and drew a deep breath.

'Kit . . . it's so many years. There's so much to explain. It wouldn't be right – I couldn't see her just now.'

Kit frowned, but felt sure the man could be persuaded otherwise. And then slowly, miraculously, Mark Mallory smiled.

'Tell me, is your mother still the most beautiful woman in the world?'

18

They say the smallest things can tip you back over the edge.

The recovered drinker, for example, who's not touched a drop for months. He wakes suddenly from a nightmare and reaches for a glass of comfort.

Or the ex-smoker, scrambling from some new terror, steadying his hand with a gulp of nicotine.

Even the entirely made-over man, new life, new love and all, catching sight unexpectedly of his lost flame, tumbling backwards into the chaos.

Last night Smallbone drank Jack Daniels before bedtime, and opened his eyes in the early hours. The remnants of a nightmare slipped through his fingers, and he was restless, scared and thirsty. He drank water to quench the thirst and then went to splash his face clean in the bathroom. His top-lit reflection showed him eyes crusted with salt.

The telephone rings early.

— *What time d'you call this then?* Julie immediately cottons on to his voice groggy with sleep.

— *No time. Morning time. Just like any other day.*

— *Don't make me laugh, Dad. You've just woken up.*

— *What's this then? Big Brother?*

— *The same. But the original version. The all-knowing George Orwell. None of this live television crap. I'll show you something much more scary.*

— *Quite so, but anyway. To what do I owe the pleasure?*

— *Just checking, Dad. That you haven't forgotten.*

— *Forgo . . .*

The sentence trails away and Julie completes it with a groan.

— *You have. Oh, Dad, you have. Lunchtime today, we're supposed to be meeting up, and you said you'd help me out with getting some stuff for New York. You said you would, promised.*

All her big-shot, career-girl accessories, and she sounds no more than six years old again. All pouting reproach for his shortcomings as a father.

— *Sweetheart, of course I haven't forgotten. I'll be seeing you at lunchtime.*

But the civilizing ritual of dining and shopping together has gone clean out of his head, and as he protests his innocence his voice is still thick with sleep.

— *Dad*, says Julie, wary now. *Is everything all right?*

The night comes rushing back to him, and it's all too late to explain.

— *Everything's fine, angel. Just feeling a little queasy.*

— *Nothing you want to talk about?*

— *Good lord, girl. You're enough to drive anyone sane.*

She laughs, and something jangles: he pictures shiny, dangling earrings.

— *See you at lunch, then.*

— *Bye, sweetheart, see you.*

Smallbone calls in half-sick. Says he'll be in, but later. Must be something he ate last night — you know, those dreaded takeaways. Feeling much better now, but it was a bit of a rough night. He'll just take it easy through the morning, make sure he's hundred per cent.

They'd have known at once, of course, in the old days. Whispers and raised eyebrows all round. Now there's just some twat he barely knows saying: OK then. See you in the pm.

And then, on the way to the station, he finds himself doing

something he can hardly believe. Edges the car out of the driveway, heads off in the wrong direction. Down through Camden, passing Holloway, and on through Seven Sisters. The roads all broad and dirty, litter-strewn: godforsaken, even in the sunshine. He veers south and eastwards towards his old stomping ground. Back towards the station he used to deal from, over the turf where he trained up Raff. Round to a little patch of barely surviving green overlooked by great grey cuboids.

Smallbone parks his car in one of the few bays where it looks like it might not get trashed. Not that you can ever be certain, but it's as good a place as any. He beeps on the alarm and glowers at a huddle of wide-eyed, waiting kids – some wearing woolly tea-cosy hats despite it being almost high summer. Then he walks purposefully to the one deserted bench.

There's an exquisite agony of remembrance as he sits back and lets the memories flow. This is the place he first brought Marianne when he asked her for the loan of her street-urchin's savvy. It was still professional then, and he hadn't even considered falling in love. Not just there, not just yet: where the flats cast ugly shadows, and sick-sweet orange peel smells mingled with shit. And not with the sad weight of Margaret on his mind, as she slow-changed into that too heavily dutiful angel.

– *Aintcha listening to me, mister?*

She turned and smiled at him archly. Though her teeth chattered and her bones shook beneath the thin skin of scarred ivory, she was wide-eyed and alive enough to see clean inside his skull. She leant closer, her shirt pleating, so he could see through to collar-bone and breastbone.

– *Why aintcha listening? Got a few things I could tell yer.*

I bet you could, Marianne. I just bet you could.

It had started there, on that bench, a love so stupefying

and distracting that he'd once spent twenty-four hours trying to compose a greeting card to send with flowers. That he'd reconjur over and over the slant of her face on the pillow after lovemaking, to reassure himself she'd come, that she'd enjoyed it, that she loved him. Or, when he suspected she no longer cared for him, how he'd smiled at the tremor in her voice, joyous that she was still tensed up and shot through with nerves for him.

Marianne: he'd barely known her, she'd passed by in just a second. Yet he'd never tasted such obsession outside the clear, sweet crushes of schooldays. She'd made him feel young again, nostalgic for a past that never was. But such love crossed over into adulthood with the slyness of pornography, its freshness peeled off of it, turning everything rotten.

He lights a cigarette, half to steady himself, but also to take him back to the old days. And then – what do you know? – he's only taken one or two puffs, but he's leaning forward, hands on knees, sobbing like a baby.

As soon as he swings the door shut behind him he sees the boy there, waiting.

He's got a thick paperback on his lap – looks like it might be some sort of guide to London – and across his knees lies a jumbo-sized half-unwrapped bar of chocolate. Something about his posture, and these accessories, makes him look like a fixture: like he's camping out for Wimbledon, or awaiting a glimpse of Michael Jackson.

He looks up as Smallbone enters, the different coloured eyes fixed, staring. There's no smile, no recognition, not even the crinkle of a brow. Maybe he thinks his presence is expected, and in a way, he'd be right. But Smallbone's not about to give this creep any sort of satisfaction.

He breezes past, not a nod, and sails into his office. Just checking in before taking lunch, saying he'll be back in the afternoon. Riffles through some dull mail, returns a few calls. Nothing urgent luckily: the morning's been uneventful.

When he goes back out, the boy's still there waiting. No one notices, perhaps because they're not looking, or maybe because the fronts of police stations are just full of people parked there. He'll ask no more questions. Nada. Better things to worry about.

But as Smallbone heads for the door the boy leaps to his feet.

— *Detective, I've been waiting for you. To have our discussion.*

Smallbone stiffens.

— *I don't believe there's anything to discuss.*

— *Mark Mallory is innocent. I told you that last time.*

— *Mark Mallory confessed and got convicted twenty years ago.*

— *But he didn't do it. He informed me as such, now that he's released. We've been having some discussions. By the way, you may well have realized of course, but I'm Kit Mallory, his son.*

Smallbone pulls away, as though from a bad smell. Partly it's the boy's stiff posturing, his pomposity. But also it's the shock of Mark Mallory having a son. Thinking back to it now, he reckons he can remember a girlfriend, striking looking redhead who attended every day of the trial. But they were children themselves, that couple, and he doesn't remember any babies.

— *I'm off,* says Smallbone, disconnectedly. *Busy. Appointment.*

— *We'll talk when you get back then?*

— *I'll be busy then, too.*

Smallbone goes out and down the steps; tries not to peek over his shoulder.

— *You look awful, Dad.*

Trust Julie to notice. What a million of his thick colleagues couldn't spot under a magnifying glass, she'd notice from a mile away, in under a second. He spins her the lie he told his

180

workmates, half believing it this time. Consistency is all, especially when you're giving evidence. The waiter shows them to the first floor, to a table by the window.

They order salads and mineral water, and Julie has a glass of dry white. Time was he wouldn't have been seen dead in a place like this. But even this gaff has memories now, inspires that odd familiar fondness. The older you get, the more associations attach to everything.

This is the place he came with Margaret, after years of silent, distant warring, for their dinner of reconciliation. They're practically sitting at the same table now, a small one in the corner, by the floor-length glass windows which seem to give out on to the sky.

— *Dad, what is it?*

A waitress comes and asks if she can take their plates, brushes the cloth down for the main course. Smallbone looks up and sees her with a start; asymmetric, choppy bangs, white skin tight over big cheekbones. It's her: twenty years on and alive, unchanged: Marianne risen from the grave.

— *Dad, what's wrong?* Julie's voice is thin with worry. He's not sure if he said, *Fuck*, out loud or not. He eyes Julie's glass unsteadily, willing himself to hold out. Julie's no fool, she'll guess something, but even to her this won't make much sense.

— *What's happened, Dad? If something's wrong, tell me.*

He reaches across the small table and clasps one of her hands. The slender length of her fingers shocks him, and the lightly scented, manicured hands.

— *Your mum and I came here. Brings back memories. I've just been thinking back that's all.*

Trying to find a way to lie and to tell the truth at the same time.

— *I'm sorry for what . . . happened. In the past, you know. There's so much I never told you.*

Julie reclasps his hand.

– It's all right. I'm grown up now. Everyone makes mistakes. You had an affair, Mum left you. That was years ago. I wish it had never happened, but you can't bring back the past.

Marianne the ghost-waitress is at their table again, laying out a cold meat selection for him and Julie to carve between them. Smallbone looks up to thank her as she rearranges cutlery and sees right beneath the clothes to the bony, white naked body; her standing in front of him at twilight, her mouth a gash of smeared lipstick, the triangular shock of dark fuzz between her legs. He blushes as the vision fades; the girl recoils only slightly. Her professionalism almost – but not quite – hides her knowledge, and her disgust.

His clumsiness knocks over his glass of mineral water, the clear liquid oozing out in a slow-moving stain. He flusters with half-baked apologies, and the waitress wipes the table, shaking her head and tutting with a sorrowful disdain. Julie's brows are drawn down, she knows something's escaping her, but she's past understanding, and is as good as admitting it.

– Dad, I don't know what's got in to you today. But promise me if you feel really bad you'll get help. Talk to someone about it – if not to me, then to someone.

Smallbone snorts, picturing some therapist living in some posh flat in Hampstead, charging a million quid for a sit down to keep stocked up in antiques. What good would that do, and how would Julie ever understand? Would she believe him if he said Margaret never left him over an affair? That there had been handfuls of girls before Marianne, which Margaret had long since ceased to count or care about. That Marianne was different, because he had loved her, but more than that, he had used her.

It was the guilt, not the infidelity, which drove Margaret away from him. And with that ghastly freak-eyed weirdo, now it's all coming back again. How he'd been thrust into the spotlight, and the Guvnor had saved his arse, but then he'd never been allowed to forget it, never been his own man again. The Laverty case, Mark Mallory, he'd never really done it the way he'd wanted to.

He had loved her though, hadn't he? Well, you never can tell. A relationship ends that way . . . you can hardly call it resolution.

He looks back across at Julie, whose eyes are full of consternation. He wants to tell her it's all right, but can't seem to find the words. They dig into their cold meat, their cutlery chinking, the whole place softly echoing on with salon refinery.

For the second morning in a row, the phone wakes him early.

The line goes dead as soon as he picks up, and he rolls on to his side, growling.

Second time it rings, he's in the bathroom, nearly cuts himself shaving. What's making him so jumpy? He half-suspects old freak-eyes. He shuffles into the hallway in his underpants, thinking the line's about to die again.

— *Jack Smallbone here.* (Trying to keep gruffness at bay.)

There's a pause, and he wants to say, *You bugger, the suspense is killing me.*

— *Jack, it's me. I'm sorry to disturb you.*

— *Raff. Well, fuck me backwards. To what do I owe the pleasure?*

Raff coughs politely, Smallbone pictures him blushing.

— *I tried to get you yesterday.*

— *Yeah, mate. I mean, go on.*

Raff coughs again, arhythmically, so Smallbone knows there's something wrong. He scoops wax from his earhole and waits for Raff to spill it.

— *It's about that case we did all those years ago, Jack. The Laverty murder case.*

— *How could I forget? We sent that lad down, Mark Mallory.*

It really is like a bad dream now, and the goose bumps are rising.

— *Well, this isn't about Mallory. At least not that I can tell right now. But, look here, I don't know if you remember a German chap called Karl Wahlberg. We spoke to him after a witness of yours was found dead, all pretty peripheral.*

Carol of Acton. A twisted corpse in a turquoise bathroom, and then that unexpected confession. So many years ago, but it all comes back so easily.

— *So what's the story Raff?*

— *Well, apparently Wahlberg remembered me from when I interviewed him about the Laverty case. And he tracked me down recently, to make a complaint. Said he'd been bothered by someone connected to Mallory. Someone sniffing around, asking questions, wanting to know about Mallory's past.*

— *Mallory's out, the case is closed. What's the deal on this one?*

— *Well, I told him, Jack, and I explained someone stalking him was a separate issue.*

— *And? The point of this is? What's it got to do with me?*

— *I just thought you ought to know, that's all. Wahlberg reported another incident. Asked for an officer to go and speak to him. But he never got to take his complaint.*

— *Well, spell it out, Raff. This isn't bloody Inspector Morse.*

— *Jack, Wahlberg's dead. And it looks like it's not an accident.*

19

There would be no more children.

Miranda knew it now, as she had known it then. It wasn't a case of being too old for it, whatever some might say: her body was still young and supple, and anyway look at some mothers these days. Madonna, even the Prime Minister's wife, for God's sake. She could give them a run for their money.

The point was, the sad truth of it, motherhood was a thankless task. Women's bodies might be built for it, but nothing in the world could give you the mental strength. You gave everything to your child, and then what did they turn out like? Ungrateful crazed delinquents, throwing everything in your face.

The worry had taken a while to settle in, but now it had come, it hit her hard. She stopped enjoying the solitude, feeling that the absence of her child was a release. She had expected some sort of disappearance, that he would meander off in his strange way. But she had thought he would return once he got cold or hungry. Or perhaps some stranger would bring him back, dirty, lost and feverish, and she'd have to bathe him like a baby before packing him off to bed.

But it had been days now: so many of them she could no longer count. Calling the police was out of the question: they'd been enemies for years. But she did wonder what they might do anyway if she had chosen to seek their help.

My child's missing, she would say, and they would ask for a description.

Six foot two, broad shoulders, 21 years old . . . and they'd put down their notebooks and smirk.

An adult, they would say. *Well, adults do wander.*

And, of course, they'd fail to understand that Kit would never be an adult, not in the true sense of the word, not in the adult way you recognize.

And then again, you see, it might all go horribly wrong. The police might intervene unbidden, like uninvited guests. They might find him wandering the streets aimlessly, be suspicious at his shambling. He might make enemies, get into a fight with those great, oafish fists of his. He might end up in a police cell, and no one around would understand. They'd start sniffing, asking questions. It hadn't mattered much before . . .

Miranda stared into the bathroom mirror, and tucked her hair behind her ears. She moistened a pad of cotton wool slowly, and began to remove her make-up.

If it had been up to Mark there would never have been any children to begin with.

At first he was uncomprehending, his green eyes dulled and slow-witted. She tried to communicate with her body, without resorting to words: rubbing her shiny palms and fingers over the still invisible bump. She thought of old black and white movies, with their breathless innuendo.

'You can guess what it is, can't you? What's happening to me – to us?'

Mark's response was somewhat more Anglo-Saxon. He backed away from her, wide-eyed, his Adam's apple bobbing. His skull shook from side to side like some life-sized marionette. Several times he started to speak, but only rough grunts came out.

Miranda had figured that, being a man, and a young one at that, Mark might well take some talking round when it came to the subject of babies. But this hostile, blind shock was something she'd simply not bargained for. Something inside her went colder, but she steeled herself against it.

'Mark' – she drew closer – 'I know this is a surprise for you. But think what it'll mean. The two of us – a family.' He was kneeling and staring up at her, his face immobile, disbelieving, but Miranda saw only a supplicant, a choirboy's angel face upturned. She lifted one hand from her belly, and cupped it round his stubbly chin. 'I know what you're thinking – we're too young – but I've got it all worked out . . .'

Mark moved her hand from his chin with a savage, staccato jerk. Something sharp caught Miranda's cheek and it took a second for her to register that it was one of her own nails. His contorted hostility had conspired to make her scratch herself. The skin pulsed hotly at the spot beneath her cheekbone where she'd drawn blood. She straightened, stepped away from him, blinking back bewildered tears. Boxer like, Mark wiped his mouth with the back of his hand. For a second she thought he might spit.

She crossed her hands over her belly: instinctively, protectively.

'Don't worry,' he told her thickly. 'I didn't mean to fly at you. We'll work out something.'

And he left her there with her stinging cheek, and the heavy aching inside of her.

Later, after swallowing aspirin and dabbing witch hazel on her cheek, she crawled beneath the covers and slept. It was already evening when her eyelids flicked open, with something ticklish rubbing her cheek. She emerged stuffily from her drowsiness to find Mark lying beside her, his body curved into an S, following her shape beneath the covers.

'Miranda, I'm sorry about earlier. But this baby' – he spread his hands – 'you must know it's impossible.'

Miranda turned her head to look at him, to will herself to fury. But she just saw his beautiful face staring into hers with sad entrancement. An attempt at reproach came out in a weak cough. She lifted her hand and ran it over his profile.

'Like you said, Mark. We'll work out something.'

He slid his hand down her spine, over her buttocks, and then inside her. Warmth suffused her dulled skin, and she had no will to argue.

Mark took her to some Family Planning Clinic attached to a big London hospital. The name of it struck Miranda as hopelessly ironic: Mark made out they were past all planning, and wanted nothing at all of a family. The place was somewhere so anonymous and central that it may as well have been abroad. Miranda protested that their GP should do.

'For God's sake, Mark, we're almost in the eighties, not the fifties.'

He was insistent they had to lie, say she was older than she was. If they knew she'd only just turned sixteen, he could get done for statutory rape. She shut up at that, not fully understanding. They counted their change and shuffled grimly to the tube station.

On the way to the hospital, she imagined them as vagabonds, or runaways. When they emerged from the underground, London rose up around them: brown and grey houses and office blocks, streets and squares and railings, all sly reminders of a city she and Mark hardly knew about. The clinic itself was in a big Victorian building, outwardly gracious, if dirty, but with depressingly unkempt corridors. They spoke to a girl behind an enquiries desk and took their seats in the waiting room.

The rickety plastic chairs reminded Miranda of primary school, and there were lots of posters with diagrams of the human reproductive system. The corner of one fell forward on to Miranda's shoulder, its Blu-tac hinge failing, sharply scratching the place she'd cut herself. She brushed the paper away, feeling even the posters were harassing her. She thought if people came here regularly, that could suffice as contraception; just an hour in this waiting room could quite kill any passion.

Miranda opened up a magazine in an effort to distract herself. 'Look out . . . coming your way this autumn', one of the articles blared out happily. As though a woman with full-up insides planning to kill her own baby could possibly care about the books, films and fashions of next season. Her knuckles tired as she turned the pages, and then she stopped mid-breath, gasping.

'One to watch out for, model and singer, gorgeous newcomer Sacha. Catch her debut single out now – *Here, There and Everywhere.*'

Pouting and smouldering for England, there was none other than the Cornflower Girl.

Miranda's hand flew to her mouth, she was afraid she might be sick. The Cornflower Girl looked older, and far more beautiful, than in any previous photograph. Had such a short while out of Hollybush wreaked such a grand transformation? Had she been disingenuous in saying casually as she sat in the common room, *I might be releasing a single*? Or had fame and glitter exploded round her this swiftly and suddenly, as steady ground rumbles and fragments just before a quake? From her preening, inanimate pose, she stared up and mocked Miranda. Her weight was slanted over one hip, and she pressed a finger to her lips: she was like a little girl with a question, or a woman with a secret. The small print drivelled rubbish about her drop-dead looks and new release.

Mark peered over her shoulder, but registered nothing.

'Away with that rubbish,' he said, flinging aside the magazine. She could imagine that's what her father would have sounded like, if she'd ever had a father.

'Miranda Laverty,' called out the nurse, and they went in to see the doctor.

Mark held her hand throughout the consultation, clasped firmly over one knee. He squeezed it tightly, almost painfully, at certain key moments. He pressed and released it as she reeled out her address at Hollybush, and the one before that with Mr and Mrs Davis. Then she found herself embarrassed at knowing so little before then, and had to explain about being given away at birth because her mother was unwell, and how difficult it could be to make adoption and fostering plans work. She found herself talking with the detached authority of a documentary programme presenter, and was surprised to feel the smarting resentment welling up inside her. When the doctor asked about her date of birth, Mark pressed her so hard she almost yelped, and she remembered to make herself a little older, as needed. The doctor appeared relieved: at least, no adults needed.

He established that she had no blood or heart problems, had not been on the pill, had regular periods and had never previously had a termination. She wondered that he could ask all those questions to so many women, and not feel embarrassed or intrusive, like a dirty old man.

Then he told her she was young and healthy and that as the pregnancy was early they ought to be able to perform an abortion without much complication. Obviously, if that was what she wanted, then the earlier the better. But she must go away and think about it – could come back again, if she had more questions. Alone, if she preferred – he shot a disapproving look at Mark. There should be no hasty decisions.

As he bid them farewell, he pressed contraception leaflets upon them, as though showering them with presents they didn't really want. Mark put his arm round her, and said he'd take her to McDonald's for a treat. He kissed her fiercely and said, 'You know I really love you.'

He bought her a huge chocolate milkshake, which dripped like sugary tar into her stomach.

'The details,' she started to say, 'the lies. Won't somebody . . .' He placed a hand over her mouth, as though to caress her, or to smother her. At a shiny, kid-sized table opposite, a pair of twin boys were yelling. Their mother was desperately trying to prevent the full-scale dismantling of Big Macs. Miranda sucked on her milkshake, and tried hard not to feel sick.

Mornings floated beneath a film of nausea and fatigue. Miranda felt as though a wall of clear but stifling jelly had sprung up between her and the outside world. Miranda and Mark could no longer stay at Hollybush, and they were going to have to see the Local Authority about getting a permanent home. In the meantime, they went into something called temporary accommodation, which turned out to be rooms in a hostel nearby which smelt of fish and chips. Not yet a couple in the eyes of the public, they were allotted separate rooms, and their companions were single wandering men and one hopelessly lost and pregnant woman. The food smells made Miranda feel all the sicker, and she longed to get out of there. Hollybush staff said they'd help, but Miranda didn't believe them.

Although no longer in the posh part of town, the hostel wasn't far from Hollybush, and Miranda popped in frequently to check post, and make sure she was up-to-date with any correspondence about the forthcoming term at sixth-form college. But now the corridors of her old home were peopled with strangers. Many of Mark's and Miranda's contemporaries had left – claimed by lost families, or halfway houses, or jails. There was another change of staff; Karl the Nazi was no longer. Nothing was as it had been. Once she poked her head round the common room door, and saw the television was new, and thought she spotted the Cornflower Girl on some trashy, tea-time, youthful programme. She placed her hands around her middle and gritted her teeth against the belly ache.

'When's the appointment?' asked Mark, meaning, When's the abortion?

Miranda looked at him squarely. 'You know we don't have to do this. I could get a job – we'd get a flat. Later on, I'll go back to college.'

He put his finger on her lips. 'You know it has to be this way.'

The world around her grew stranger, but she no longer tried to make sense of it. On Saturday, as she made her way out to the shops, a tall, thin dowdy woman pushed past her on the pavement. Her neck was slumped down inside her collar, and her eyes were covered by huge, clumsy sunglasses. She kept her gaze glued to the ground, and her shoulder knocked Miranda's.

'Oi, can't you say sorry,' snapped Miranda, but the woman did not reply.

Miranda dwelt briefly on the subject without any real curiosity, but as she came back from the shops she heard a noise from within the house. She heard a high, Germanic accent – a voice thick and scratched with anger. And a softer voice answering to it – young and broken up with pain. She heard the thud and shunt of shifting furniture, and then the slap of flesh on flesh. The younger voice bleated.

Up the stairs Miranda bounded, as though with a following wind; two steps at a time, despite the fullness in her belly. At the top of the landing she turned right, to where Mark's door stood open. Mark slouched in a corner, a line of blood streaming from his mouth. Karl the Nazi stood before him, his back to Miranda, his feet squarely apart, hands resting on hips. If she could only have seen his face, she guessed he would have been sneering. She took a step forward, and then a twinge of sharp pain halted her.

'Toe-rag, pervy cunt,' spluttered Mark. 'You've got it coming, you'll see.'

'Just keep out of it,' growled Karl. 'You don't know what you might run into.'

His voice was hard but calm, and he slapped Mark again, fiercely. Then he turned and stormed out, not seeing Miranda. She trod into the room, trembling, and knelt down in front of Mark. He stared with rheumy, half-blind eyes, as though barely seeing her.

'What's going on?' she wailed. 'What was he doing here? What has he done to you?'

Mark made as though to straighten himself, then crumpled like a flower. He sniffed loudly and roughly to stem a trail of snot.

'What's going on with the Nazi? Why did he come here?'

'Shut it, Miranda. Just don't ask me too much right now.'

And she left him there snivelling.

Of course, it gave her the perfect excuse. Mark was in pain for days afterwards, and he wanted to sleep late. On Monday, she left early, and wrote him a note.

'Darling, I didn't want to wake you. I've got to do this on my own.'

She slid the note inside an envelope, and left it under his pillow. Very tragic fifties movie queen, she thought, not without satisfaction.

She spent the day wandering round the shopping arcade, popping in and out of the various stores. As she rested and sat staring at the giant indoor, coloured fountain, she spotted a ring of earnest little girls mouthing and wriggling to the piped music. She was able to match their words to the soulless background litany: *You're with me baby in my heart/With me coz I care,/Where ever I may go, baby/Here, there and everywhere.*

No matter that this audience was between six and eight years old: it was little short of tragic, thought Miranda, that the Cornflower Girl could worm her way so quickly into their fickle but fragile worshipping hearts. The thought triggered a sharp rise of nausea in her gullet, and she quickly rushed into Mothercare to try to distract herself. Here, thankfully, her mind soon turned to other things, and she even managed to lift a Baby-gro, without a single person noticing. The security tag must have been faulty, it was all so delightfully easy. Back at the hostel she admired it with a mixture of dread and excitement.

'How did it go?' asked Mark, coming to find her in the bedroom.

He looked at her darkly and she looked up without answering. He sat beside her and leaned towards her and she took his head in her hands and kissed his lips hard, biting into the flesh.

'Mark. I want this so much.'

He pulled away, spread his knees, placed his palms on them stiffly. The breath he sucked inward made a sibilant hissing.

'You didn't do it, did you? You know if you wait too long it'll get dangerous.'

'But I don't *want* to do it. I want us to be a family. We'll go away from here, find a place together, put Hollybush behind us. We'll go where no one knows us. Start everything afresh.'

Mark stared at her so hard his eyes grew like glass. At first she thought he might have snapped a nerve, so still was his gaze on her.

The memories faded into the shadows of the little square living room. All her controlled adult life, Miranda had been waiting for this time. It had taken the most subtle balancing act of privacy and enterprise to get her this far. She'd never wanted Kit to know about his childhood and his father, until he was old enough to hear it from her told slowly and sensibly, without sensation. So they'd kept moving, and stayed away from the thick of things, and she'd prayed each time he wouldn't be squawked and pointed at. She'd even tried to tell the staff at the units he'd been in – that there were things he didn't know, that only she herself could tell him. And she'd kept close and yet distant, thinking that way must be best for Kit.

And the money! How she'd scrimped and saved. The early days had been the hardest, as she'd swallowed both her pride and her sickness every time she removed her clothes in front of customers. That was never a dream she'd fashioned in her wild, scheming days at Hollybush: selling her skin, and bones, and the small, nervous bunched up muscles, opening up every inch of flesh for strangers even as the scent of Mark had yet to be washed away. And then making the sale over and over again, because there were so many willing buyers, at such ludicrously high prices.

Oddly, though the prostitution had made her retch at first, by the time she'd saved enough to stop she had almost grown inured to it. But then – at least for Kit's sake – she'd decided to get respectable, and had earned her money with only the most tentative of footsteps into public, latterly doing sub-editing for *Country Brides* and *Your Home, Your Garden*. She'd learnt to survive because she believed the prize was worth waiting for.

But now . . . she got up, wandered round the room, and then into the hallway, picking up small objects, not turning on the lights. She felt like an intruder in her own home, inspecting random items, looking for clues as to who might be living here.

Perhaps all this worry was needless, and he'd be back any minute. The dark house creaked willingly, the gurgle of pipes answering to the rattle of windows. It was too noisy for a new home. Surely that sound must be a person. There! Wasn't that footsteps?

Miranda rushed to the front door in a thrill of relief. Out on the doorstep, she breathed in late summer grasses. Memories swarmed back to her, but there was no sign of anyone. She retreated into the hall.

Miranda went and sat in the little side room, the one she usually kept locked: her 'office' she sometimes called it, as she sub-edited pieces about wedding hats. Absently, unthinkingly, she picked up her old letter box. It opened without the key and she sifted its contents with her fingers. Letters and cuttings she knew so well, she could identify them almost by touching.

It was only then, in the thickening evening, that she started to understand. That Kit might be heading for the city, and then what nightmare might be unfolding? She shut her eyes tight to stop the ghastly flow of thought; then flicked on the light switch with a sharp, vengeful purpose. She started calculating furiously how much money she had: what she had saved from her recent jobs; could she work while on the move?

As the possibilities of things became plainer, she realized the need for swift action. Kit would not be coming back, and she would have to go and find him.

20

He reaches the house quickly. There's a couple of police cars parked up outside, and an officer at the door, ready to shake his head severely at the odd encroaching stranger. No junk mail today, then. But there's nothing spectacular in the air, no sirens, no rubbernecks. Just your average bog-standard, everyday dead body.

The place itself is a narrow slice of those flat-fronted Victorian terraces, once an artisans' cottage, perhaps, now a series of flats for yuppies. Probably couldn't swing a cat inside, though it'd cost you a small fortune. Looks like Wahlberg had the basement, or the Garden Flat as they'd now call it. If you peer through the shallow front bay you can see through French doors into a garden.

Smallbone flashes a card at the sentry, who doesn't seem all that impressed. Then Raff comes out and nods him through. Brings back a twinge of the old days. Him training up his junior, the Laverty case their public triumph. These days Raff's moving upwards, he's a real star, despite the accent. Smallbone might even have mustered some jealousy if all of that mattered at all any more.

– *Thanks for coming.*

Raff grips Smallbone's forearm in a move halfway between bear-hug and handshake: that hybrid gesture for fond men who aren't quite liberated enough to embrace.

– *Looking good, mate*, says Smallbone, pulling back just a little. And it's true: the faint lines around Raff's eyes have conspired to lend him a helpful ruggedness: finally he looks like he's been about a bit, could tell you a few stories.

— *Good to see you too, Jack*, but the pleasantries are embarrassing them both.

— *What can I do you for, Raff? Let's have the low-down.*

Raff leads the way into a narrow hall that smells musty, like in winter. The dead body's been moved but the signs of male solitude are everywhere. A sparse unfilled kitchen, with cupboards that tell you they're half empty even with the doors closed. A pair of leather driving gloves for men by the angular black telephone in the hallway. An enormous widescreen television where the living-room hearth might have been. A glass coffee table with some waxy stains on it; a fixed chrome shelf for a mantelpiece.

Towards the entrance to the kitchen, at the back of the flat, they'd found the body slumped with a noose round its neck. A chair had been tumbled over; a cord hung from a broken light fitting. Wahlberg looked in his early forties, strong and healthy for his age. Looks like he'd been single, and in the PR business, pretty small-time but doing all right.

The shelf with the photographs displays several framed pictures of a white-toothed, tanned man. Usually he is leering as his arms wrap an assortment of young females. Protégés, no doubt, each one the Next Big Thing. But there's this one photograph that's much older, and in it Wahlberg's a handsome youth. Must still be in his twenties. And there's no mistaking the girl with him. Smallbone picks up the photograph, frowns at it narrowly.

— *Louisa Laverty, if I'm not mistaken. I see what you meant about the connection. But what makes you so suspicious? This is a suicide, isn't it?*

— *Well, we don't know for sure yet, but it is a possibility. But there are signs of a forced entry, perhaps some kind of struggle. The lock wasn't broken, but the door frame has been damaged. There's some chipping to the internal door and some paint scrapings which seem fresh. One of the neighbours reports hearing raised voices some time last night.*

— Could be Wahlberg had a row with someone, personal problems. Maybe it all got so bad he went and topped himself. Doesn't take us any nearer to Laverty.

— But, Jack, Wahlberg was being bothered. There was a connection to Mallory. And suddenly he's dead. Perhaps someone came here, killed him, and tried to make it look like suicide.

— Well, who was the one bothering him? Have we managed to establish that much?

— Trouble is, he got snuffed out before he could make his complaint. But he talked about a youth, maybe a relative of Mallory's. Obviously we'd like to talk to him, though I'm not sure how we'll find him.

Smallbone starts to speak, then stops: instead gathers up photographs.

— We'll seize all this, look through it. Maybe it'll lead somewhere. And that boy you were talking about. I'm not sure yet, but I think I might know who he is. Might have some kind of lead. Don't you worry, Raff, we're going to sort this.

But he's seen someone else in one of the photographs, and a cord's twitched inside his brain. A gnarled woman with a smoker's mouth, standing alongside Wahlberg and Laverty. All three of them grinning hugely, like they've as good as won the lottery. And he remembers a turquoise bathroom, and dolphin shower curtain torn in two.

Is his memory playing tricks on him, or is this his long-lost witness: Carol of Acton?

Julie's fixed the date, she's flying at the end of this month. Smallbone awaits the day with self-pity, as though she'll be taking the summer with her. There'll be a farewell party, of course, and a quiet dinner with the parents. He asks her what airport she's leaving from, says he'll be sure to see her off.

— You know I'm going to be fine, Dad. No need to go out of your way.

He gazes at her earnestly.

— Wouldn't miss it for the world.

They're lunching round a tiny table on a crowded pavement not far from his flat. It's been a promise of theirs to do this as much as possible before she leaves, in the little time that's left to them together, in this city. He tells her of the mind-pictures he's been forming of her apartment: high-ceilinged and airy with vast windows giving out on to the jagged Manhattan skyline.

— White carpets, he says. *And lots of pale wood and chrome. Glass coffee tables and a white sofa. Watch yourself with the red wine.*

She laughs at him, her head thrown back.

— Let's not get too precious. I'll probably end up in some hovel with brown carpets and no kitchen.

He watches her watching him as he reaches for the mineral water.

— Gonna miss you, Ju.

His fingers find hers on the other side of the bread basket. They make a swinging cradle of hands and she says suddenly, *Come with me.*

He stops, splutters for a second, and stares at her with raised eyebrows. It's a strange moment, almost like hearing those words from a lover or a mistress, offering you the escape you've dreamed of but can't accept. He touches her face.

— What a lovely idea. But you know it's not possible.

— Why isn't it possible?

They pay the bill, scrape their chairs back, wander up towards the park.

— Me, Manhattan, my age. Whatever would I do out there?

Julie links her arm through his.

— You wouldn't have to do anything. Just come with and be. You're almost retired anyway. Why not take time out?

— I wish it was so easy. But I do have some commitments.

And he thinks of Raff's bubbling new ideas, the grey filing

cabinets in his office, the slatted blinds in the bedroom, and wonders if that's really true.

On the way up to the park they duck into a newsagents so that Julie can buy herself a pocket-sized bottle of mineral water. He stops by the paper shelf, half concentrating, half dreaming, wondering vaguely what's what in the world, as if it really matters.

He picks up something middle-brow, unable to stomach the more demanding stuff, and little glossy, booklet supplements tumble out from inside. He and Julie bend together to gather in the straying sheaves of paper, and as her smooth hands rest beside his knotted ones, they both see it together. Or at least he supposes she sees it, because at that moment everything goes still, and he feels as though a magnifying glass is honing in on those few words. Not quite on the front page, granted, but all of a sudden foregrounded.

'Dead Man Raises Ghosts of 80s Model Murder.'

The article's about Wahlberg, for fuck's sake. God knows how that got to the newspapers. Stuff about him being found dead in 'suspicious circumstances' *though at this stage we're keeping an open mind, added Detective James Rafferty.*

And of course, the sly coda, the sting in the tail,

. . . *Mark Mallory, the man who pleaded guilty to the killing of model Louisa Laverty two decades ago, has recently been released.*

No comment, no inferences, but there's an editorial spread about lost children and paedophiles and speculation about that old chestnut, *should life really mean life?* So either the whole Laverty case was mishandled and the wrong man went down for it, or the real killer's out too soon and the system's failed again.

You can't win in this game, every which way you're a loser.

Julie shakes his shoulder: it's like an awakening, so he guesses he must have been wandering off a bit. She holds his upper arm as he straightens and he feels like an old man.

Customers have been clogging up the aisle, impatient to get to the counter.

— *I saw what you were reading,* Julie says once they're outside. *Has any of that been bothering you?*

— *Well,* he replies evenly, *Raff did fill me in a bit. Bit of a blast from the past, of course. But not much to do with me any more.*

She presses his arm again, as though he needs comforting.

— *What's it doing in the papers anyway?* He goes off on a bit of a rant. *Beginning of an investigation of a death that may or may not be suspicious, that might be distantly linked to the murder of some model twenty years ago. I mean a nice girl, maybe, but who the hell cares.*

The night heat rises off the pavements. Smallbone's got a window half open, and one of those rotating fans blowing an artificial cold. He keeps forgetting whether or not it's a good idea to have both on at the same time, like having the windows down in the car and the air conditioning on. Then he remembers, it's not a car, and he can do what he bloody well likes.

He's got piles of papers on the desk and he's trying to make sense of things. It's been ages since he's worked so late, shown half this dedication, but there's an uncomfortable restlessness driving him.

The papers on Wahlberg show he was obviously a dodgy sort. Started off as a social worker at some kids' home called Hollybush – he thinks he vaguely remembers Mallory spent time there too. Then he left, chucked it aside, for a more glamorous career in PR. Managed Sacha – or Laverty, whatever – moulded her in the early days, although it's clear just as she was really making it big she'd cast him aside. And looks like he must have added a couple of years to her age, so the model agencies didn't get too uppity. Those photos of them smiling. He's probably some pervert.

You can tell the bloke's not all above board, because there's early letters he's written to her modelling agency passing himself off as her uncle. Called himself John Laverty. Smallbone thinks back to all his enquiries, a dead girl without a past. He was already out of her life when she met her early death. But it looks like he went on to manage a few more in his time, probably they flashed their tits once for the Sundays and then went on to become bank tellers.

It's not clear why he conspired with Laverty to obliterate her past. Publicity-wise you'd have thought there'd be gold dust in that rags-to-riches malarkey. Unless there was too much secret vice from the children's home to risk uncovering.

Did Wahlberg top himself to bury some secret, or was his death the result of some revenge killing? Smallbone's not seen the strange boy lately, and he wonders if he'll be back. But his head's starting to ache a little, and nothing's getting any clearer.

– *Fuck it*, he says out loud to an empty room. He reaches for his jacket, swings his arms into the sleeves, then shrugs it off again because it still feels too hot.

On the way home, he stares up at the night sky. Closes his eyes for a second, because the air's all summer sweetness. Thinks of Sunday in bed with Margaret, and her lips against his shoulder blades. The deliciousness of knowing it's morning, but not having to get up. Julie, no more than a toddler, jumping up at the door handle. No traces yet of the ghost of Marianne, stepping in between cool sheets.

He opens his eyes. The sky glistens beyond a film of moisture. Why not pop into the pub? A couple won't do any harm. His memory's heavy but his head light as he floats up to the bar, and he couldn't say how many he's had by the time he's come out again. This blurred world is so much easier, none of those nasty, jagged edges. He stops at the off licence and buys two bottles of wine. Top of the range, naturally. Some weird double-think about not being a lush if you only drink the classy stuff. The summer sky's so clear and starry, he could almost enjoy himself. If it weren't for the case; for being an old alcy; for Julie going; for being alone . . .

As he opens the door of his mansion block his brain's starting to feel lighter. He heads for the staircase and footsteps echo somewhere above him. Quite a light tread – tripping, if you will – he tries to match it to one of the neighbours. Perhaps Jenny, the girl who lives opposite, or either Bob or Geoff, that gay couple.

– *Hallooo*, he calls out playfully, pissed before he's even started. Wondering if someone'll call back, wanting to put his guessing to the test.

The stairwell is silent but for his own, crazed echo. He reaches his door and fumbles for the keys.

It's at that point everything changes pace. It's one of those mad, distracted moments when you're being so utterly stupid that it takes a while to understand. Like the time he couldn't open his car door and spent a good few minutes jangling keys before realizing it was the wrong car and there was already someone else in it. It's not quite like that this time: this is his own place all right, but why doesn't the damn key turn, and why can't he steady the lock?

It seems like minutes – though it's probably seconds – before the truth drunkenly hits him. The door's already open: someone's been in before him.

He steps inside, swaying slightly, telling himself it's just some burglar. But his mind is doing cartwheels as his eyes whizz round the room. Nothing taken, looks like – telly intact, and DVD player. He holds his breath so his ribs hurt and there's a rush of blood in his ears. He can't seem to hear anything else, and everything's gone into slow motion.

The desk on the far side of the room holds all his papers,

work and personal. He notices one drawer pulled out and starts grabbing at the others, taking in the chaos of messed up letters, documents strewn about and disordered. A thief rummaging for valuables, or an amateur detective looking for clues? You'll have to get the boys in, he starts to tell himself, can't deal with this alone, Jack. He slides across to where the telephone perches, hears the low growl of the dialling tone. And then just before he hits the key pad there's a nearby, tinny clatter.

The handset almost slides out of his fingers and his whole body stills and freezes. He counts to three, then draws breath.

    — *Come out, come out, wherever you are.*

His feet slide silently towards the bathroom. A film of sweat coats his forehead.

    — *Come out. Game's up. Whatever you want.*

He's approaching the bathroom, sees the closed door in front of him. There's no sound from beyond it. Apart from that moment of clumsiness, this one's light-fingered and stealthy. But there's something else, a low-pitched banging, the blunt clack of wood on wood. He turns — it's just the front door, flapping ajar on its hinges — but his eyes are averted, his skull angle-poised on his neck.

And then he feels it. The sharp slicing of pain at the back of his head. His eyelids batten down instantaneously, as little pin-pricks of quiet agony burst at the base of his skull. Then they expand and get blunter and his knees go from under him. Someone's tying him, he can't breathe, rough cloth's stuffed into his mouth. He tries to force his eyelids upwards, but they're blindfolded too. The fabric's clean and oddly sweet-smelling. He feels the cloth being pulled tighter. The pain beats blunt, and then sharp again, as though his tender skull will turn to pulp.

He raises his blind head, hands flailing drunkenly. With another thwack to the back of the skull he falls forward heavily. His nose bangs on the floor and a trail of mucus and blood spills out. It mingles on his top lip and he tastes it sickly on his tongue. The tripping footsteps are receding and he spreads his arms out in front of him. His breath comes out in loud belches, rich with lager after-taste. He hunches on to his knees and manages to loosen the gag and breathe, then he pushes up the blindfold so it's on his brow like a bandana.

— *Come back, you bastard. You're going to pay for this.*

The patch of pain on his skull is warm and wet, the hair matted. God knows what he looks like as he lopes out on to the landing. He doesn't know if he's still drunk but he thinks he can still hear footsteps. He's panting, wheezing and belching and he's dimly aware of Bob and Geoff. Their whitened, worried faces peer from their open front door.

— *Gotcha, you bastard*, he whispers as much to himself as anyone, all the way down at the front door now, standing breathless and bloodied.

There's an echo in his brain of those light, tripping foot-steps but out on the summer pavement there's just the emptying night.

Kit had taken to sleeping on pavements, or on the open planes of parkland. The summer season was ending, but it was also at its hottest. He loved opening his eyes and catching sight of the stars, or shifting beneath a makeshift blanket to the soothing chirp of crickets.

He had bought himself a special notebook to record the details of his progress. It was purchased with some of the money he'd gathered from the street and then saved up: it had a spine of spiralling wire and covers of cardboard in marbled taupe. There was a special patterned pen to go with it, too, so he could write down all his exploits. Wherever he slept, he kept pen and notebook safe, sometimes falling asleep with them almost crushed by his flank. One fellow wanderer had unwisely tried to grab them, and though Kit did not wish for violence he had no option but to punch the other near-unconscious.

Although words did not come easily to Kit, he had long enjoyed writing, as placing his thoughts and experiences on paper gave them extra permanence and validity. Initially, it was true, the significance of this document had reminded him unpleasantly of school. But then he began to understand that this was something he was in control of: a way of reflecting *his* memories, of making his own thoughts permanent. And he comforted himself that by the time his work was published, he might have achieved such widespread fame and glory that the rest of the world could adopt his vocabulary.

The chronicle began with the first encounter of his father

outside Wandsworth. After a few words exchanged in early sunlight, Mark Mallory had begun to walk and Kit, his son, accompanied him.

'I must repeat,' Kit said, as their path curved round in front of the shops, 'it really is a pleasure and delight to meet you.'

Mark Mallory looked at him with wide eyes and furrowed forehead. 'It certainly is incredible,' he said finally, after a pause. Kit warmed to the compliment.

They walked in continued silence, with a quick closeness and friendship. Bearing this in mind, Kit felt words largely unnecessary.

'For fuck's sake,' said Mark Mallory, 'these boots are killing me.'

'Killing you?' said Kit, in alarm. 'How can a pair of boots do that?'

Again the wide, green eyes were on him with that staring fixed intensity.

'If you say something kills, you might not actually mean it.'

Kit considered his father's words: labelling something a killer did not make it true. Was this his father's way of underlining that he was innocent: no murderer. Kit made a mental note and said, 'Where are you going to live?'

'I've got a mate from inside who'll put me up for a few days.'

'And where does this mate, as you put it, live?'

'Leyton. Right on the other side of town.'

'Ah,' said Kit wisely, 'E10 or E15.' Mark Mallory did not respond. 'Perhaps I could stay with you?'

His father shook his head. 'I don't think that would be very wise.' The traffic hummed about them. 'But you do have somewhere to go, don't you?'

'Naturally,' said Kit. 'I have many friends in high places.

But the point is . . .' Mark Mallory waited, 'I'd very much like to talk to you further. There's so much to discuss.'

'There certainly is that.'

Mark Mallory sighed, and Kit guessed he must be tired, and then he said, 'Why not give me a day, and then we'll meet at my mate's place?' He offered to write down the address, but Kit assured him he'd remember it.

'Ten a.m., then,' said Mark Mallory. 'Day after tomorrow.'

The road was dirty, and it wasn't hard to guess that this wasn't where rich people lived. Kit had found the address, a door with chipped paint, between a hardware store and a cafe. He positioned himself in the street and waited for the allotted hour to come. He didn't like this place as much as Regent's Park, or anywhere in Central London. But at least it wasn't stifling, like places where people peered from behind their curtains.

Kit did wonder, momentarily, if his father would come down to meet him, or whether he would have to pluck up the courage to knock on the forbidding, dowdy door. But not long had ten o'clock passed than Mark Mallory slipped out on to the pavement. He didn't smile, or embrace Kit, and Kit found this entirely satisfactory, for he found too obvious fondness uncomfortable, even (these days) with his mother. His father jerked his head towards the cafe and the two of them stepped inwards.

Kit wasn't all that keen on the smell of bacon, or the sight of workmen in string vests. He claimed a table by the window while his father mumbled something at the counter, and then presented them both with tea and plates of toast, eggs and bacon.

'I took the liberty,' said Mark Mallory, lifting cutlery with gusto. Kit eyed his plate with suspicion. He didn't like eggs and he was sure the bread had seeds. He chased a crust round his plate, but in the end could only manage the tea.

'Not hungry then?' asked his father, who'd already polished off his own plateful. Kit shook his head, feeling guilty, but Mark Mallory didn't seem to mind. He swapped plates greedily, and then sat back and belched, after which he smiled sheepishly.

'Sorry, but you've no idea how good it feels to eat breakfast on the outside.'

Kit didn't bother to ask *outside of what*. Thinking time was limited, and he had an important purpose.

'You won't mind if I ask a few questions?'

Mark Mallory looked at him squintingly. 'Kit, I know this must be strange for you, but let me just say this. What happened between me and your mother was a very long time ago. I loved her very much, perhaps more than life itself. And deep down I still do. But we were little more than children.'

'How did you meet my mother?'

'We lived together in a children's home. We were your original childhood sweethearts. When I first laid eyes on your mother, I knew there was something joining us.'

His eyes had misted over with the sentiment, which to Kit was quite unpleasant. He had a mission, after all, and was in pursuit of facts.

'Were you still living at the children's home till right up to the trial?'

'No, we were living by ourselves then. We had to get out of there.'

Kit nodded sympathetically, envisaging two childhood tearaways.

'I expect there were social workers there,' he said wisely. 'Who made you do things you didn't want. I had one once called Paul. Horrible. Did you know anyone like that?'

Mark Mallory frowned. 'There was one guy, yeah. The

Nazi, we called him. Right bastard, excuse my French. What he did to Debs . . .'

'Debs?'

'The girl who died. She changed her name to Louisa, then Sacha. All those years ago . . . Kit, this isn't the right time to discuss this.'

'This is really tremendously interesting,' said Kit, to his father's continued frowning. His brain was ticking furiously. 'The Nazi . . . was that a nickname?'

'Yeah, Karl Wahlberg was his real name.'

'Would you mind writing it down?' His father raised his eyebrows at the pen and notepad pushed towards him, but Kit pleaded with him, insistent: 'This really is important.'

Mark Mallory looked sick as he scribbled on the paper. His face had turned a greenish colour: perhaps it was the two breakfasts.

'Look. This is all of a bit of shock to me.' He pushed the pad away, distastefully. 'Perhaps I'm not yet quite ready for this. Why not call it a day and meet again in a while?'

'How can I find you?'

'Can I not find you, Kit?'

'No, I'll find you.'

'Then same place. Three days' time.'

It hadn't been difficult to find the Nazi.

Once again, Ray assisted with telephone directories and streetfinders. Wahlberg turned out to be an even rarer name than Smallbone, at least in that part of London. Ray, whose fortunes were turning and who was on the waiting list for a council flat, offered to help Kit in his continuing mission. But Kit thanked him and said this was something he'd rather do alone. He took an *A-Z* and a guide to Rough Justice and went off to prepare.

Next day, he had made his way to a cluster of streets just

south of Shoreditch. This had once been a no-man's-land, but was now dotted with smart houses. He found the street he was looking for, the house number and the right door. Then in a manner to which he was now accustomed, he took up watch across the street.

At 9.30 the door of the basement flat opened. A broad-shouldered, sandy-haired man emerged, with hard lines around his mouth. As he reached the railings at street level he kept his gaze on his shoes. Kit went closer, wondering if this could be the man. The stranger scraped a sole along the pavement, then raised his eyes and looked at Kit. They exchanged glances, Kit curious, the other man purposeless. He looked away, vacantly, but Kit's memory churned. The man walked off, indifferent. Kit waited, triumphant.

It was after six when the stranger returned, but Kit hadn't minded the wait. The man walked fast towards his front door, still keeping his head down. Kit hurried across the street, matched up to his footsteps.

'Mr Wahlberg. Excuse me. Excuse me, I'm Kit Mallory.'

The Nazi stopped in his tracks, stiffened, then turned to look at Kit. His face was blank, but Kit thought the lines round his mouth showed cruelty.

'Can I help you?' he said. His voice wasn't quite English. He spoke as though looking down from a great height. Kit prickled.

'I believe you once worked at a children's home in London called Hollybush. A girl there, Louisa Laverty, was murdered twenty years ago. I wonder if you know anything. I'm making some enquiries.'

The man froze there on the pavement, then raised a hand carrying the paper. He stopped himself mid-motion, and stood still as a statue. His hard mouth was open, but no sound came out. Then he snapped his jaw shut.

'Who are you? What do you want?'

'Mark Mallory is innocent. I'm making some enquiries.'

'Leave me alone.' And the stranger turned on his heels. But long-legged Kit was able to match his stride easily. He followed him down the stone stairs, and up to the front door. The man flapped the air with his paper and turned around fiercely. His spat out cross words and spittle.

'Explain who you are or get away. Or I'll call the police.'

Kit stayed where he was and the man opened the front door. Kit tried to slip in with him, but the door slammed in his face. His head snapped back on his neck and he saw an outline through the door panel: a fist scraping the glass, and an angry mouth moving.

That night, Kit had slept beneath the stars again. He dreamed of his childhood home and his mother with a tall, straight-backed, angry man. He saw their outlines from the garden through the shallow bay window. He woke briefly before the dream ended and stared up at the skies.

Kit knew when he'd remembered something and his memory rarely failed him. He could see his mother arguing with the tall man as clearly as if it was yesterday, and then the same man coming to their house in the North, speaking in a voice that was not quite English. A man who was handsome, but with a hard, ugly mouth.

He'd seen the Nazi before, long ago, and guessed he would do so again.

The next time he met his father, they stayed away from the cafe. Mark Mallory led Kit up a flight of carpeted stairs, guided him into a flat and walked heavily to the refrigerator. His mate was away, he said: there was room for them to talk. He offered Kit tea and a cigarette, and Kit requested, instead, chocolate biscuits. He got Swiss roll as a compromise. They sat down at a table.

'Kit,' said his father, 'there's something I have to tell you.'

Kit's hand tightened on the pen and notebook which he kept safe in his pocket. He itched to start recording, was sure he was nearing his great discovery. His father's shirt stuck to his back, a patch of sweat between the shoulder blades. He breathed heavily, but said nothing. A curtain flapped in the dry breeze and there was a low buzz of house flies.

'I wanted to say . . .' said Mark Mallory, but could not finish his sentence. He gulped down his tea in one go and went to make another cup. He was on his third cigarette now, in almost as many minutes.

'It's about me and the dead girl,' he started mumbling, as though he half didn't want to be heard. 'Louisa. Sacha. Whatever. She was very beautiful.'

'But not as beautiful as my mother.'

Mark Mallory smiled weakly. 'Perhaps not, no, Kit. But the two of us were close. You see . . . it's difficult to explain. She gave me something your mother couldn't give me.'

Kit shook his head blindly. This was some terrible mistake. He had expected to hear of the dealings of some evil grown-up. He didn't wish to listen to sordid tales of Mark Mallory's straying appetite.

'But you still loved my mother . . .'

'Yes, Kit. But you have to understand . . . Debs — as she was to me — she was like a breath of fresh air. Things were so closed in the children's home where your mother and I grew up, having someone new like that was like a blast of something different, something promising.

'She was so full of ambition, she had this burning desire to make it from the start, and for a while I felt it was as though she could take the rest of us with us. She'd had this social worker, Carol, who'd befriended her when she was in an abusive foster home, and Carol said to her, *Debs, this isn't you, you're made for better things.* And she encouraged Debs to find out who she really was, because once she knew where she'd come from then she could move forward. So Debs tried to find her father, but she wanted a friend to join her, and I was dead chuffed because I fancied her so much, I didn't think . . .' oh God, Kit, I didn't think . . .'

And then Mark Mallory started to shake, first his shoulders, then his wrists. He raised the tea-mug to his lips but hot little droplets missed his mouth. His eyebrows twitched, his lips trembled.

'Kit. This is impossible. I fancied Debs, but I didn't love her. I went with her, you see, to escape from your mother.'

'*Escape from my mother?*' Mark Mallory's words were blasphemous. Kit jumped to his feet. 'Why did you want to leave her. You told me she was beautiful.'

Kit stood from his chair, and pulled his father up with him. He pulled the older man's body inwards, till Mark Mallory's eyes were bulging. Moisture poured from his forehead, saliva ran from his mouth. Kit pressed his hands to his father's throat.

'You can't be my father then. Perhaps you *are* guilty.'

'For God's sake, we're all guilty. Every last one of us.' His father pulled away spluttering, and banged a palm on the table. 'Don't you see, I had to go. Our love . . . It should never have happened. For God's sake, Kit, you're a freak.'

'Don't you dare call me a freak.'

Kit pulled Mark Mallory up once more, then flung him down on to the carpet. He looked at him withering, whimpering, and aimed a kick at his stomach. Then he aimed a globule of spit at his eyeball, just missing the socket, and turned and ran from the flat, leaving the older man weeping.

Outside he continued running as the sickness rose from his stomach, and at the first public lavatories he stopped and vomited hard, loud and long. Salt tears ran down his face as he stared at his streaming reflection. His freak's eyes stared back at him, and he threw back his head as the sobs came.

22

He feels soft fingertips at his temples and knows them at once to be female. There is the lightness of the touch, the occasional sharpness of a nail's edge. At first there is just blackness, then red-purple smudges like blood oozing from a wound. The pulsing against his skull confuses him initially. Then he understands it is his brain, and learns the heaviness of his pain.

Smallbone opens his eyes.

A harsh beam of yellow makes him close them again, instantly. The fingers smooth his matted hair as though to say, *It's all right*. The wounded are like children: constantly forgiven their failings.

So he lies back, his tight and tender body informing him that he is on the couch: the proximity of cotton and viscose a clue that he's still dressed. A subdued distant hum through the window, the artificial yellow just glimpsed, are signs it is still night.

The fingers massage his temples, and he opens his eyes again.

Julie smiles down at him.

– What happened, Dad?

– Julie, what are you doing here?

He has forgotten – or lost the instinct – to be grateful, but it's all right. Julie's wide, worried mouth laughs, not in mockery, but forgiveness.

– Your neighbour Geoff called me. Sounded very worried. Apparently you chased an intruder into the street. Then you came back in and collapsed. Delayed loss of consciousness.

He tells her his head feels like a polar bear's and she passes him the Panadol. He heaves himself upright, his body's hesitation an irritant.

— *How long have I been out?*

— *I'm not sure. I came quickly.*

Stale breath fills his mouth, he can remember the past evening, but if Julie's spotted any of that she has the grace not to comment.

— *You should go to hospital, really. You know, with a head injury.*

— *Don't fuss. It's just a bump.*

He laces his fingers round one of her hands, while the other holds a compress to his forehead.

— *Who was it, Julie? Did anyone see?*

— *I reckon your colleagues'll be round soon. Take fingerprints and all that. Probably just a burglar. Dad, try to relax.*

But it's not like that, he wants to tell her: this wasn't just another burglar. Call it detective's intuition, but he's a feeling he's a target. Why, he doesn't know, and his skull aches with fatigue.

Officers from the local nick arrive about forty minutes after Julie. Smallbone doesn't quite know whether to feel personal pride or professional shame. Whatever, what does it matter? They won't find anyone now. They move like shadows around the flat, dusting, lifting, banging at drawers. Did he ever look that amateur, searching a crime scene?

— *Nice place you got here*, says one, who looks about twelve.

He's already caught the sly snickering of two of them — *Innit posh for a police officer?* — and Julie's been getting the once-over, which makes his blood boil. But mostly he's impatient, certain this drudgery will lead nowhere.

— *Nothing taken, then. Nothing much disturbed. Looks like you've been lucky.*

He rolls his sore eyes and gives a brief rundown of what happened. Lucky seems an odd way of putting it, but he doesn't say this out loud. In the midst of the slow chaos, the telephone gives a distant shrill.

— *It's for you, Dad*, says Julie, needlessly. *Shall I say you'll just call back?*

Smallbone raises an eyebrow.

— *No, no, love. I'll take it.*

She slides the receiver into his hands and he listens to the anonymous static.

— *Hello, anyone there?*

Julie's frowning with concern, and then he hears a voice he recognizes.

— *Jack, everything all right?*

— *Raff. Don't say good news travels that fast.*

— *I called you at the station, thought you might be working late turn. One of the boys told me something had happened round at your place. Just wanted to make sure you're OK.*

— *In the safest of hands.*

— *Jack, this can't be coincidence. Mallory just released, Wahlberg, and now this.*

— *Raff, a man after my own heart. Spot the conundrum in everything.*

His laugh turns to a cough, and then a wheeze.

— *Jack, just be careful. I'm going to get the speculative searches on the Wahlberg scene fast-tracked. In the meantime, get well. Stay calm and keep your head down.*

Daylight bludgeons him awake.

Julie wanted to stay the night, use the sofa, but he wasn't having any of it. Not a little kid any more, darling. I can look after myself. But that's exactly what he feels like – a child too sick to go to school – whose mother's given him a sick note, but won't stay home to look after him.

The air about him is thick with a misplaced, too-perfect quiet. He slides and staggers to the kitchen, the eerie, tidy stillness mocking him. How can a savage intruder and a team of clumsy, jobbing coppers leave the place so damned untouched? He is like a ghost in his own home, wondering if last night really happened. From second to second his vision blurs, making him further doubt everything about him. The tenderness on his scalp, the bruising over one browbone, strands of hair matted with blood – these are the only forensic reminders.

Daytime heat gathers once again. Smallbone forces open the window. A slow-moving shaft of warmth creeps over him: no refreshing summer breeze. He stares down at the morning pavement, which blurs and wavers in the sunlight.

And there he is. Unmistakably him. A tall, thin, broad-shouldered youth with shiny copper hair. His back is to the apartment so Smallbone doesn't see his face, but there's no question about it. Smallbone clocks him from a distance. A tumble of thoughts is unleashed at the tender spot beneath his scalp. Wahlberg reporting a boy stalker, and those creepy, freaky eyes.

Smallbone's breath pumps through his throat in light, irregular gasps.

– *Oi, you.* He's shouting out before he's had time to censor himself. Embarrassed, he backs away from the window – then grabs his keys and hurries out.

Out on the pavement the street blurs, sharpens, blurs again. Sweat rivulets down his forehead. *Oi, you,* he shouts again, to no one in particular, but the boy seems to have vanished and people are starting to turn and look. Then he sees him again, the thick head of auburn glinting. Smallbone's as good as dived across the paving stones, like a dog foaming at the mouth. His whole self is greedy for revenge and resolution.

The boy turns his eyes towards him: uniform, calm, uncomprehending. Smallbone stutters to a halt. It's not what he thought.

– Sorry, mate. I'm so sorry. Wrong . . . mistake . . . Take it easy.
The world blurs and focuses once more.

Whoever's knocking on the door has found his or her own way in this far. Call this a security-conscious block, seems to take nothing to make it past the front door.

– Yes? Smallbone calls out, shocked at the tautness of his own voice.

– It's me, Jack, answers Raff. *I've come to see how you are.*

Smallbone sighs and goes to answer. Raff stands there in the hallway, staring with unsettling intensity. A housefly buzzes at his nose and he flaps at it angrily. The damp heat melts around them.

– Jesus, Jack. You look awful.

Smallbone leans against the doorpost, a high-pitched dizziness in his skull. Raff fades in front of him, turned to sepia: he sees the boy, and then Mark Mallory. He shakes his head and blinks.

– Well, I have to say I've been better. Don't you want to come in?

Raff makes his way in easily, sits lazily on the sofa. They sip sparkling mineral water: a show of virtue without an audience.

– What's going on, Raff? Has the world gone mad?

– This boy, says Raff. *The one we've been talking about. We've got to find him.*

– Yeah, I reckon Wahlberg's stalker might be following me. I told you I thought I knew who that boy was. Kid who says he's Mallory's son. He's on a mission, I swear to you. To clear his old man's name.

– So maybe he'd hurt you as part of his revenge. Sending the wrong man down. But that doesn't explain Wahlberg. Or why he's so convinced his old man's innocent.

– Perhaps he thinks Wahlberg's the real culprit and I'm the dirty copper. Either way, same fate for both of us. Smallbone draws a hand across his throat.

— Not to mention the fact that Mallory himself is now on the loose. On which happy note.

Raff chucks the early evening papers on to the coffee table in front of them. It's fallen open at page 2, a small article but a big headline.

DETECTIVE ATTACKED AT HOME AS MODEL MURDERER WALKS FREE.

Julie's gone. Got the plane out to New York, and he didn't even get to see her off at the airport. Tried to get his shit together, but the old vision kept going wobbly. In the end the hammer beneath his skull simply made it impossible. Julie wanted to postpone the flight, but he wouldn't hear of it. At least Margaret would've been there, given her a good send-off.

It's only a few days since the attack, but he's starting to feel the long-term invalid. The nagging pain, the lack of clear sight: now just another fact of life.

The heavy heat of evening cannot disguise the shortening days. The thought of September unfolding fills him with dread: the end of summer is like a little death, not to mention this pain and no more Julie. He half wishes he'd let her stay, but that would have been cowardice winning.

Smallbone flicks on the telly. As the natural light dies about him, the sporadic flicker of brightness makes the room vibrate. He reaches for the Jack Daniels, swallows and savours its warmth. His eyelids are half-closing now, the distinct voice of the newsreader fading into his half-dream. More than twenty years on now: the killing of the girl-woman.

Half of him is here, on this cool, comfortable sofa: the other half back there, enclosed and entrapped with her, Marianne. Her room was tiny and dirty, the crying of babies born to child-mothers ripping through paper-thin walls. She thinks he's come to ask her more questions: the alley stabbing, the estate shooting. Probably bored about the enquiries, but getting all prepared and coquettish for him. Thin body and kitten eyes going all sly and hungry.

But what she doesn't yet know is that he's come to say goodbye. That it's too much, he can't go on like this, it's no good for either of them. He's got the speech all prepared in an odd, melodramatic way. He won't tell her he wants to keep Margaret, because he knows Margaret will leave him anyway; nor will he say, *Marianne, I love you*, even though he surely does. He will be too afraid to tell her that his obsession is making him forget himself, so he lies for hours in cold bathwater unaware why he's shivering. So he'll make it seem like it's low-key, two people moving on. Dignified, restrained, even altruistic.

But the speech never quite gets off the ground, because her thin hands are all over him, feeling down into his trousers, tickling a reluctant spark into his crotch. She is sad and hungry and alive on seeing him: her tongue forces its way between his lips and teeth; she ruffles his hair, pulls him down on to her, digs her nails into his back.

What with the quickness of it, the hot heart-beat of desire, he never hears the door open, the click of another's presence.

He never heard it then and he doesn't hear it now.

There's an almighty crash inside his skull, and it must be that remembered gun blast. Marianne tumbles limply off him, her white, bloodless, death face fading. His anger and thirst for revenge and both swelled by his guilt: the whore's pimp come to silence her, the disloyal grass struck dumb and useless. And all because Jack Smallbone couldn't keep his trousers zipped up. He wrestles the gunman, gets the gun, and then kneels where she lies bleeding. Torn skin exposes blood and tissue near her messed-up, slowing heart.

But fuck! This pain is fresh. His own head is still splitting.

He puts his hand to his skull, feels the wetness of a few days ago. The healing wound has burst again. He opens his eyes slowly.

Thwack! the room bursts and fizzes about him, white sparks rebounding off the walls. Something heavy hits the back of his head again, but this time he wriggles forward. A rising tide of nausea in his throat escapes in little dribbles.

Smallbone heaves himself upright, and turns to face his attacker.

— *You lousy fucker. What d'you want from me? Coward, why not show your face?*

The figure's all in black with a long coat and a cap – something that's halfway between Oliver Twist and a Greek fisherman's headgear. The peak's pulled down so far Smallbone can't see his eyes, and a scarf's all bandaged up round his nose and mouth so it's as good as a mask. He bobs between the shadows: lighter and nimbler than Smallbone expected, but it's difficult to tell in this half-light, and with his own pulsating vision. Smallbone flaps the air with one hand, like a tightrope walker floundering, and the two move slowly, half-crouching, like wary Sumo wrestlers.

— *Just tell me what you want. You know there's no point hurting me.*

His attacker stays silent, hovering. In a wild burst of confidence, Smallbone dives for the light switch, desperate to illuminate things. But his attacker's there before him. Thin, swift fingers claw his hands, drawing blood from the skin. And the fucker's kneed him in the groin: he doubles up and crumples.

— *Not so fast*, slurs Smallbone, to his silent, faceless assailant.

But drink and pain have made him slow, and he can't raise himself up again. The bastard kicks him away from the wall, like so much unwanted rubbish, and now he's in this little, indeterminate heap with sharp fingers at his neck and a pulsing agony at his groin.

Survival instinct comes late to him, and he opens his lungs to scream.

The attacker's there before him, stuffing fabric in his mouth, pulling tight at the cloth's edges so pressure gathers on Smallbone's teeth. He gags, but makes no sound. His brain throbs fit to burst his skull.

The thin fingers, cruelly efficient, trace their path with a sharp nail's edge, pressing coldly at his throat. The noose hurts his Adam's apple; the killer's palms are dry and cool. A rheumy moisture fills his eyes. He sees a heavy, Moroccan vase, skewed sideways on the floor, and decides to make one last lunge for it.

The noose reigns him back, no more than a hapless pony. It tightens on his throat.

— *A little obvious, isn't that, Detective?*

At last, the voice. But it's a whisper, so low, so hidden, that it's impossible to place. *Who are you?* Smallbone wants to say. *Why is it you hate me?* But a pathetic trail of spittle is all he can manage.

— *Think your last thoughts, Detective. And if you're a religious man, now's the time for prayer. And learn not to go snooping.*

The last remark doesn't make sense to him, but he's too far gone to question. The room swims about him as his stomach rises to his mouth. There's a wet heat at the back of his head and a searing ache behind his eyeballs. His brains must be spilling out. He wants to say, *Just end it now.*

But this killer wants to pause before the final tightening of the noose.

— *Your child will be so sorry. Pity you've learned your lesson so late.*

Perhaps it's the mention of Julie which gives him one last surge of strength. Perhaps it's the attacker's strangely chosen words of strength and pride. Either way, there's a lull. Small-bone leaps for the vase. The weight of his surge breaks the fabric, he tumbles forward and free.

Now he's sprawled like an angry, wounded big cat on the floor. His fingers are on the vase but his attacker's standing over him. He sees sweat on the thin eyebrows. Sharp finger-nails zoom for his eyes. He jolts his face away just in time and at the same moment lifts the vase. He delivers a heavy blow to the thighs which sends his opponent tumbling.

Now the two of them are skewed, limbs splayed akimbo. The impact of the blow has flattened Smallbone himself, and he struggles to straighten himself, battling the endless, throbbing pain. He loosens the gag and noose and stumbles upwards, towards the figure in black.

If his attacker had a gun or a knife, surely now would be the time to use it. But something tells him there are no weapons. This is a killer by stealth. He's got him on the retreat now, dancing towards the door. Smallbone stumbles forward, still the heavier on his feet.

And then, before he knows it, his assassin's behind him once more, disappearing into the shadows, unable to resist one last try. Smallbone wheels round with all his weight and the two of them collapse. He pins the black-clad figure down beneath him, but now the thin fingers are in his mouth, working beyond his teeth and tongue, scratching his throat, strangling him from within. He swallows, his throat con-stricting, his windpipe about to implode. But the wrists are thin enough to snap. The skin up close smells fresh and sweet.

— *No, you don't, you bastard.*

He spews the fingers out again, the hands stop clawing, the attacker's energy subsides. The figure's so small and light. Smallbone reaches for the cap, readies to unwrap the makeshift mask.

— *Why does something tell me this isn't the first time you've done this?*

The intruder's body has gone limp, yielding entirely to Smallbone's bulk. Smallbone reaches for a low sidelight, and pulls the cap and scarf away. He gasps.

The face is strange, yet familiar. The auburn hair, the pale fine skin. Beautiful eyes, a piercing blue. This isn't what he expected. Here is his stalker, so often wrongly imagined. And though up close the face is lined, and contorted by cruelty, you can't help but wonder at such hatred coming from such a beautiful woman.

23

If you had asked Miranda how it was she had kept her secret for so long, she would probably have misunderstood. Once the dirty facts were out, she absorbed them so quickly, so much as though it could never have been otherwise, that there was no real secret to be hidden.

She and Mark had lived through their childhood without parents – without blood ties, at any rate, without the certainty of that flesh bond. You didn't count the prosthetic parents who hit boys or fingered girls. Mark and she complemented each other: they were made to be together. Her love for him was absolute: their child its natural extension.

The baby was to be born in the spring. Mark and Miranda moved away from the hostel and from Hollybush to a dirty pocket of London somewhere south of Brixton. They sought foreign streets in districts with alien-sounding names, and to their young, untravelled minds, south London was like the other end of the world. Miranda sometimes called herself 'Mallory' and pretended they were married. She had occasional dreams of white dresses and churches sweet with scented flowers.

They lived for a while in a bed and breakfast full of the sounds and smells of others' filth. Then they went to a lawyer in the high street to talk about housing. The lawyers' offices were above a butcher's shop and you had to climb a damp, smelly staircase to reach the reception. Mark rolled his eyes when they first went there, and Miranda knew what he was thinking: fed on years of late-night American B movies, this wasn't exactly what they expected. But the lawyer, who wore glasses, and a pink floral maternity dress, actually turned out to be well worth the visit.

She said Miranda, in her expectant state, was definitely a priority. The couple were young, with no other ties or protection, so the council would look to house them. She got Miranda to sign a green form and scribbled in a notebook. Twenty years her senior, thought Miranda, and at least twice her size. Every so often they'd lock gazes in a sort of confused, disparate conspiracy. Miranda was relieved when they left the offices behind them.

It did the trick though. They were not long moved from the B & B to a flat of their own. It was a one-bedroomed flat in a low rise, just a stone's throw from more menacing tower blocks. But one of the neighbours had window boxes and a hanging basket over the front door. You had to make an effort. At least the place had potential.

Mark found a job labouring and Miranda scraped together extra money by waitressing. It was agreed she would work till too swollen and exhausted. After the baby was born they would think again about college. Miranda occasionally sat in the local library and flicked through manuals about grants and scholarships. Sometimes she thought of the broad horizon of possibility and a faint, sour sense of longing would tighten round the baby. And then she thought of Mark: his blazing green eyes and taut body, his low murmuring when they made love and the way his absence cut up her insides. The knot of longing left her, and she thought only of him.

If not for that fierce love, she would surely have found pregnancy unbearable. The first shock and excitement of it gave way to a heavy slowness, and she deeply resented her body's independent yielding to its weaknesses. Nor did she recognize her inflated belly, or claim the heavy, veined breasts as her own. She was shocked to catch her reflection in a shop window one day, to see the clear, backward stoop of the expectant mother, one elbow poking outwards, hand cupped in the crook of her back. She was a fat mother from a nursery rhyme. A tear sprang to her eyes.

At first Mark threw himself into practical tasks, as though in search of some comforting oblivion. He spent hours stripping wallpaper and re-plastering, hammering plywood and scrubbing surfaces. He was neat, efficient and industrious, and showed all the makings of a good father. Once she caught him taking a break in the kitchen, standing with one shoe raised, resting on the footbar of a stool, his back to her as he gazed out at the tower blocks on the skyline. He raised a heavy mug to his lips and the muscles in his upper arm bunched and tightened. When she went to kiss him and he turned she could see that he'd been crying.

Of course, by now Miranda knew all about those long afternoons back in Hollybush when Mark had disappeared with the Cornflower Girl. In so many ways more than one, he had been trying to find out who he was, and she had to stifle the bitter laughter, because it had a habit of turning to coughing, and hurting her insides. She had always suspected, mockingly, that 'personal history' was just one more remedial lesson, a social worker's babble of self-discovery, and an excuse for Mark to spend more time with Debs. What she had never quite appreciated was how precise and specific their goals were.

It was Debs who had started it, urged on by Carol. She had so many problems with her foster parents she became convinced she could salvage her lost self-esteem if she located one or other of her parents. Not that, to Miranda's hardened gaze, she looked like she was lacking in the self-confidence department. But sure enough, once she embarked on her project, she enjoyed a measure of success. She had located her father, an ex-long-serving prisoner. Perhaps he had been the man whose black and white photograph she'd once so coyly shielded. He'd shown little interest in meeting her. Having made the effort, she'd resolved to forget her past.

The project took quite some time, what with the research, the counselling, the secrecy, the preparation for joy or disappointment. Debs had urged Mark to join her, unravel his own history so they could work on parallel projects, compare notes and be conspirators. At first he strongly resisted. Looking back, perhaps he'd always been afraid.

Eventually, though, Mark decided to find out: spurred on by capricious, seductive Debs and his own sense of sharp foreboding. As the information started unravelling, he felt as though he were watching a scary movie, which he knew was going to sicken him, but which he simply couldn't walk away from. His mother had been young when she'd had him, a wild outcast, a suicide risk and mentally unstable. She'd had two children very close to each other, and it was clear she couldn't keep them. Adoption for both together proved too difficult – perhaps it was the dubious pedigree of the mother – and Mark had been fostered out from early on. There had been attempts to adopt the younger of the children, but there was a suggestion this hadn't worked and she, too, had had to go into fostering. The counsellor had said it wasn't unusual for children like this to go through a multitude of 'replacement' families. It was as if once you started on that road, you could never get off it. Sometimes such children could never trace back their origins.

Mark had let the pieces of his own story unravel gradually, until he no longer really had to ask to know what the very last piece was. It had been last summer when he'd found out – just before exam time. That his younger sibling had been a sister: a little girl named Miranda.

They had been lying together in the hostel bedroom when he had told her, Miranda's fingers clamping his to her palpitating belly. For a second, she had dug her nails into the skin beneath his knuckles, feeling the little emerging beads of blood slightly wet at her fingertips. Mark winced, but he was talking still. He hadn't wanted to believe it, he was saying, but it all made horrible sense.

Miranda slouched against the headboard, her face half-turned aside. She felt a bitter sense of bathos, that it should all turn out like this. That Mark should be taken from her because of a rotten biological coincidence. And of course, she had read *'Tis Pity She's a Whore* and even *Oedipus Rex*, if only in translation. The literary precursors for this love were far too well-worn and melodramatic for her liking, and it had never been part of the scheme that she and Mark should resort to terrible destruction and self-mutilation as a result of a doomed union. Much safer and yet grander, she thought, to stick to Heathcliff and Cathy.

But as she spread her fingers over Mark's cheeks and brought him still closer, his beautiful eyes stared back at her and she took in his broad, sharp-planed cheeks. It did make sense, but it wasn't horrible. Hadn't Heathcliff and Cathy, too, first known each other as children? Weren't all great loves star-crossed, forbidden – even Romeo and Juliet? And of course, for all practical purposes, no one need ever know.

Mark, for all his protestations, finally fell into step. Realizing that Miranda was still determined to have the baby and make it work, seeing her unstoppable energy, he agreed to go along with it, support her as best he could. Perhaps he just got exhausted, and lost the will and fight to challenge. Let events take their own course, knowing he had nowhere else to go.

Or perhaps he simply loved her. He never really explained.

Now Sacha – model and singer – intruded on their world only rarely, from increasingly glossy and adult magazines, on pop programmes and the occasional chat show. Meanwhile, Miranda's belly swelled beneath her flattened palm, and she slept more deeply and heavily. Mark started to leave her alone some evenings, and come back late without explanation. He would go for long, solitary walks and simply say that he'd been 'thinking'. She sniffed for alcohol or cigarettes, or anything else besides, but his body gave away no clues. If she clawed him too hard, asked too much, he would click his tongue and shrug her away.

One night, he didn't come back till after three in the morning. She heard him open and close the door, and pretended not to wake.

Miranda realized she no longer had a choice. The uncertainty about Mark's escapades brought back ghastly memories of Hollybush. She had to find out where he was going. One afternoon, she decided to follow him.

A pregnant teenager with swollen ankles and cramps in her belly made for a somewhat unlikely sleuth. But curiosity and adrenalin made Miranda lithe and cunning. She waited until Mark had left the house and caught the direction of his journey. Then she hurried down to where she was to start shadowing him in the street.

It was the strangest of sensations to spy on her own lover and brother, yet it came to her easily, perhaps because she knew him so well. Her sense of his presence was so strong she could almost second-guess him. And he was so intent on his journey he never stole a backward glance. She moved at a distance with him into the underground and then back out on to the pavement.

As the afternoon faded to twilight, they had reached a part of town Miranda knew nothing of. She followed him through an ugly, shiny shopping arcade, past a chip shop and a launderette. Now he had disappeared into a maze of grim, grey streets.

The pavements were emptier and Miranda's footsteps

echoed. She halted, her heart beating, when Mark appeared to stop and wonder; paused behind a dustbin until he settled and moved on. He headed for a terrace of dirty, flat houses and fumbled for keys to one of the doors. It looked like a door nobody in their right minds would want to open. She couldn't see the hallway but imagined a smelly, mildewed carpet. Mark closed the door behind him and disappeared from view.

Half-crouching, half-slouching, Miranda stayed where she was. Her brain ticked disbelievingly, as she tried to think why Mark might be here innocently. She could not leave until she knew. And then she heard the second set of footsteps.

The figure that approached was not at all as she expected. Tall, with skinny, knobbly ankles, but made shapeless by dull and frumpy clothing. She wore heavy, sturdy lace-ups and a thick and lumpy coat. Her hair was colourless but so heavy it looked almost artificial. Apart from that, though, the woman was unremarkable. She could easily merge into the faded, soiled neutrals of the street.

The woman, like Mark, disappeared into the house, and Miranda stayed there crouching, her sickness growing within her. But something was troubling her, beyond merely what was obvious. She kept thinking she'd seen the strange, frumpy woman before. She had a flashback to the hostel, several months ago, when she'd just found out she was pregnant. A woman brushing past her with her head down, and Mark screaming at Karl the Nazi.

The nightmare was deepening, and Miranda couldn't leave without understanding. And as evening turned into night, she stayed still waiting for the woman. When the frump finally re-emerged, Miranda impulsively sprang from her hiding place. Perhaps her rival would disappear once she discovered Mark was spoken for.

And then the bizarre, ugly enemy slipped. Her hand flew

to adjust her hair, as good as replacing it on her head. Miranda saw then the reason it looked so thick was it was a wig. In a flash of terrible comprehension, she saw the woman was in disguise. She ran a few steps closer, looked more carefully, and saw this woman's profile was beautiful. And even from the side, she could see her eyes were a clear, cornflower blue.

By now Miranda's heart was beating so fast it sent reverberations up through her throat and onto her tongue. She straightened from her hiding place, strode out to face the other. Two sets of footsteps quickened down the pavement. But the disguised Cornflower Girl didn't recognize her, or else didn't see or understand.

Miranda quickened to a run, her big-bellied body now weighing nothing. She could almost touch the other girl. And then she called out the false names.

'Louisa, Sacha, Debs.'

Whoever she was, the Cornflower Girl turned. Her breath jolted through her nostrils and face visibly whitened. Both of them stood staring, rooted to the spot. Miranda shook her head with what she hoped was an intense and icy scorn. She displayed her belly proudly, an unbreakable bond to Mark.

'You . . . fucking . . . bitch. Stay away from my man.'

Her words hung between them in the dull air, exciting no response. And then the Cornflower Girl threw back her long white neck and parted her lips. Her teeth shone with a garish brightness. She gave a throaty, raucous laugh.

'You fucking witch, Miranda. You know what Mark is to you. You've trapped him, with your perversions. But I'm going to free him, take him away from you.'

Miranda went for the other girl's throat, the blood rushing to her brain.

'Don't you dare. Don't you fucking dare.'

The wig slipped from the girl's head, and she lifted a trembling hand to save it.

'What sort of woman are you?' cried Miranda. 'Coming here dressed in all this shit?'

The other girl sneered at her. 'Mark won't come with me into my world, so I have to come into his. Bless him, he's still not ready to go public with our relationship, and this is his way of keeping things as low-key as possible. Me – I'm a highly valuable commodity these days, I've got people watching me all this time, have to have disguises. But then you don't need telling, do you? You should know all about secrets. Still just give it time, Miranda, one day soon it'll all be out in the open. And when that happens you're history and Mark's coming with me.'

'Oh no, he isn't. Don't you know I'm having his baby?'

Sacha lowered her lids and looked up and down Miranda's body. 'Don't kid yourself, you poor sad bitch. Your child will never live. It's a crime against nature. And don't you dare try to hurt me, Miranda. Don't forget what I know about you.'

Miranda stood there, breathing heavily, and let the other girl go. Tears exploded behind her eyeballs and escaped down her cheeks. Her stomach hurt her, but reminded her of Mark's beloved, breathing baby. She wasn't going to lose Mark, and she wasn't going to lose her secret. And this was one thing she knew Mark could never help her out with.

It would take time, she knew, she would have to wait till after the birth. But once she had her body back, she knew what she had to do.

24

Smallbone's brain throbs as one more ghost fills his night-mares. Looks like he's fated to dream for ever of these pale, troubled women. Marianne, Sacha, and now this malevolent beauty. Already, he's been jolting awake to the vision of her murderous eyes. She is unbalanced, past her first youth, and a would-be assassin. But he sees the fine skin, the sharp bones, and imagines what she was like when just a girl.

It is no longer worth guessing how long they will hold her at the station: what they will say to her, how she will answer. Just thank Christ that now, as victim, he is spared the role of interrogator. Raff will probably head it all up, put the puzzle together. Step into the skipper's shoes just as he was itching to do all those years ago.

Mark Mallory, the kid who didn't seem quite right. Con-fessed to something he didn't do, as Smallbone suspected all along. Spent the best years of his life inside just to protect the woman he loved. A witch woman to be sure, prepared to kill for her filthy secret. But how could he not have loved her. His lover, sister, baby mother. Or maybe he was atoning for another crime, just not the one he was charged with.

Perhaps he was so fucked up, prison was his only escape.

In the aftermath of the attack, news filters back to him from the station. The woman's confessing to everything – spewing out all the poison. Her dirty secret turned her rotten, and she turned killer to try and erase it.

And then Smallbone does something weird. He gets hold of Raff, says, *Bring me a copy of the tape.* If they'd been speaking face to face instead of over the telephone, he could just imagine Raff's face, slanted quizzically, not quite getting him.

– *Why d'you want a copy of the tape?*

– *This is still a major investigation and I did handle it when it started out.*

– *But now . . .*

– *And now . . . I'm the fucking would-be victim, the last-in-line, if you will. Look, Raff, just do it for me. I'd like to have a listen.*

These last words are an absurd, domestic trivialization of what he really feels. It sounds as though he's expressed a preference for spinning a few desert island discs, when in fact he's got a hunger, a huge, hollow-bellied need to hear his assassin confess. He gets the tape, eventually, (*all very irregular*, says Raff) and in the privacy of his bedroom he listens to the disembodied voice.

The voice of the woman who tried to kill him is calm and clear, almost actressy. Oh, and she's mad as a hatter, you can tell that straight off. Not in the clinical sense, of course: not like she'd be parcelled off to Rampton, or diagnosed as unfit to plead. But there's that streak of underlying mania which he recognizes from having interviewed so many killers in his time. And she's terribly grand, this one, keeps showing off with how much she's read. Probably has a little trouble drawing the line between fact and fiction.

First off, she talks about Laverty, beauty of many guises. That one came too close to Mark Mallory for her own good, and it's clear the bitter, arch love rivalry never stopped hurting. But the threat of revelation, of the brother-sister secret, was what really did it. Poor Sacha, in her glittery world: she must have thought she'd finally escaped. Only to be snuffed out by another nowhere child.

The voice on the tape doesn't need much prompting. There's hardly any intervention or coaxing from Raff and his colleague. It's like she's reading from a book or performing on bloody *Jackanory*. Now she's explaining about her next conquest, Carol.

That old lush, quasi-mum and boozy depressive to boot. Miranda had known Carol would have been close to her charge, might have known about the secret. Wasn't she the one in the background, urging them on, when it was just plain Mark and Debs trying to find out about their parents? So Miranda goes to visit her, to console her about Laverty. Turns out she unearths the address from a scrap of paper Carol gave her a while back. Found out, as expected, that the old dear was devastated at the news, and after much soul-searching was on the verge of speaking to the police. Soul-searching, because Carol knew her favourite protégée had always wanted to keep her past private. Still, a murder was a murder and the police was the police.

That was the cue, of course. Actressy little killer-kid didn't trust the boozy old cow, and who knew what might come out once she started spilling her guts. Miranda had acted: Smallbone still remembers the aftermath.

And finally Wahlberg, the longest survivor of all. Altogether a tougher nut, and much less likely to squeal, what with so many skeletons of his own. Exploitation of young girls, deception, under-age sex and God knows what. Must've been why he'd kept the police away from Carol's death, and in that way he'd helped Miranda. But Miranda makes no secret how she'd hated him, because he'd hunted her, chasing her from refuge to refuge. Didn't matter how far she moved, changed her name, her clothes, her lifestyle. He'd wanted her to sell her story, make a nice little earner for both of them. Paint her as heroine-victim, with Mark as the banged-up, ogre-ish villain.

Sounds like it had been enough, at first, just to keep away from him. To shut the front door in his face when he pitched up unannounced on the doorstep. But when Miranda realized

Kit had gone to London, she understood he was looking for Mark, and knowing her son as she did, she knew he would try and piece together the past.

Ever the watcher, the finder, as sharp as when she'd been a teenager, Miranda returned to the capital, tried to follow Kit's footsteps. Finding Wahlberg was easy, he even looked pleased to see her. When she materialized at his basement flat, he let her in unguarded, smiling like she was an old friend, wishing they'd kept in touch. And then he told her he'd been thinking of her because he'd this strange telephone call, and a visit, to boot, from this peculiar young man. Raking over all old stuff about the Laverty murder case. Miranda knew she'd arrived not a moment too soon. Someone else who knew too much, who'd never talked up till now, but you couldn't leave things to chance. She'd taken him by surprise in the hallway, when he'd thought he was showing her out. Smallbone imagines the strangling, a noose like the one she'd tried on him. Dragged him back inside and rewrote the scene: murder made to look like hanging.

The tape clicks towards its close, Smallbone doesn't want to hear any more. What, in the end, had she wanted with him? His head aches with it, blood bubbling in his ears with the memory of that night. Did she think he also knew too much, or was on the brink of knowing? Or had she just got so used to killing it was impossible for her to stop?

One thing was certain, after all: Mark Mallory *was* innocent. Or as innocent as you can be in that world of double-dealing cover-ups.

August turns into September, but the headaches won't disappear. He's on a sort of indefinite sick leave, doesn't know when he'll be going back. Not totally sure he ever will, in fact. Doesn't seem much point. If the next big case takes twenty years to solve, could be in his grave by the time they've wrapped it. And who's got that amount of time to spend chasing one ordinary, sodding murderer?

Julie calls from Manhattan: he tells her only half the story. Sure, a twenty-year-old case has been solved all over again. And yes, his hunches were right, but still he sent the wrong man down. He has to tell her something, in case she sees the papers and worries. But he can't tell her how hurt he is, about the headaches, and the nightmares. What would be the point – she must have better things to think about.

– *How are you, Dad?*

– *Fine, princess, just fine. More to the point, how are you? How's Manhattan treating you?*

– *It's tough out here. And I am a little lonely. Everyone works so hard. But it's all very exciting.*

– *Well, just make sure you take care of yourself, allow time to settle in. And don't work too hard, sweetheart. All that glitters is not gold.*

For days he doesn't even wander out of the flat, not until the last sop of milk's gone sour at the bottom of the carton. Even then, he ventures out only to restock on the most basic provisions, like a marooned man braving the shallows round his lonely, desert island. People turn and look at him, it looks like: is it recognition or paranoia? Lurid billboard headlines hint at the story he's become part of, but they jockey for pole position with some young actress's divorce. Did Sacha aspire to be like that actress once, instead of winning her fame through death? Did Marianne? Did Miranda? Who fucking cares anyway?

Out on the pavements, he keeps seeing tall boys with auburn hair. Kit Mallory, it must be him, coming back to say *I was right, wasn't I?* But it's always a trick of the light or his own screwed-up, wandering vision. Smallbone falls asleep in front of the TV, and dreams of Julie and Margaret in Regent's Park.

*

Over a week into September, and he's still not back to work. Just about plucked up the courage to go for a walk in the park. Starting to feel alive again, at least, to enjoy the smell of autumn grass and fresh bread from the bakery. There's a woman out jogging who reminds him of the young Margaret; he feels a piercing twist of nostalgia and wonders if he'll ever fall in love again.

Another jogger with a bandana passes: the scarf reminds him of the gag, the blindfold. He sits abruptly on a nearby bench, his breathing quickened and tightened.

– *Are you all right?*

A concerned woman stands in front him, wearing an expensive-looking linen jacket. He wheezes, *Fine*, and stays sitting, prays the vision passes.

Back at the mansion block, a figure hovers at the doorway. For a second he recoils with scarred nervousness, then thinks it's a colleague from the station. But it's someone unfamiliar. Couple of seconds later, turns out to be another journo.

– *Detective! How are you feeling? What are your views on the Laverty murder case?*

Smallbone pushes past him, but the man presses against him.

– *What does it feel like to send the wrong man to jail for twenty years?*

He suppresses a 'fuck off' and manages to close the door behind him. Now he's running up the staircase and collapsing into his living room. How does it feel to send the wrong man to jail for twenty years? Old, that's what he should have answered. It makes him feel old.

Smallbone flicks on the television, the world of empty, afternoon chat. An escape here, at least, from his own, niggling troubles. The screen is bright, but blurred: a fierce blue and orange. He leans forward where he's sitting, tries to adjust the set.

A frantic newsreader's voice babbles in tones that remind him of racing commentaries. He leans closer, sees buildings falling, smoke and filth billowing into the sky. A digital clock in the screen's corner tells him the time and the date. The screen goes blurred: he squints and focuses, then turns up the volume.

The dreamscape of Manhattan burns and crumbles on the small screen. The camera shudders, like it's an upmarket blockbuster, only stranger and more terrible.

Now it's a news studio, but even the talking heads are baffled. Buildings crashing, thousands screaming, carnage on the city streets. Politics and polemic and planes falling out of the sky. The biggest terrorist attack ever. His head is hurting, splitting open, like when the witch-woman tried to kill him, but there's something else this time, freezing him: a sharp, dry-mouthed dread.

One thought flashes in his brain.

Julie.

Smallbone rushes to the phone, keys her home number, then her office. He dials and redials frantically, but there's no way of getting through. Information is flashing up on the telly about numbers to ring for concerned relatives. Everyone in the world must be ringing those numbers.

After an hour he stops, gives up, his shirt sodden in sweat. The stench of his panic disgusts him, and he washes it away. The fierce pummel of water on flesh is a blessed distraction.

Then the telephone rings and he jumps out of his skin.

— *Yes?*

— *Jack? Have you heard?*

Margaret's voice — sharp, pleading, intimate, taking him right back to the old days.

— I've been trying to get through. No reply. You?

She makes a strangled, gulping sound, trying to feign strength and good humour but failing.

— I'm sure there's no need to worry. Just yet. Julie's offices . . . they're not . . . are they?

They babble uselessly into the void between them. Neither he nor Margaret knows Manhattan. They couldn't say where Julie lives, or works, where she might have had her breakfast. Just that her life is now in the centre of New York, horribly close to the heart of the danger.

Both of them run out of words. The line crackles with anxiety.

— Look, says Margaret. *I've got things to do. But why don't I come over in a little bit. We can try again later. See where it gets us.*

Smallbone nods, then realizes she can't see him, and talks stupidly: *Yes, that'd be good.*

Then he tries Manhattan again, without even expecting a connection.

The afternoon's still bright, so he goes out for another walk. The first emerging, homebound commuters have their eyes glued to papers, or the pavement. Everyone's reading, looking: both the twenty-year-old murder case and the divorcing actress have been wiped clean off the front pages.

He buys food at the local deli and returns to the mansion block. Not a sign of any journos who've been bugging him recently. Inside the phone's ringing – he reaches for it breathlessly.

— Just me again, says Margaret, *checking what time for later. Eight-thirty suit you? Shall I bring wine, or . . .*

Her voice trails into uncertainty and he laughs at the old/new awkwardness.

— Yes, wine. Why not wine? As long as it's expensive enough.

While waiting for her, he paces the flat restlessly, watching endless re-runs of the news. Bush and Blair on television, thousands in a dirty-faced street crowd, weeping. He thinks back to landmarks in his life, as though groping for distraction. First love, lost love, the red-haired assassin: none of it even scratches him.

Margaret's round in time at 8.30, and they pour wine and chink glasses. It's been so long since he's seen her like this, cooking, moving in the kitchen, frying mushrooms, grinding pepper, it's like moving right back in history. They talk little, but the food tastes surprisingly good.

— *Well cooked, Margaret. Cheers.*

— *You look like you need it.*

He raises his eyebrows.

— *You do. You've lost weight.*

— *So have you, Margaret. But you're looking good on it.*

She gives a quick, embarrassed laugh: a laugh he hasn't heard since Marianne.

And then, the shrill awakening. The sound they both dread and fear. They stare into each other's eyes to the ring of the telephone.

— *Shall I get it?*

— *No. I will.*

He scrambles for the receiver. The line crackles with static.

— *Dad? It's me. Dad?*

Joy and relief strangle him, but he's still embarrassed to find himself crying.

Afterwards, when they have both wept, Margaret runs her fingers through his hair.

— *Take care of yourself, Detective. You need to get out more.*

— *You going quite so soon?*

She pushes him gently away from her.

— *I'll call myself a cab. Nice seeing you, Jack. This place is so nice. We must do this more often.*

He guesses, as she puts her coat on, as she heads for her taxi, that they probably won't, but perhaps it doesn't matter. The ecstatic relief of Julie's call is enough for one day.

Next morning he sleeps late, and wakes with a headache. Thinks he'll treat himself to a cooked breakfast, and pops out to the corner shop. Is he imagining it or is the street eerily quiet – the whole city muted, blanketed by disbelief. Finally, surely, the journos'll leave him alone: in the aftermath of real tumult, they must've found something to occupy them.

But don't you believe it, even today of all days. There's one leaning against the entrance door, a lonesome wheeling figure. He straightens and paces in circles: you can tell the man's anxious.

– *Get out of my way,* Smallbone wants to yell, *why don't you leave me the fuck alone.*

And then he's nearer, and the figure stops, and turns to stare him in the face.

– *What the – ?*

It's him, Kit. They stand eyeballing each other, not speaking, and it's like their first meeting all those weeks ago, when the whole world was more innocent. And now two decades' worth of misplaced history have slipped in between them, and the crossing of their paths is both clearer and more crooked.

Smallbone no longer has words for this most lost of all boys. White noise blurs out the street's silence, and then he hears Julie's voice inside his head.

– *Dad. It's me. Can you hear me. Just calling to say I'm all right.*

Who will this boy phone at such moments, to share such joy and relief? Surely not his witchwoman mother, headed for a lifetime in Holloway? Or the father he barely knows,

245

cowed and coarsened by incarceration, stumbling and inarticulate, ill at ease with liberty.

Smallbone breathes, prepares to speak, but no words come out. The boy has dark rings round his eyes; his cheeks are hollow and haunted. His jaw moves silently, the teeth grinding; and then he funnels his mouth and spits. A globule of sputum lands square on Smallbone's shoulder.

The older man's throat catches in anger and disgust. The word's he's been groping for start to bubble out in fury.

– *You dirty little –*

He pulls the boy inward by the collar, by the scruff of the neck. Sees the big, bewildered face up close, with those ugly, creepy-coloured eyes. And then he stops short. The strange eyes are crying.

Smallbone lets the boy go. He brushes awkwardly at his shoulder, though the heat's already dried the spittle.

– *I'm sorry.*

The boy lifts a fist in rage.

– *I was right you see. Mark Mallory was innocent.*

– *Is that what you came here to tell me?*

The boy doesn't answer.

– *Kit*, says Smallbone, softly. It's the first time he's said his name. *Do you know where Mark Mallory – where your father is?*

Kit prepares his answer formally, you can see him working out the words.

– *I believe he is currently of no fixed abode.*

No need to ask where his mother is, and perhaps no need to ask, either, why Kit has come here. In this unloving, ungiving city, the merest sliver of familiarity helps.

– *I'm sorry for what happened, Kit. I don't know . . . if there's any way I can help . . .* The boy straightens, wags a finger.

– *Oh, I wouldn't say I need any help as such. I have many friends in high places. But you might be able to assist me.*

– *How's that, then?*

— I should like to find out about the forthcoming trial of Miranda Laverty. I'd very much like to follow proceedings at the Central Criminal Court, EC4.

Smallbone smiles, in spite of himself.

— Well, I can understand about that. That won't be a problem. But what about that discussion you kept talking about? Perhaps we should have that after all. It's the least I owe you.

The strange boy pauses for thought.

— Yes, that would be very interesting. But I have a very busy schedule. Perhaps we could leave it till tomorrow?

— No problem. Same time tomorrow. You can come up to my flat.

— Now that would be interesting. I shall look forward to that, Detective. Things have been rather changeable for me lately. And you seem like a very interesting fellow.

Smallbone's not sure — but could it be? — Kit Mallory smiles.

The lanky outline recedes leaving Smallbone, frankly, baffled. But what can you do? Got to make an effort, haven't you. Takes all sorts to make a world, and who's to say what's normal. And anyway, those less fortunate, etc, etc.

And then he smiles to himself, shakes his head in near disbelief. This is the first time in years he's let himself admit to any countable blessings.

Yet his would-be assassin's stymied, and Julie's been saved, after a genuine global disaster. He feels an odd kindness when he thinks of Margaret, both foreign and familiar, either way something that's been missing for as good as two decades. He closes his eyes and thinks of Marianne, but a strange sequence of sensations jostles: he can trace her outline, and smell her smell, but no longer quite make out her face.

A soft, low sigh escapes his belly. The long nightmare is fading.